Summoned
to
Destiny

Realms of Wonder

Summoned to Destiny

Fantastic Companions

Mythspring

Nothing Less Than Magic

Summoned
to
Destiny

Edited

by

Julie E. Czerneda

Fitzhenry & Whiteside

Published in Canada by:
Fitzhenry & Whiteside, 195 Allstate Parkway, Markham, Ontario L3R 4T8

Published in the United States by:
Fitzhenry & Whiteside, 121 Harvard Avenue, Suite 2, Allston, Massachusetts 02134

www.fitzhenry.ca   godwit@fitzhenry.ca

10 9 8 7 6 5 4 3 2 1

Library and Archives Canada Cataloguing in Publication
Summoned to destiny / edited by Julie E. Czerneda.

ISBN 1-55041-861-0

1. Fantastic fiction, Canadian (English) 2. Short stories, Canadian
(English) 3. Canadian fiction (English)—21st century.   I. Czerneda, Julie, 1955-

PS8323.S3S82 2004   C813'.087660806   C2004-903853-2

U.S. Publisher Cataloging-in-Publication Data
(Library of Congress Standards)

Summoned to destiny / edited by Julie E. Czerneda.–
1st ed.
[292] p. : cm.
Collection of short stories by Marie Brennan, Ed Greenwood, Kevin G. Maclean, Jana Paniccia,
M.T. O'Shaughnessy, Ruth Stuart, Karina Sumner-Smith, and Michelle West.
ISBN 1-55041-861-0 (pbk.)
1. Fantasy fiction. 2. Self-realization – Fiction.   I. Czerneda, Julie E.   II. Title.
[Fic] dc22   PN6071.F25.Su   2004

Fitzhenry & Whiteside acknowledges with thanks the Canada Council for the Arts, the Government of Canada through the Book Publishing Industry Development Program (BPIDP), and the Ontario Arts Council for their support of our publishing program.

Cover Art and Design by Kenn Brown and Chris Wren, Mondolithic Studios
Text Design by Karen Petherick, Intuitive Design International Ltd.

Printed in Canada

Contents

A Special Introduction

by Tanya Huff

≋•≋

The fantasy genre has often been criticized as being escapist literature. Personally, I'm not sure why that should be considered a criticism. What's wrong with having somewhere to go where duty and honor and sacrifice and courage and truth are still strong? There are a billion places, a billion people, trying to teach us the small lessons – fantasy creates a place where we can safely learn the larger for, if people learn by example, can there be better examples than stories where doubt and fear are defeated? Where the greater good wins? Where hearts and spirits are strong?

"But it's not real!" fantasy's detractors proclaim.

Not real?

Good and evil and love and hate aren't real? Trying your best in spite of enormous odds isn't real?

Ah, but I know what they mean. They mean magic isn't real.

Well, they might live in a world where everything is explained and wonder has vanished, but they don't have to. They, like all of us, can choose to see the magic around them. Maybe not the magic that gives a girl the shape of a white raven or sets dragons flying, or crafts a sunset out of dreams, but all that is merely the outer shape of magic. The inner core of magic is made of belief. And trust. And being open to the infinite possibilities in art and music and words.

In *Touch Magic*, Jane Yolen writes of how Albert Einstein believed that imagination was more important than knowledge and then she goes on to ask, "And in what literature, that bond between writer and reader, do you find the template for imagination more palpable than in a fantasy book?"

Duty. Honor. Sacrifice. Courage. Truth. Good and evil. Love and hate.

Imagination.

Magic.

You're holding magic in your hand right now.

Go ahead, escape into it.

And when you come home, bring something back.

Tanya Huff

Tangled Pages

by
MT O'Shaughnessy

Raal pressed a stray curl of dark brown hair back into place behind his ear, wishing he'd combed it. Head Page was probably going to notice. And he'd end up running errands all day from North Tower to South Gate again.

Back straight, he dropped his hand to his side again quickly, watching the reflection in the dark marble floor ripple. Raal hoped no one saw, but of course Dara was already smirking. Raal wished he'd picked some one better to bunk next to in the dorm. But how could he have known she would instantly dislike him?

Raal could see out of the corner of his eye that Head Page was in front of Sheena, three people up from Dara. The line of Page Initiates stretched beyond them, each in silver and black uniforms. The row produced odd ghosts in the gleaming stone walls and floor of the dorm, every inch mirror bright from endless hours of cleaning. While some of the more studious Page Initiates claimed to have evidence that their dorm had once been a meeting hall, Raal thought the simple lines of the black marble too plain. He suspected the long narrow room had once been storage.

But even here in the Outer Courts, a simple storage room was more magnificent than anything he had ever seen, coming as he did from a small farm. And there was the ever-present hint of centuries of history seen and set within these walls.

Raal pulled himself back to the here and now, ignoring the itch of curiosity as he thought about what ancient magics or battles might have started in this room. Most likely it really had been storage and the only history this place had seen was what foods had gone moldy first.

Head Page's inspection was lasting longer than usual, which meant she was being very particular. Raal didn't have many points left to lose. With Dara doing her best to get him sent away, he wouldn't need his recent streak of fumbling and awkward lessons to have his remaining points vanish like so much dust on the wind.

Hands behind her back, Head Page leaned close to Sheena and said something that made the Page Initiate blush slightly. Immediately she straightened an almost invisible crease in her uniform's collar.

Head Page moved to Drake, who had a slight scuff on his left shoe, then to Dala, who surprisingly got off with a mild nod of approval. Raal waited with dread as Dara was looked over. Somehow she always found a way to talk out of turn. And get away with it.

Today turned out to be no different.

"Is my hair correct, Head Page?" Dara asked sweetly. "I was uncertain when I saw how Raal has his done this morning."

He almost closed his eyes. He had to admit Dara was good; it even sounded like a valid question. But it set him up for trouble.

"Page Initiate Dara, I don't remember you taking the time to be concerned with your grooming beyond the requirements before. How nice for you to have finally found some interest and pride in your position. One point loss for talking out of turn, three loss extra for not remembering Page Initiate Raal's title," Head Page said. Turning, she looked over the row of Page Initiates.

"Remember, people. No matter how high, no matter how low, a title is a title. A position is one that a person was specifically given and trained for. Respect, even for each other, is not mandatory, but the appearance of it is. Remembrance."

The Page Initiates all chorused, "Remembrance!"

Standing before Raal, Head Page looked down at him and sighed. Quietly she said, "I can't very well ignore her, you know. So…"

The words were delivered in such a way that only Raal heard them. Originally he had thought Head Page harsh. But the tall, older woman in black and gold ran the Page Initiates coolly, calmly, and with a normally even hand. He had to admit that Head Page treated him fairly, if listening a little too often to Dara for his liking.

Raising her voice, Head Page said, "Raal, I'm sorry but two point loss for sloppy grooming. You have five points left. I think you should spend time considering that fact. I'm giving you the day off to think over your options."

Without another word, Head Page turned and moved on to the next Initiate in line.

Silence folded around Raal. It seemed like he was wrapped up in a blanket of it, nothing seemed to come through it. Nothing but those words.

"Think over your options."

⚜

Dazed and not paying attention, Raal soon found himself standing at the West Gate. Tears of frustration in his eyes, he watched a blurry crowd pass through the massive stone arch. Beyond lay the empty fields of grain and the southern edge of Draden Wood. The land was pink in the early morning light, stretching on for leagues and leagues. Somewhere out there was his parents' farm.

How could he go home? It would kill them.

Raal had been sent to Celadan Rath two years ago. The "City of Lights" had offered a chance for a farmer's child to move up in the world. And with every last bit of savings that his parents had had, they'd entered Raal into the Outer Court's Page Initiate School.

Standing in the dust and shadows, Raal realized he had wasted his parents' hopes as well as their money. He was never going to become a Page. A year to go and only had five points left to lose? Even if he was incredibly careful, with Dara's ever-helpful presence there was no way he'd have them past a month.

If only he was more graceful or more skilled at speechcraft. But Raal fumbled with the language lessons almost as much as he did with the Court's posture requirements. He couldn't even walk smoothly like the others. They seemed to glide through the massive stone halls and corridors as if on ice. Just like a Page was supposed to, as they had been taught. All he could do was stumble or lope. Something about the Outer Court offices always made him slightly nervous and on edge.

He took a slow step toward the West Gate.

He often muttered when he was supposed to speak clearly, confusing titles and forms of address that he should have long since memorized.

He took another, slightly quicker, step toward the West Gate.

Next month, Raal knew the Page Initiates were going to begin training with the Wards and Sigils of the Outer Court. He dreaded what would happen when he had to face dealing with even the most simple of them. Older Pages hinted that if you so much as misspoke a Ward's Unsealing, you could be killed by the magic it contained. And if he wanted to become a Page he was going to have to be able to deal with Wards every day!

Raal began to run through the West Gate.

Celadan Rath had stood for several thousand years, a city of stone and magic that had endured wars, plagues, and natural disasters. Magic held the city together, magic glittering in every stone and in every street. It was what gave it the name "City of Lights." Celadan Rath was no place for some one who made mistakes. The ancient power that flowed through its streets had helped shape a very old culture, and with it a set of strict traditions. The expectations of generations of people rested on fulfilling those traditions.

Raal was running toward the nearest edge of Draden Wood before he realized it. His uniform's jacket flapped open and he shrugged out of it, sobbing. Another betrayal of his family, of the simplest requirement of a Page to the Outer Court.

⚜

Jael stood and watched her charges scuttle through the halls of the Outer Court. As Head Page of the Initiates, she was responsible for making sure they were trained and honed to a fine edge of skill before they ever saw true service here.

The Outer Court was made up of the apartments and meeting halls of the lesser nobles and functionaries of the city. While not as important or as influential as the Inner Court, there were those here who could reach the ear of Matra Dalena. The Queen of the City of Lights, Matra Dalena was the center of all decisions and law for the people.

Even this removed from the Inner Court, these children were closer than any commoner was likely to come in their lifetime, unless they committed some horrible crime. Which meant there were many eyes on even lowly Pages.

With a gesture, Jael summoned one of the Page Initiates and passed on orders for Dara. The brat got under her skin, and if she could she'd break her down. Dara's attitude might work for her in some small holding in the country, but it had no place here. She needed to learn to either play her games more subtly or to grow up. Jael preferred that she grow up.

As it was she couldn't figure out what exactly made Dara dislike Raal so badly. Whatever it was, she was doing a fine job of getting her fellow Initiate kicked out. The little…

Jon came up to her and watched as several Page Initiates scurried in to report on their errands so far today. He quietly stood at attention in his full Page uniform of gold and black, impeccably neat where her Page Initiates looked barely held together.

Nodding at the last Page Initiate, Jael dismissed them to their next round of errands. Dara, she was pleased to see, was jogging past. She had a rough day ahead of her with messages to each of the four Gates. It would take a good hour of such jogging to get from one to the next. It should tire out some of that temper. And give Jael a bit of quiet.

Turning to Jon, she smiled at her good friend. "So what brings you here?"

She lost her smile when she realized that Jon wasn't returning it.

"You need to come with me. I've something to show you," he said.

Jon led Jael quickly through the halls to a guard station. Inside one of the station's small rooms Jael was introduced to a guard, a Foot

Patrol. Looking a little worried, the guard explained how he'd been on his rounds when he'd seen something in the wild grasses near the Draden Wood.

Carefully he pulled out a crumpled Page Initiate's coat.

Jael almost cried. It was Raal's. "The boy was down to five points," she explained, not hiding her disappointment. "Losing his coat? Jon ... Raal isn't a bad Initiate. He could have made it, if..."

Jon and the guard exchanged a look. "You don't know then?"

"Know what?" she asked.

"Today the Outer Court is holding a Hunt in Draden Wood." The guard's voice was hushed as he spoke. "The Magii have created a series of entertainments for them. Including a Tangle. A full one."

Jael's hand went to her mouth. "Gods have mercy!"

⚜

Wind whispered in the leaves, mottling the ground with sunlight and shadow. A stream flashed into gold where the sun made it through the trees, laying like dark glass where shadows held.

Back against a twisted cedar, Raal stared at the stream for a long time. He had stopped crying some time ago; now he was just numb.

There definitely was no going back now. He couldn't go back to the city, nor could he go back to his parents. He wasn't sure what he was going to do. But sitting here felt fine for a start.

He had always loved the forests around his home, often frightening his parents by spending whole afternoons in some glade playing by himself. He hadn't had time to explore even a little bit of the Draden Wood since he'd arrived. Maybe he should have; it was so calming to be here now.

But then, when could he have? The life of a Page Initiate was filled with work and lessons and errands. There wasn't time for anything else.

Raal chuckled to himself. It was actually a little funny. The one thing he'd needed was time to himself, but it was the last thing he had been likely to get.

He dug his fingers into the ground, feeling the dirt cool his hands.

The scent of the wood was clean and crisp. Autumn wasn't far off. He could almost taste the last of summer in the coolness of the air.

Here was where he was at home. Here he was most happy. Alone, out in the world beyond the stone walls and the snarls of magic and Court life.

Raal sat up straighter. There was something in that thought that tugged at him, but it was quickly lost as a ripple seemed to go through the air.

Under his hands the ground seemed to shiver. Something shifted and the air darkened somehow. He couldn't quite figure out what was wrong before a second wave hit. Instantly the woods around him changed.

Vines appeared to erupt from the ground while trees leaned in toward each other. Branches somehow changed, looking sharp and jagged. The clean air vanished and a dank smell of age flowed down cold winds. Leaves and needles were kicked up into the air before that wind, small whirlwinds appearing and vanishing.

It was when the witchlights began to flicker into being that Raal knew. He was in a Tangle.

Everyone had heard of them. They were the dangerous pasttime of the rich and powerful. It was so powerful a magic, it took at least three Magii to create one. They bent a place into a kind of maze of magic and confusion. The more complex a Tangle, the more power it took.

From where Raal sat, it looked like this one was very, very complex. He couldn't see an edge to the changes. They went off out of sight.

Of course that could be an illusion. Part of the "fun" of a Tangle was getting through it and out the other side. He'd heard the Courts of the city often liked to populate them with creatures, both summoned and illusionary.

One of the small balls of blue witchlight floated past his face. For a moment he could swear he saw a face in it, looking out through the heatless flames.

Raal got up, his back pressed against the tree. The quiet of the woods had changed completely and he didn't have a clue what he should do. All he knew about Tangles were that they were considered sport, not how to get through one without getting hurt.

Out of the bark around him thin blades of thorns slowly began to sprout. Carefully, he moved away from the tree, checking the ground and branches overhead. Raal looked around for a safe place. Maybe if he could just sit still until the Tangle was done…

A coughing screech echoed through the trees to the north. It sounded close and it sounded like a creature that was hungry. Or angry. Or both.

When the sharp explosions of branches and underbrush started to sound as if they were moving toward him, Raal decided sitting still wasn't such a good idea.

The magic of a Tangle might be new, but surviving in the wild wasn't.

Rather than racing straight south from the clearing, Raal cut east. He knew the city had originally been in that direction so there was a chance, if his sense of direction hadn't been fooled by magic, he might just leave the woods and find safety. As well, he knew most wild animals on the hunt tended to travel in straight lines rather than turning sharply. So unless whatever it was tracked his scent, he was going to get out of its path.

Hopefully.

Moving as quietly as he could, Raal focused on what he had to do rather than the shaking in his legs and arms. As quickly as possible he moved through the altered woods; avoiding a hissing vine, a series of half-hidden holes that could have broken an ankle, and two fallen trees that blocked his path.

At one point he began to realize that not only did he have to avoid whatever the Tangle was made up of, he had to avoid those who "played" in it. Raal wasn't sure but he imagined the Courts didn't appreciate failed Page Initiates enjoying their "sport." It probably was illegal for him to even be here.

So when he heard voices he crouched behind a tree and waited.

"I told you that these fellows were good!" said a man's voice.

"Fellow is a bit off. There were women there too, you know," replied a second man's voice.

"Franken, I did notice, but who cares. They are still going to be saying 'Duke Treto outdid himself by having five full Magii make this

Tangle.' I imagine even the Inner Court's hunters will be envious. They don't use more than four all that often," boasted the first voice.

Franken disagreed. "Du … Joshua, I don't think it matters as much as you seem to think. Skill is more important than brute strength. I hear when Magi Dr'Karth weaves a Tangle, it can stretch for leagues and even the best hunters take days to get free of them. I don't think these five could get the Tangle larger than this patch of Draden Wood. Which is impressive, grant you, but…"

The voices of the two men faded as they moved off.

Raal continued to crouch, dazed.

"Days?" he whispered.

⚜

"What? A failed Page Init… why am I even listening to this? Head Page Jael, I expect better than this from you. This is not worth interrupting my meeting with Under-Minister Millan. I need those contracts with him for the trade routes to the south and it's taken two months to set up this meeting. One little boy is not worth my time. Now off with you…"

Jael watched as Functionary Davis turned away and walked off. He had been her best hope.

For an hour now she'd been trying to find someone who would help get Raal out of the Tangle in Draden Wood. But so far no one was willing to so much as lift a finger.

Which wasn't surprising. Most people wouldn't give a second thought to a Page in trouble, let alone a Page Initiate and a failed one. Even though Raal might be killed in the Tangle, he just wasn't important enough to matter.

Frustrated almost to screaming, Jael stood in the corridor and wondered what to do next.

"I tell you, Master, that there is no need for your inspection… I mean the other four and I are quite capable…"

"Pupil Haren, I do understand but I am still interested in seeing your work for myself."

The two voices echoed from a side corridor and Jael almost didn't move in time. The two figures were walking with surprising speed considering one of them looked old enough to be her great-grandfather.

Both were obviously Magii, although it was easy to see who was a Master Magi and who was still a Pupil. The younger of the two dogged the steps of the older, a worried look passing across his face each time his Master wasn't focused on him.

Looking at the plain white robes of the Master Magi, Jael didn't need to see his face to realize it was Master Magi Dr'Karth. He was the center of gossip's tales for his scorn of the ornamentation and grandeur many expected of such an esteemed Magi.

Dr'Karth looked up from listening to his Pupil. Surprisingly he actually saw Jael; most people above the rank of Page tended to treat them as invisible. Something of her worries must have been plain because he stopped and held a hand up for silence.

"My dear young lady, whatever has given you cause for such a long face?" he said.

"Master?" said his Pupil.

"Hush, Haren," Dr'Karth said.

Bowing low before she even bothered to open her mouth, Jael replied, "It is nothing a Worthy such as yourself should be bothered with, Master Mag…"

"Oh, stop that now. I'm no more worthy than you, so up and eye to eye. Now tell me, what is it, child?" Dr'Karth's voice held a hint of humour and warmth Jael wasn't quite used to hearing in the voice of someone high in the Courts.

Jael hesitated. Only for an instant.

"Well… sir… there's a boy…"

⚜

Raal panted, sliding down a boulder to rest on the ground. He'd avoided two more bands of Court hunters and three unseen beasts. He'd just run from what he thought might have been a cross between a bear and a deer. Something had enraged it and after a good fifteen minutes it had finally stopped chasing him.

He thought.

Digging his fingers into the ground around him, Raal leaned his head against the boulder and wished he was invisible. Or not here. Or something.

He sat up, for an instant sure he had felt another ripple in the air. It reminded him of when the Tangle had been created. A bit anyway. It was a little different, but he didn't know how.

Somehow he felt some one was looking for him. He could just imagine a kindly face peering through the trees, looking to find him.

Shivering with an inner chill, Raal wished harder he was anywhere else. Who knew what that illusion actually hid, but he highly doubted a kindly old man was looking for him.

The feeling got closer and closer to him. He unconsciously clenched his hands tighter and wished over and over that he was invisible. Almost sobbing, he closed his eyes and tried to press himself into the boulder at his back.

For a moment the sensation hesitated, then moved on.

The feeling of being surrounded by a presence, by a searching, passed. He held himself rigid for as long as he could, worried it might turn back and find him.

Eventually he felt strangely drained, falling exhausted into a dreamless sleep, never noticing the clear sunlight that for a moment rested on the boulder next to him before the darkness of the Tangle swallowed it up again.

⚜

Dr'Karth hummed to himself, frowning.

He, Pupil Haren, and Jael stood in a room at the top of a tower Jael had never seen. Apparently the Magi Quarter held more secrets than she'd ever known, including this series of open-topped towers that one could only see from inside.

At the center of the floor a large metal bowl filled with dark water sat on a stone base. The three of them stood around it while Dr'Karth stared at the water. From time to time Jael saw flashes of motion in the water's reflections, but she had no idea what they were.

Pupil Haren seemed intent on watching Dr'Karth while the older Magi was intent on the water.

"Well. That's interesting." For the first time in some time Dr'Karth spoke. "Are you sure that this Raal is indeed there, my dear?"

Jael blinked in surprise.

"Yes, sir. We're positive. We found his uniform coat at the edge of the Wood…"

Dr'Karth snapped his fingers. "Of course."

Turning slightly, Dr'Karth drew a line of light in the air and made a quick motion with his hand. Suddenly he was holding Raal's coat and the line of light was gone.

"This should help."

Frowning he let the coat go. It floated unsupported where he left it. Quickly he sketched more lines of light, through and around the coat. With a final gesture from Dr'Karth a column of light erupted from the bowl of water and passed through the coat, casting a bright golden glow over everything.

"Interesting indeed." he muttered. He glanced up at Jael, his expression puzzled. "Well, I can safely say he's there. But. Somehow I can't find where. I can feel his essence through this coat, and around that essence I can feel the Tangle. But I can't locate where in the Tangle he is." Frowning, Dr'Karth gestured and the coat collapsed into his outstretched hand. "He seems to be… shrouded. But how?"

Jael was stunned. "But… Raal has no experience with magic! He's not even been taught the basic Wards for the Outer Court yet!"

Dr'Karth laughed. "Well, that's not really experience with magic so much as learning passwords. I am surprised to hear that, however."

He turned to Pupil Haren. "I think this is a good test for you. Transport to the other four Pupils' Masters and ask them to join me at the edge of the Tangle."

Pupil Haren paled slightly and nodded. "Of course, Master."

As he removed himself to one side and began to draw on the air, a bit too carefully Jael thought, Dr'Karth turned to her.

"You and I, my dear, are going to Draden Wood."

With a single word that rang Jael's ears and a simple snap of his fingers Dr'Karth created a large doorway of light in the air. Holding his hand out to her, he smiled. "Join me?"

Hesitantly Jael put her hand in his.

⚜

For a moment, Raal's world spun. Something was all around him, in him, but he couldn't see it. Whimpering he had balled himself up and rocked on the ground. He just wanted to be left alone.

The original rush of fear had faded, replaced by concern and now fear again. He went back and forth between feeling he could do this, to absolute terror of the Tangled woods around him.

Raal had stopped moving through the forest, instead deciding to stay in one clearing that seemed safe. He had no idea how long it had been since the Tangle had started, nor did he know what time of day it was now. But he was starting to get hungry.

As the sense of something else in the clearing faded, he slowly straightened again.

Wiping tears from his eyes, he laughed. "And I used to think this morning was the worst thing in the world…" His voice was quiet and low. He didn't want to draw attention to himself.

The two men, Franken and Joshua, had passed his clearing twice. Raal worried they might eventually decide to pass through it rather than around it, but so far they hadn't.

Thinking about them made him smile again. At least someone *else* was having as many problems with the Tangle as he was. In some ways it made him feel better. Not so alone. Even if being discovered by them might be almost as dangerous as being caught by whatever else was in the Tangle, Raal was happy to have real people nearby.

Even if there was something about Joshua that made Raal think he should know him from somewhere.

Tired, but afraid to even nap, Raal listened to the sounds around him. They weren't the normal restful sounds of wildlife or a quiet wind moving through the trees. Now the animals had gone or had been silenced, replaced by the creaking of rotting trees as they swayed in a cold wind. Or by distant howls and faint yelping. Or sometimes by the truly frightening sound of the trees being shouldered aside by some massive beast.

As he listened, Raal heard the two men talking again. Arguing actually, from the sounds of things. He worried they might be getting a little too loud, drawing attention to themselves. Then he realized they were moving toward him.

Willing his senses to be better he listened hard and tried to search out any indication that they weren't alone.

Something prickled along his spine. Raal suddenly *knew* they weren't. Something was out there with them. Listening as he was listening.

Tracking them.

Jael blinked to clear her eyes after the bright light of the gateway that Dr'Karth had created. As she looked around, she saw several pavilions with colourful pennants flying in the sunlight. Crowds of Outer Court functionaries and nobles milled throughout the area, laughing and lifting silver goblets of wine to smiling lips. Four Pupils stood to one side, quietly talking amongst themselves. Or they had been, that is, until they turned to look at the Master Magi.

Seeming surprised but not alarmed, they moved together to meet Dr'Karth and Jael. Ignoring her, they bowed to him.

"Master, we obey."

Dr'Karth didn't appear to enjoy their formality any more than he had her own earlier. Waving it aside, he quickly asked: "There is a boy in that Tangle, not of the Outer Court. Why was the Wood not scryed for people?"

Paling, one said "But all knew there was to be a Tangle toda..."

"In fact, I had not been aware of the plans for a Tangle. I hardly think it reasonable to believe 'all' knew anything," Dr'Karth said.

Haren appeared with a small crowd of Magii. They were the annoyed Masters, from the looks on their faces.

As the Masters strode towards their small group, Dr'Karth held up a hand to forestall their comments. "Apparently, I'm not the only one who was unaware of this little enterprise. I think it time to remind you that while Bans are placed, not everyone pays attention. And Masters, despite evidence to the contrary, are not all seeing. We too need to be informed." Dr'Karth's voice now held a chill that Jael had never imagined hearing in the short time she'd been talking with him. Pointing at one of the Pupils he asked curtly: "What is the Order of Phal?"

She stammered "The... uh... the Order of Phal is the edict that 'Safety is first,' Master."

"Indeed," Dr'Karth said. "And in safety is the realization that assumptions are often false and proof is the best determination of truth."

They looked as uncomfortable as any of Jael's Page Initiates during inspection.

"Now. I assume you had a Limit on the Tangle. What is the time?" he asked.

Jael watched without understanding most of what Dr'Karth said. She didn't need to. From the now-worried expressions of the Pupils, she knew instantly something was wrong.

"Well, uh... Master..." said one.

Dr'Karth actually looked ready to snarl. "Of course. Outer Court. Let me guess... Duke Treto? I'm betting he didn't want to have his 'fun' end before he could prove he could beat a five Magii Tangle. The fool. And let me also guess that you were instructed to Key the Tangle to him?"

They nodded.

"Five more fools!" Turning to Jael, he explained: "A Tangle is a spell. It normally has limits on how long it will last and how far it will reach, as well as other things like how much energy it uses, how many creatures are in it, so on, so forth. It's often Keyed, that is attached to a specific person so when he wishes, or if he becomes injured, the Tangle ends. Duke Treto apparently didn't want this one to end before he could best it. Knowing him, he won't accomplish that any time soon."

Sighing, Dr'Karth looked at the wavering border of the Draden Wood.

"So we're going to have to wait until the Duke either falls over and hurts himself, or he gets free. We can't stop it."

❧

Franken and Joshua were only feet from where Raal hid. Now he could see them, hear their breathing, even the muttered cursing about vines that twisted around ankles and earth that shifted underfoot.

To the west, Raal … felt… something waiting. All he wanted was to get out of here, now!

But the two men stepped into the clearing, looking around.

"Stop for a bit?" Joshua asked.

"Of course, Si…" Franken began to respond when there was a roar.

The ground shuddered as a figure bounded through the trees and into the clearing. Some sort of scaled flesh flashed past Raal as it whipped its thin body toward the men. It ignored him completely, although he had no idea why.

The two men immediately raised their swords in efforts to deflect the creature's rush. But it was too fast. Something like a tail, maybe, slapped against Franken and sent him sprawling out of the clearing. A gleam of tooth sparkled in the gloom before Joshua yelled in pain. Raal couldn't see everything that was happening, but he didn't think it was good.

He rocked with tension, willing the beast to leave them all alone. He clenched his fingers into the ground, teeth grinding as he tried to keep silent. Raal barely noticed a flood of … *something* as it rushed through him. Instead he focused on willing Joshua to be all right, for him to stand up.

Jerking upward, the man did just that. He looked pained and surprised, but the pain vanished from his face as he brought up his sword.

Franken stumbled back into the clearing, holding his ribs. He feebly lifted his sword in the direction of the creature as it twisted and snarled back at him. As quickly, it stopped attacking.

It lifted its blind head and sniffed.

Still now but for its breathing, the creature looked like a nightmare. Its skin was scaled and gray. Overall it was slim and well-muscled with four legs, each ending in thin claws. It almost looked fragile standing still.

Raal was thinking this when he realized the creature was slowly turning toward him, growling low in its chest. It had scented him. And now was focused solely on him.

It roared violently and sprang!

Raal yelled and threw up his arm to fend it off. Thunder sounded and the world rocked. Thrown backward, Raal collided with a tree.

Dazed, it took him a few tries to focus again. He was surprised he had the time to, that he was still alive. He couldn't figure out why. Looking around, he also couldn't make sense of what he was seeing.

The trees around him were snapped as if they had exploded. There was a column of smoke rising from a patch of ground close to where he had been, and the two men were easing themselves from a knot of limbs and weapons at the far side of the clearing.

A dull ache flowed through Raal as he sat up and looked into the eyes of Franken.

"How... did you do... who are... what..." Joshua was rambling.

Franken smiled. "What he means is, lad, who are you and how did you just throw that monster away from you, then burst it into ashes? Though we might be more grateful should you next time decide *not* to include us in the explosion..."

Raal looked around, beginning to understand. "Oh... my."

Splints of wood fell to the ground where some of the trees had been damaged. A patch of clear sunlight streamed down around them. The clearing didn't hold any trace of shadow or twisted plant life. It was as if the Tangle ceased to be in the small area where the beast had ... exploded.

Raal blinked, almost missing Franken's next words.

"Duke... Joshu... Sire. I think it's time to call an end to the Tangle."

Explaining why the other man's face had seemed familiar, Raal realized distantly. Raal had never been good with the faces of the Treto family, only knowing them by their uniforms and arrogant actions. He had learned to keep his head down while avoiding them as much as possible.

"Well, Franken… I think it's actually not a matter of my ending it," Duke Treto said. "It looks like our new friend here helped us defeat the last beast."

There was a shiver in the ground that spread to Raal's sight, a soundless echo of thunder. Where it passed things altered and shifted. It was as if some nightmare image was revealed as merely shadow on a wall.

Where branches twisted and clutched, they unbent and spread thick leaves, their lines once more clear of the Tangle's magic. The vines that formed mazes along the ground slumped and quickly merged into the earth. The scent of decay vanished like it had been a dream, replaced with the healthy smells of an autumn afternoon in a forest.

Trees lifted from stooped shapes, cliffs of stone shrank back into boulders and beasts returned in shimmers of pale light. A deer fled from the group, startling the three of them into laughter.

"I think, Sire, that next time you want to have a Tangle… I will find other things to do," Franken said with a small smile.

"And I think next time Duke Treto decides to have a Tangle, he best first consult either with myself or one of the other Master Magii before enlisting our Pupils' help."

The deep voice surprised the two while Raal just laid back and gave in to shock. A group of people stepped from nothing. One moment they had not been there, now they were.

When Raal saw one of them was Head Page, he almost started to cry in relief. Some one he knew!

"N..now, Master Dr'Karth…" Duke Treto stammered.

"Oh, hush. I'm here about this one." Dr'Karth pointed straight at Raal.

It was then that Raal started to laugh uncontrollably.

In Dr'Karth's study the light came from crystal spheres hung from the ceiling. Their glow was golden and reminded Raal of early summer mornings. Happily wrapped in a blanket, sipping warm cider, he listened to the Master Magi and Head Page… Jael… talk. His head was still spinning from the day.

Outside the night city glittered, seeming almost unreal to him.

"… so all this time, in a city filled with magic, the boy never noticed that he was sensitive to it?" Jael was asking.

"He would only have problems near the Warded and Sigiled areas of the Outer Court," Dr'Karth answered. "I think every time he came near one of those permanent magics he instinctively tried to shy away from it."

"Which explains a few things. Like a promising Page Initiate who was perfectly fine in the classroom lessons but all thumbs on errands." Jael smiled at Raal.

He smiled tentatively back. Then frowned. "What does all this mean, though?"

Dr'Karth smiled broadly. "Well, my dear boy, it means you won't have to worry about being a Page Initiate any more. You are officially relieved of duty."

Raal froze. Everything had been a bit hazy and he had felt safe with these two. But somehow he was being told he had still failed.

"But… I have… five points!" he cried.

Jael blinked at him in shock and the Master Magi laughed.

"My dear, dear child! You didn't *fail*. You simply were never meant to be a Page. You, my boy, are a Magi!" he said.

The swirling thoughts, the strange conversations of the afternoon and evening all clicked into place. Raal finally understood.

"But …" he said. "What will my parents say?"

Jael smiled and patted his hand. "Raal… or rather, soon I suspect, Pupil Raal… I think they will be most proud. There are few honors higher than being a Magi in the City of Lights."

Mouth open, Raal looked from one to the other. Then, before he whooped with relief, he laughed.

"Dara is going to be so mad…"

Stormsong

by
Ed Greenwood

Bright and blue the flame danced, flickering and leaping in time to the two sweat-drenched women who danced around it. Their unbound hair swirled around them as they spun and arched, their singing growing hoarse but their movements ever more insistent, building … building …

One of the dancing Oerbele flickered her fingers in the gesture all of the Saeren had been waiting for. Amnaedra bowed her tousled head momentarily to swallow as she'd been taught – as all poor singers in the Arculum were taught – so her voice would ring out clear and rich, holding her lone note in the swelling chorus.

There was a swirling of emerald-green robes as the kneeling Saeren all around the chamber raised their heads in unison and sang, every one of them gazing at the flame dancing in its central brazier.

The flame that was now growing brighter, whiter, stabbing higher into the air in time to the rising crescendo of the dance … rising like a leaping, wriggling fish or serpent, leaving the brazier behind entirely to reach up …

Rising in splendour, a blinding white brightness now, to lick at the gemstone hanging in its web of cords.

Amnaedra stared at the gem as the white flame curled around it, singing as hard and as clear as she could. The cords caught fire and curled swiftly into ash, receding from the gem as if recoiling from it.

Her own dusty-black hair was stirring and curling just as those cords were. As she watched, the shrinking strings seemed almost alive, and it was tempting to gaze unblinkingly at their slow writhing and dying, as the elaborate webwork melted away – but the proper thing for all Arcrae in a flame chamber at such a time to do was to watch the gem awakening to its enchantment.

Flames were raging around the gem now, holding it in midair where no cords remained, and Amnaedra saw the faceted stone blink with the radiance of the flames, wink again more brightly – she was sighing in the satisfaction all Stormsingers felt at such a success, joining in the great gasping hiss that was washing over the chamber around her – and then seem to *swallow* the flames.

Abruptly all bright fire was gone, at just the right moment, as the song reached its high, final note. Out of its triumph the gem, all aglow, rose higher into the air by itself ...

And the song ended. Amnaedra did the same as every other Saere in the chamber: let her gaze fall to the brazier. Now empty of flame, it spilled out a last few drifting wisps of smoke, as the two spent dancers collapsed to the floor on either side of it.

Involuntarily every Saeren looked back up at the hovering gem – and then at the woman striding smoothly towards it, her rich blue warden's robes somehow stately at this moment if no other, holding the chalice before her. Through the ring of Saeren she passed, as deftly as if no green-robed women had been kneeling there at all ... and Amnaedra found herself gazing at the chalice.

It was old and battered, its once-ornate chased decorations so worn and pocked from falls and blasts and ungentle handling that it looked like the ancient armor that hung in some of the older halls of the Arculum. It was as large as the warden's torso, and she staggered under its weight and let it fall back against her body as she let go of it with one hand, raising that slender arm to the floating gem as if in supplication.

Many small jewels winked on her fingers and across the back of her hand, strung on their lace-like net of wires – and the gem high above her flashed white spell-light back at them.

Flashed, quivered once, and then descended like a softly falling star, dropping into the chalice so gently that no sound of its landing could be heard.

The warden turned slowly, her expressionless face lit from below by the glow of the stone, and bore the chalice out of the room, treading slowly. Proudly.

Amnaedra felt that same pride as she watched that blue-robed back dwindle down the passage. The Call of the newly-enchanted stone thrummed within her with an echoing song of its own, and as always, there was a lump in her throat. Truly, there was nothing more glorious than being a Stormsinger.

The woman in the blue robe had set a slow, steady pace up from the harbour, but she slowed even more now, in the shadow of this frowning cliff on a high shoulder of the Stormfang, where the path lead up to a tapestry as large and high as a great castle gate.

She turned to watch the throng of dusty, travel-robed women trudge up to assemble before her. Silent, faces weary but alight with a wary excitement, they gathered close together under her silent gaze, here where the steep path levelled out. None of them dared to stray past her.

When they were all close-gathered, the woman of the Arculum turned again to face the tapestry. Storm-grey it was, as wind- and water-lashed as the rocks around it, and of like hue. It hung within an arch as rough as any cave-mouth, and bold across its weathered expanse was a device in silver-blue on black, of a feminine human left hand reaching up for a hovering gem.

The woman in blue raised her hand and murmured something – and tiny gems set here and there in the tapestry winked with sudden light, silent flashes that heralded a soft rising up into darkness.

As that great curtain ascended, a plain pair of tall, stout iron-strapped wooden doors was revealed – and promptly parted, opening inward with no chain-rattle, shouts, nor visible guards, to reveal a huge chamber beyond, like a great cavern let into the side of the mount.

More than one of the women gasped. Many-pillared and high-ceilinged it was, floored in glossy, unbroken black tile – and aglow with the lambent gleam of thousands of gems set into the walls and pillars.

The warden led them into the room and then slipped to one side, gesturing open-armed to bid them continue across the great, gleaming expanse.

A few heard the doors softly close behind them, and looked back to see the blue-robed woman standing calmly beside the closed way out.

At about the same time the utter darkness at the far end of the hall melted away into cavernous dimness, to reveal a lone figure standing facing the throng.

Another woman, this one in robes of black. She looked tall, imperious – and unfriendly. Silence and apprehensive stillness fell together.

Into it she of the black robe sent her voice, flat and confident and cold. "Behold the Hall of Stars. Here traders and those who would gawk may come, but no farther. You have professed interest in joining the Arcrae, and some few of you may be fit to do so. Disrobe, every one of you, and leave all you brought on the floor about your feet. You'll have need of nothing from the wider world here in the Arculum."

There came uneasy silence after her voice stopped. No one moved.

Though she moved not a muscle, the black-robed woman seemed to grow taller. Her voice came again, its sharp thunder magnified by dozens of flaring gems on the walls around her. "*Disrobe!*"

Everyone flinched, and some of the women even shrank away, covering their faces with their hands. The hall plunged into a sudden flurry of hastily letting fall satchels and kirtles, unlacing and unbuckling – all save for one figure among the travelers, who stood trembling.

Light stabbed out in a beam as bright as the noon sun, straight across the room like a speeding spear from a gem at the throat of the black-robed woman, to strike the full-garbed traveler … who was seen to be caught with fingers on the hilt of a half-drawn knife.

"Did you truly think to deceive us?" Her voice dripped with cold contempt. "Are we seen as such witless mystics as that? *Who sent you?*"

The thunder of command rang in that demand, but the traveler's reply was inarticulate, choking in the thrall of the bright magic that now lifted one boot and then the other, thrusting the struggling form into the air above the heads of the staring, half-undressed women all around.

"Ah," the black-robed woman said scornfully. "Thannard. Again."

She sighed, waved a disgusted hand – and a dozen beams of gem-light lanced out from her fingers to smite the traveler. Boots, belts, clothes and all melted away from the arched, convulsing body, a ragged cry of pain rising as the drawn knife flared into flames ... and a naked man hung in the air, blackened fingers falling away from him with the molten metal that had been his weapon.

The crowd of women gasped – and in the next instant the man was hurled the length of the chamber, tumbling along above their staring faces trailing a despairing cry.

He crashed into the doors hard enough to shake them, and abruptly fell silent. The warden calmly stepped aside to let the broken and bloody body fall.

Something larger than any man promptly flashed down out of the darkness overhead, swooping on bat-like wings to pounce on the huddled remains. It lifted a featureless, many-fanged face to regard the watching women for all the world as if it had eyes, blood wet on its long, cruel talons.

Some of the women trembled in silence, but others wept in fear as it seemed to *loom* towards them, leaning and stretching – and then was gone, bounding back up into the gloom above as swiftly as it had come.

The dead man was gone, leaving behind only a small pool of blood where he'd fallen.

The blue-robed warden stepped calmly forward and held out one hand, fingers spread and palm down. There came a brief glow of magic from the gems on her fingers ... and the blood on the floor simply melted away.

The women stared at where it had been, or fearfully up where the great gargoyle-beast had gone – and then spun around as if slapped with a whip by the cold, calm voice of the woman in black.

"No man may pass beyond the Foredoor," she observed, "for it is the Way." She stared back at them, her gaze as sharp as any sword drawn in challenge, and added softly, "I am of the Marae, what folk down in town call 'the Masters.' I gave you an order – and in the Arculum, orders are obeyed."

She fell silent and glanced at one traveler and then at another, obviously waiting – and there followed a sudden frenzy of movement as fearful hands stripped off a last few garments … and promptly clutched bared arms and shoulders, amid much wincing and trembling.

The black-robed woman smiled thinly. "I am Mara-Daethele. Years ago – many years ago – I stood as you do now, shivering. The Hall of Stars is always cold, for some reason. I chose to pass the Mara that day, walking on through the Foredoor to join the Arcrae … and I was found fitting."

She gestured into the darkness behind herself, and then added in almost kindly tones, "If you'd rather not walk past me, take up your things and depart. There's no shame in reconsidering, only in doing things without sufficient thought. If you hope to become what the wider world calls a Stormsinger, walk on past me, and follow the gem-light."

Chilled bodies wavered. Swallowing, some of them still trembling visibly, women here and there in the crowd started forward. One lingered to trace the slender golden gleam of a neck-chain – a family relic or remembrance – and then reluctantly laid it back down, took a deep breath, and followed, as the Mara watched. Then all the women were moving.

None turned back.

When the chamber was empty, the Master nodded across the strewn floor to the blue-robed warden, who inclined her head in silent answer and lifted her hand in a signal – and as the doors began to open, the winged monster swooped down once more.

Cradling the gnawed and dripping remnants of what had been a man, it flew out through the opening doors with blood-wet fangs. The warden waved her hand again, and in its wake, all the droplets of fresh blood flared into little puffs of flame and were gone.

Amnaedra had discovered the ledge high in the vaulting of the Hall of Stars only this spring, but now the long and torturous route to its high vantage-point was one of her favorites, for even when dark and deserted of all but the ever-present perching frozen garaunts, the great chamber almost hummed with restless magic. Thousands of enchanted gems were embedded in its pillars; their collective power was enough to make the skin of one skulking Saeren tingle all over.

When a Mara stood in the Hall and called the gems to life, the surge was enough to make Amnaedra gasp in ecstasy.

Pressed against the cold stone in her leathers, she watched it all, slipping away like a nimble spider only when the last of the newcomers passed through the Foredoor. Small and slender, she moved as swiftly as she safely and quietly could. It was a long way back to where she'd left her robe, and still longer to her study, even for one who knew the hidden ways that honeycombed the Stormfang as well as she did.

Countless passages – natural fissures whose walls were scored with many ledges, as if the gigantic hand of one of the Watching Gods had long ago taken hold of the Stormfang and half-torn it wider, as a man scorning to save the sweet juice starts to pull asunder a maggoth-fruit – linked the caverns and carved chambers to the sky outside the mountain, and with pools deep beneath the earth.

Amnaedra had found a fallen glow-gem long, long ago, and with it spent years exploring. The passages were where she liked to go to study tomes of magic, or to be alone, or just to wander. Garaunts in plenty sat frozen and immobile here and there in these hidden ways – but as long as she avoided the oldest, deepest passages beneath Old Tower, she never saw anything more dangerous gliding or lurking.

Feeling excited and restless in the echoes of magic still washing through her, Amnaedra came to the ledge where she'd left her robe and swiftly stripped off her leathers, ignoring the dozens of motionless perched garaunts all around her. She bundled the leathers hastily together, thrust them in a ball deep into the crevice that one end of her favorite ledge dwindled into, scraped her soft slippers dry of mud on the rough edge of the ledge, turned to pluck up her robe – and froze.

It was gone.

Gone, and – she looked around for it wildly, knowing it couldn't have fallen from where she'd left it, but hoping that someh –

And then gem-light kindled out of darkness and rushed up to snatch her.

Her body sang involuntarily. In a soft white cloud of spell-radiance, Amnaedra found herself flying from the high end of the cavern, where the ledge was, to its lower end … where someone stood holding her robe.

Someone all too familiar: a tall, thin figure known and feared by every student in the Arculum. The most senior Master of all, Mara-Themmele, her rod of office gleaming dark and severe in her hand.

"For purposes of your continuing education, young Naedra," the Mara said in dry tones, "be aware that at any Intaking, a second Mara always farscries the first, ready to raise alarum or provide magical aid should there be wizards hidden among the arriving postulants. I could not help but notice the presence of a certain Saeren whose frequent absences from her study have been noticed – and remarked upon – even by such busy and mighty personages as the Marae of Arculum."

A familiar emerald robe drifted into Amnaedra's grasp. "Uncontrolled curiosity is a good thing in no one," Mara-Themmele added, "and neither is restlessness. You must tame both these failings if you're ever to become a Stormsinger … and master at least one of them very swiftly, merely to be allowed to stay in the Arculum. No, don't stare at me with those great eyes, girl – put your green on, and make sure you fulfill the task I'm giving you as punishment just as well as you know how."

Amnaedra quickly slipped on the robe and belted its sash, her blue-eyed gaze never leaving the Mara … and her mouth never opening.

The corner of the Master's mouth crooked. "Good. You're learning *some* control. Your punishment is thus: you will help Oerbele-Nurmurra show these new postulants a flame chamber, so Nurmurra can give her full concentration to observing their faces as she speaks, and not miss anything interesting."

She looked Amnaedra up and down as the short, sleek Saeren stepped forward to stand before her, hands clasped and tousled head bent in the correct posture of submission, and sighed soundlessly before snapping, "Look *up*, child!"

When their gazes met, the Mara added warningly, "My eye will be upon you."

Themmele waved her rod gently, and it was suddenly surrounded by a cluster of gems, all orbiting it lazily in various directions. They flared into magical light, illuminating the smooth flows of the rod's carved knobs and grips, and its own inset gems – and then suddenly those circling gems all became so many eyeballs, staring unblinkily at Amnaedra. The effect was almost comical, but Amnaedra's throat was too dry for laughter, even had she dared.

Mara-Themmele shook the rod, and all of the flying eyes came to a staring stop in midair, to glare in chorus at the wayward Saeren. "Your conduct had better be perfect, little Saere. *Perfect*, or time as a garaunt awaits you."

Despite herself, Amnaedra shivered.

The Mara's nod was slow and firm in promise ere she murmured, "It's best you please me, Amnaedra – and see to it that nothing happens to me. More than one garaunt has worked mischief on the Mara who forced them into gargoyle-shape ... to be trapped that way forever, because the only person who knew their true nature was dead or enraged at them."

In sudden, icy terror Amnaedra found herself staring at the garaunts perched on ledges all over the cavern – impassive, faceless, and frozen with their wings folded around them – and then quickly looked back at Mara-Themmele, her eyes very large and very blue, and managed her own nod of promise.

Warmed within and without – by a rich broth and brown robes that had been wrapped around fire-heated rocks – the postulants walked wearily into the chamber they'd been directed to by another blue-robed warden.

It was a high-ceilinged, conical cavern, its arching walls and bare floor smooth-carved out of solid rock, and was flooded with light that came from no visible source. At its heart, a great fang of stone jutted up into the room – a fang that had been carved into an exquisitely-detailed model of a many-towered building, or complex of inter-connected buildings, perched on a pinnacle of rock.

The Stormfang! The brown-robed women peered at it in wonder, their hesitancy forgotten as they crowded around the carving to peer and marvel.

"Good, isn't it?" a pleasant voice asked, from the back of the chamber.

The postulants looked up in time to see a last fading twinkle of the gem-light that had heralded the speaker's appearance out of the empty air.

She was a barefoot woman clad in clinging garments of rich ruby red, and was striding towards them with cat-like grace.

Fearfully, the nearest postulants shrank back, retreating from the carving entirely as the woman in red smiled lazily and strolled around it. Her smile broadened. "You are now here," she announced, pointing at the top of one miniature tower, "in the upper levels of Garaunt Tower."

As she spoke, there came a deep thudding sound from high above, somewhere beyond the ceiling, followed by a brief shriek of stone grating on stone. More than one postulant glanced up apprehensively.

The red-robed woman smiled again. "The garaunts are usually as still as stone, but they *are* alive. They are our guardians, our errand-runners, our sentinels, and – though they cannot speak – our heralds. I'm sure you've heard of them. Folk across the Dozen Realms spin gory fireside tales about them: faceless winged creatures of stone with jaws and talons, who swoop down to rend, or lash with long whips. True enough. Yet despite what you may have heard, they serve us, and slay only at our command."

She straightened, and her voice became suddenly brisk. "There's much to learn here in the Arculum. I am Oerbele-Nurmurra, which is to say I am of the Oerbele, commonly called the Dancers, and so my robes are, as you can see, of the hue we call 'dragonblood.' You are novices, so your robes are brown. Get used to being called 'Novice,' or nothing at all, until you become accepted as students."

"When will that be?" one of the boldest newcomers asked, a little hesitantly.

Nurmurra smiled again, and spread her hands in a "who knows?" gesture. "When we deem you ready."

She began to slowly circle the carved model of the Arculum, her every step graceful. "All advancement within the Arcrae occurs when 'we' deem someone ready. Everyone begins as brown-robed Novices, and then become Saeren, and wear robes of emerald green. When a Saere has mastered enough learning to work simple enchantments – and the right temperment to be allowed to do more – she'll be given robes of flame – what folk of Dlethdrake call 'oraunge'– and be called a Laeraeke. If a Laera masters enough magic to work complex enchantments, she becomes a dancer, like me."

She stopped, striking a pose apparently out of unthinking habit, and added, "You'll see Arcrae in other robes of office, who outrank we Oerbele: blue for the Starmae or Wardens, who enforce discipline and represent us down off the Stormfang –" she waved at the model of the mountain – "and Black for the Marae or Masters, who keep our most powerful secrets, and teach them to a few. Then there is one of us robed in white-and-gold, which we call 'sunfire.' That one is the Raegrele, master over us all. Absolute master. The Way tells us that no Stormsinger shall defy the Raegrele and remain of the Arcrae. In the days ahead you'll be firmly informed of many rules, great and small, and you'll grow very used to hearing the words 'it is of the Way.'"

The boldest novice frowned. "What is this …'Way,' exactly?"

Nurmurra nodded approvingly. "Life here in the Arculum is governed by rules, enforced by the wardens and set by the judgements of the Raegrele and the Marae. For instance, the Way decrees that no man – not even the Arculum's trader, Stanmaer, whose ship brought many of you here – may enter our towers. Men have their magics, the spoken spells of wizards … and we have our gems. In smaller, everyday matters, the Way allows us to wear storm-grey overcloaks when weather is harsh, but our sashes must be of the hue of our rank."

The dancer took a step towards them and added firmly, "I know the wider world says many harsh and wild things about us, and that some of you have come here because you're unhappy with the laws of your lands or the strictures of your elders. Know that defiance and wayward willfulness are not tolerated here. If you find this unacceptable, speak to any warden to regain your belongings, and freely depart."

She turned back to the model, and plucked off the upper part of another tower, holding it up in the palm of her hand.

"Now this," Nurmurra continued, smiling at the delighted gasps of the novices as they stepped forward for a better look, "is Sea Tower – where you'll live for the next few seasons, at least." She spun back to the model once more, to point into the miniature room revealed by the removal of the tower. "And this is the Long Hall, where the Arcrae assemble when the stones sing. When you hear the walls moan, move quickly. Unless they speak of another place, this is the room to which you should come – as fast as you safely know how."

"What's in the other tower?" a novice asked curiously through the murmur of consternation that followed Nurmurra's words, bringing her hand down to hover above the thickest, lowest miniature tower.

The dancer's smile turned wry. "The Marae, and our oldest secrets: the libraries, the Nightvault, and the flame chambers where we Oerbele work. That's Old Tower."

Although she hadn't touched the model, the novice snatched her hand back from it hastily, as the room resounded to a collective gasp of indrawn breath.

Nurmurra's smile became more crooked. "I see you've heard tales of our hauntings. The lurching, slithering, all-devouring Thob, long dead but yet alive. The moaning ghosts of the women we devour."

Pale faces stared fearfully and mutely back at her.

The dancer sighed wearily. "Know this: *none* of us eat the flesh of novices or anyone else. Not even with sauce."

High King Harule of Dlethdrake had six sons, and in the opinion of the grey-bearded man who sat facing them from behind his gleaming desk, that was at least three too many.

Like young lions they strode about his study, black-browed and imperious, hands never far from gleaming golden sword-hilts, magnificent in their silks – and strutting in their restless power. Full of bluster, but empty of attention and comprehension … and all too short of wits.

For the fourth time, the wizard tried to drag them back to the topic that mattered.

"The women are *dangerous*, I tell you!" he snapped. "Every season they're left undisturbed is more time for them to weave their magics, and build an army of garaunts! Someday – someday *soon*, I fear – they'll storm forth and lay waste to all the kingdoms of men! And we let them be! Here, at our very gates!"

One of the princes clutched his gold-hilted blade and looked involuntarily over his shoulder at the west window, but the others threw up their hands in exasperation.

The eldest, Prince Haelur, leaned forward and planted hairy-fingered hands that glittered with massy rings of worked metal on the wizard's desk. "*Enough* doom, Tharammus! Tell us plain, leaving out all the terror-tales: what exactly is it that these women *do?* We never see them outside their towers, they do no mischief I can see, they buy fish and meat and maggoth-fruit in the markets of Sespral just as we all do, in markets across the Dozen Realms, and the years pass, and the gods strike me down if *we* see any army of flying talon-beasts! *Speak*, Tharammus!"

"They work strange magics," the wizard said sullenly.

"So do you," another prince snapped. "D'you just want to be rid of rivals in magic? Or do you look to seize what they have, to make your own lore – and hire-price to my father – greater?"

"Lord Prince Laram," Tharammus said stiffly, "you have wits enough to need not *my* lore to know how much good gold flows from the treasuries of Dlethdrake each year to buy glow-gems, and healing stones, and clearwater crystals."

"So you'd have us sword those who make them, and be left with *no* supply, hey? Beggar our lives in the realm to make the vaultkeepers of the treasury happy?"

The youngest prince said loudly, "We always end up snarling at each other like dogs. Let this cease. *Now.*"

It was rare to hear the high voice of Renthus raised when his brothers were in the room, and a surprised silence fell. Into it, Renthus

said crisply, "Tharammus, pretend we're outlander traders whom our
father has ordered you not to deceive in the smallest way. We know flat
nothing of the Arculum, and you must answer our stupid questions
simply and clearly, but holding no shred of the truth back, and twisting
nothing. So: how do the women of the Arculum work magic?"

The greatest wizard in Dlethdrake regarded the young prince
thoughtfully for a moment, and then nodded and replied calmly, "They
sing and dance, building enchantments within flame, and putting these
magics into gemstones."

"Which they sell?"

Tharammus raised one finger. "Only three minor sorts: stones that
can be commanded to give light, stones that can close wounds and heal
by touch, and stones that purify what they are immersed in: glow-gems,
healing-stones, and clearwater crystals."

"The rest?"

"They keep, to unleash magics as they desire."

"And do they come here to do so, or to any other of the kingdoms
of men?"

The wizard hesitated, and then said reluctantly, "Not that we can be
sure of, no. But we suspect –"

"All men suspect things. All wizards suspect much," Prince
Renthus said flatly. His brothers watched him with arms crossed,
nodding and frowning. "So tell me how this Arculum came to be."

Tharammus did not – quite – sigh. "More than a thousand years
ago, a she-wizard fled the kingdoms of men. She was the One Who
Sang Her Spells, Tsangara by name. She spell-tamed the garaunts, and
they built a tower for her on the bare rock of the seamount we call the
Stormfang. Malcontents and witches came to her, outlaws and hags,
fleeing the laws and rule of many lands, and in time a house of spell-
weaving women came to be."

"While our warriors and wizards did – what?"

"Went up against the Arculum to scour it out, and were hurled
back, time and again, by the storm winds they called up, singing together
– and by ravening blasts of hurled, exploding gems, and by the claws
of the garaunts."

"So they've had power enough to withstand every attack?"

"Yes," Tharammus admitted unhappily, seeing full well where this was heading.

"Yet," Prince Renthus said, as softly and as dangerously as his father the king was wont to, "you expect us to succeed now where we've failed before? *Why?*"

The wizard drew in a deep breath, and said carefully, "I – I fear that if we tarry longer, their power shall be ungovernable. Nothing stands between the Stormfang and Sespral Bay, and we of Dlethdrake, but a barren, rocky shore –"

"Save the fishing-ports of Wael and Pelruus and Tsimbur's Spar," Prince Laram murmured, leaning back against a pillar. "But continue. Our Westmarch begins at Starmshar harbour, and men standing on its wharves can see the Stormfang, yes. We are closer than Thannard, and Tarsarma, and Brasenoy – but the Realm of Dragonkings has always been mightier far than those lands, and bids fair to remain so. The Arculum belongs to no kingdom, and keeps to itself; why should we thrust at it now, and risk it allying with our rivals against us?"

"Indeed, how can a few women shut up in stone halls do aught else, if we come against them, but look to other lands?" another prince growled.

"Tharammus," Laram asked, "do you hound us now because our father sent you forth burning under the lash of his tongue, as it uttered these same objections?"

The mage slammed his hand down on the desk, eyes kindling. "Will none of you *see* it? These women work magic *anyone* can unleash, who holds one of their gems and knows the right Word of Unleashing! Any killsword in the hire of Thannard could come to court a-hunting your father, and –"

The largest and most darkly handsome of the princes pounced. "Aha! So *that's* it! You hate these women because they can hand magic to any of us to use, without our needing *you* – and other overpaid, overbearing wizards like you!"

"Lord Prince Meldar," Tharammus said icily, "have a care for your tongue. Were such words fall from the lips of one not of the Blood Royal, I would smite that speaker down in any instant. I outline a clear danger to the realm, and you –"

"*Cease* all snarling," Prince Renthus said sharply. "We can all think of many clear dangers to Dlethdrake, and we spend much time guarding against some of them. Yet this spell-college of women sits alone and quiet, and I still know too little about it to call it a clear danger, just because Mage Royal Tharammus rages and cries doom once more. Let us return to simple questions, and clear answers! Why, tell me, are these Arcrae all women? Because this Tsangara made it so, aye, but why?"

The wizard shrugged. "Better singers. Better dancers. And because, I suppose, she had drunk more than her fill of having men with swords and crowns telling her what to do."

Prince Meldar frowned. "Singers? Dancers? Do they truly work magic by dancing about, then?"

"They do."

"So all we'll find, if we burst into the Arculum right now, are a few lonely-for-men dancing girls?"

"No," the Mage Royal said patiently, "they have what they call their Bound Beasts: work-trolls, griffon steeds, doorserpents – and the garaunts I cannot warn you about strongly enough! I've seen a garaunt tear a man apart with one taloned hand, plucking him from his saddle as casually as you snatch ripe sarnrinds from a passing platter! I –"

"Yes, yes, the stone gargoyles are formidable, we grant ... and yes, I grant we know not their true numbers. Do you?"

"Ah –"

"*Tharammus!*"

"No."

"Can you not spell-scry into yon few towers, then?"

"No wizard can. They have some magic that cloaks the entire Stormfang in darkness, to all spells that peer and pry."

Prince Haelur waved a large and capable hand. "So before we sharpen our swords, send in some women to join these Stormsingers, and spy on them from within."

"Oh, Princes of Dlethdrake," the Mage Royal said with a sly smile, sitting back and regarding them across the gleaming width of his desk, "believe me: I've already done that."

"Not all of the Arcrae come to us as you have," Nurmurra told the novices, as they assembled around her in another room.

This one was just as conical and smooth-walled as the room with the model, but held no central rock. A brazier stood at that spot instead, burning with smokeless deep blue flames, and a long table curved along the far wall with several old, thick, well-used books laid open on it.

A short, slender young girl with dusty black tousled hair and emerald green robes stood a few paces beyond the brazier, as if guarding a wooden box that rested on the floor behind her. She gave the novices a silent, friendly smile, her blue eyes large and bright.

"This," the dancer told the brown-robed women, "is a flame chamber – which is what we call the heavily-spellbound rooms where we work magic, experiment with enchantments, and practice casting them. And this is Saere-Amnaedra, who was born to one of the Arcrae, and has grown up among us."

Amnaedra let her smile grow, nodded her head in greeting, and told the novices, "As is the Way, I know not who my mother is, nor my father. I'm a Saere, and have a rather, ah, raw singing voice – so if *I* can work magic, so probably can all of you."

"You've all heard that we capture magic in gems here in the Arculum," Nurmurra continued. "It's a process both difficult and deceptively simple. If we were going to enchant a gem, it would be suspended a certain distance above this brazier right now, resting on a web of fine cords." She lifted one long arm gracefully to point, and added, "Notice the hooks set into the walls all around the room."

Amnaedra went to the table, and laid her hand on one of the books there. "Particular woods must be used in a brazier when working gem-magic, and the flames seasoned with the right mixtures of substances. Successful mixtures are set down in books like these, as are notes about songs and dances that have worked for some Arcrae."

Nurmurra smiled. "And that's why no wizard can control us, and no realm need ever fear Stormsingers riding to war against them. For every dancer – or group of dancers working together – the dance is different, the song also. We all enchant gems in slightly different ways, because our bodies make our dancing and singing subtly distinct from each other."

She whirled her body around in a sudden flourish, dancing around Amnaedra as the Saere came back towards the brazier, and added, "A dancer must *feel* the flow of the magic. Those who cannot become our cooks and chambermaids and artificers, retaining their brown robes lifelong."

By then the boldest novice, of course, had a question. "Who decides what magics we ... ah, you ... work?"

"All of us are allowed time to experiment, and assigned time to practice under supervision," Nurmurra replied. "The Laeraeke and Oerbele must all produce certain numbers of gems that heal, purify, or glow, in a given time – for these sorts of gems bring the coins that keep us all fed and supplied."

"Do magics ever go wrong?"

"Of course. That mark on the floor by your foot is all that is left of one overly ambitious Laeraeke."

The boldest novice almost jumped back from the small stain, amid murmurs of alarum.

"And this," Amnaedra added brightly, lifting the empty and bottomless box aside to reveal that part of the floor that had been hidden under it, "is – or rather, was – Mara-Joadyl."

The novices stared. There were gasps, at least one shriek, and the sounds of someone being sick.

Something protruded up from the floor, frozen forever in a desperate clawing motion. It was a human hand, the slender fingers covered in dust.

The stores-cellar was so cold that breath curled out from the mouths of the people standing there like winter smoke. The light was blue and dim, and fell not upon the grim faces of the eight Marae who stood in a circle, like so many menacing black monoliths, but around one grizzled man in homespun.

He stood impassive, in much-patched, flopping seaboots and a weathercloak that dripped storm-wet. His belt-sheath was empty of its dagger – which was floating in the air, its point hovering nigh his throat. As usual.

"Well, Stanmaer?" Mara-Themmele's voice was impatient. "*What is so important that you must needs speak to us directly, and not merely to our warden at the docks?*"

"Lady Marae," the ship-captain growled, "there's talk in Starmshar of women who rode down to the inns under royal guard – and some of those same women boarded my ship and came here."

"So we have spies among the newest novices," a Mara said coldly.

"Again," another commented.

"How droll," said a third bitingly. "For this I was called away from the Everflame?"

"*Enough*," Mara-Themmele said sharply, bringing abrupt silence. Into it she said more quietly, "You were right to tell us this, Stanmaer. Know that you enjoy more of our trust than any other man living … but take care that you continue to deserve it. The Warden-Bursar shall grant you an additional nine gold greatwheels."

"Lady Mara-Themmele, y'are most generous," Stanmaer replied, bowing his head. "Have you … instructions?"

"None at this time. Return to your ship, and await the usual wardens."

The seacaptain bowed again, turned, and strode away down the cellar, his dagger following him. He did not look at the two black-robed women he passed between.

As silent and unmoving as statues, the Marae watched him go, until the door that bore the badge of the Arculum – The Hand and the Gem in silver-blue on black – closed behind him.

"You will watch," Themmele said simply, "and if you've the slightest suspicions: do the garaunt dance."

The other Masters nodded, and Themmele stretched out her left hand, fingers spread, towards the floor, indicating that the moot was at an end. Black robes swirled as the Marae turned in unison to ascend the dark passage that circled Bowra's Well. From there it climbed to the Nightvault, and the familiar chambers of the Old Tower beyond.

"Between unruly students and spies," Mara-Ylounra commented tartly, as they went, "we'll soon have this army of garaunts Thannard and Dlethdrake are always crying doom about."

"Between troublemakers, spies, and Ylounra's rivals, more like," one of the Masters purred in the chill darkness, but whoever it was took care to disguise her voice. After a hiss of rage from Ylounra at both the remark and Mara-Themmele's subsequent silence, they climbed on without another word.

There were, however, a few chuckles.

The room the novices beheld this time was small, circular, and low-ceilinged, almost cozy. "This," the dancer Nurmurra announced, waving one slender arm in a gesture that included the curtained-off privy and wardrobe, a central table, three chairs and three simple beds, "is a study. You'll live here, and in others very much like it, in threes, for some time to come – at least until you wear the robes of a dancer. Even then, some of us among the Oerbele prefer to live as we are used to. The loneliness is less, but you must take care to get along with your study-mates … and work no unauthorized magic, for fear of severe punishment."

She took a step towards the door, and then spun about, hands on hips, and added, "Which reminds me: the Marae and wardens have rods of office. If you see something that looks like a carved stick floating in a doorway, don't try to pass it, for it will only be left in such a place to bar passage with harmful magic."

She pointed again, and added, "Yon bell sounds for dinner – a long peal – and classes: two sharp strikes. Have you questions?"

There was some hesitation, and then a short, pock-faced novice asked hesitantly, "Uh, the Nightvault … why is it called that?"

"A great magic was worked there long ago, and now no flame will kindle in it. Only spell-glows give light there. Working magic is normally forbidden in the Vault for fear of … unforeseen results."

The boldest novice jumped in. "The one who started all this, Tsangara – when did she die, and what happened to the Arculum after she did?"

Nurmurra shrugged, her smile faint. "She may not be dead. No one knows her fate – she simply vanished, some seven hundred winters ago. The most senior of those teachers of magic she'd named Mara, a lady by the name of Raegra, took her place. Raegra *did* die, almost sixty winters later, and all who lead us take the name 'Raegrele' in her honor."

The novice glanced around at the walls. "And are there ... tombs?"

Nurmurra chuckled. "Probably. When an Arcrae dies, her body is carried off by the garaunts, none know where."

"Why not?"

The dancer shrugged again. "It is the Way."

Amnaedra crouched on a high ledge in the darkness, listening intently, fingers spread on cold stone as if touching it could tell her things. She suspected the Marae *could* learn things in silence, by touching the stones, but all the rocks told this particular Saere was that they were both cold and hard. Which was hardly news.

In the passage not far below, one warden had just hailed another – and that second one, Amnaedra suspected, had been following the trail of a certain wayward Saere who liked to skulk off along the dark ways alone.

"Trouble?" That was Ilnra's voice. Tall and dark-eyed, no friend to any Saeren.

"It's that Amnaedra again." The softer tones of Bethrauma. "Missing from her study. Off exploring, as usual."

"Again? Sometimes I think she must be a spy for some realm or wizard – she's always *skulking*."

"Part bored cave-worm, part mischief-monkey, more like," Bethrauma replied. "She *can't* be a spy: she grew up here, she's never been outside our gates, and the Watching Gods alone know how many times the Marae have put shield-spells on her mind, to prevent any wizard reaching in to her. The fading tatters of at least a dozen shields must be riding her right now!"

"Well, find her, or we'll have Mara-Ylounra gnawing on our behinds again!" Starmae-Ilnra said wearily.

"*That* woman likes the lash, and finding reasons to use it, altogether too much."

"Mmm, but she seems to especially hate little 'Naedra, for some reason."

"D'you think the brat's hers?"

"No, the Raegrele's, more like."

"*No!*"

"No?" Ilnra's voice was arch. "Remember, she does seem to have a soft spot for sailors … and all the Marae know spells to shift muscles and innards, and so can turn the bulges of pregnancy into a larger bulk all over their bodies."

"I – no, I *can't* believe it!" Bethrauma sounded scandalized. "Marae often cast such magics on their friends and favorites to make them look … better; any of us could have bargained to have a pregnancy thus concealed. The Raegrele? No."

"Well, why else all this attention for one little wandering Saere? She's done more duty-cooking in her young life than some of the oldest kitchen-crones!"

"I've never liked that particular punishment. What if she takes it into her head to poison us?"

"Huh! Not a tureen or a platter, my dear Bethrauma, leaves the kitchens without *three* clearwater crystals being dipped into it!"

"Well, that's a relief … and I suppose our having only a handful of younglings among us – and only one who dares to go wandering through the dark passages alone! – is another."

"You're easily relieved just now, Starmae. Daughter of the Raegrele or not, she's not yet found, is she?"

"So do we seek out Mara-Nevrele, say, or Mara-Olone, and get them to command a garaunt for us – they'll listen to both of us, where they'd tell me to go do my own looking, and so thrust me aside – to hunt her down before Fireroar Ylounra hears of her latest vanishing?"

Warden Ilnra sighed, rolled her eyes, and then said firmly, "We *do*. I think I know where Olone is. Come!"

They hastened together – and like a silent shadow in the darkness, Amnaedra followed, keeping to the highest darknesses, on long-forgotten ledges where books mouldered unseen.

The torch flickered again wildly, and died. Mara-Themmele dropped it and called forth bright white gem-light to make sure the Nightvault was deserted.

It was not. The Raegrele had reached the great chamber before her and stood waiting, looking neither patient nor happy. She beckoned the most senior Mara with an angry sweep of her hand.

As Mara-Themmele strode hastily forward, the Talking Stone at the Raegrele's throat – the palm-sized gem that could translate speech, greatest treasure of the Arculum, enchanted long ago by Tsangara the Founder herself – flashed, and the whispering began.

It built into a roar before the Mara reached her superior, a whispering chorus that would ensure utter privacy for the two women, blocking all magics and the ears of anyone not bold enough to burst in and stand between them.

Themmele was almost a head taller than the Raegrele, but the Mother of the Arculum impatiently used a gem to lift herself off the floor until they were nose to nose, before Mara-Themmele could work a like magic for her. By unspoken accord they let the light fade, and stood breast-to-breast in a darkness that was incomplete only because of the faintest lustre-glows of the enchanted gems they both wore, reacting to the presence of other strong magics only inches away.

"So. Spies. Tell me more."

"Our trader Stanmaer has brought word that sailors who sailed from Starmshar to Sespral after he did believe that our latest group of novices conceals a spy or spies. Apparently some of the women who took ship here were brought to the Starmshar docks under royal guard."

"Will it never *cease?* Gods hurl down Dlethdrake, and Thannard and the rest, too! Bah!" The Raegrele growled deep in her throat, her breath hot on Themmele's cheeks, and then hissed furiously, "I want those spies found and slain – *not* bound into garaunt shape! I grow increasingly uneasy about the number of those who do not wish us well whom we have cast into winged stone-shape and clasp to our very bosoms, *inside* our shields and rock walls, here in the Arculum."

"Wholesale bloodletting sits not well with me," Mara-Themmele muttered, "but I'll do what I can."

"No, Themmele, none of your spending two seasons skulking and spying! Who's to say a woman can't be a wizard? Or handy with a sharp knife in the dark? I want all Marae – and the wardens, too – to mind-scry these novices, right away."

"But the risk …"

The Raegrele shrugged. "So a few lose their wits, or all of them – do you want the Arculum destroyed? Turn their heads inside out if you must!"

"And we lose – worse, we wantonly throw away – the talents of all these women who came to us in hope, just to find and pluck out the few bad fruit among them."

"Themmele, hear me: this is a firm, simple, direct *order*," the Raegrele said grimly. So strong were her emotions that the teardrop gems on her brow flared into light, flickering between the red fire of anger and the yellow-green flames of fear.

Themmele stared into the blazing eyes so close to hers, nodded, and said with a sigh, "I hear and obey, Raegrele. Yet it will be no comfort, if we bring disaster upon ourselves, to know that the mistake was not mine."

The Raegrele glared at her – and then whirled around with a snarl and strode away, treading air as if it were stone. The whisperings suddenly died, leaving the senior Mara standing alone in the chill silence.

A very long time seemed to pass before one of her gems winked, and a ghostly whisper arose from it: "Sorry, Themmele. Remember, please, that I must make all the decisions – not just the easy ones."

"Hunt her down? I should think so!" Mara-Olone sounded angry. "I've half a mind to let it slash her rump to ribbons, to give her something to *really* remember us by! Sneaking all over the Arculum like some sort of thief when she should be studying? *How* long has this been going on?"

"Mara, *please!*" Bethrauma pleaded. A warden does not shush a Mara, but only a fool could have missed her desire for a lowered voice and the swift sending of a garaunt.

"All right, all right," Olone said with a sigh. "When *I* was a Starmae we didn't go all kindhearted, look now the both of you! Naetheless, one of my favorite stoneheads is perched right above us ... *amrael! Soloathyn!*"

Amnaedra stiffened almost as much as the garaunt beside her did, and scrambled hastily back from it as its eyeless stone-hued head swung towards her. Then it spread its wings and hopped from the ledge, arrowing down feet-first so abruptly that Ilnra squeaked in alarm and stumbled back to give it room.

"So-soane," Mara-Olone said firmly, placing a hand on the garaunt. It bent its head until its fangs were almost touching her forehead, and she moved her hand to its snout and added, "*Alossrae Arculum tharandur! Ammathrae Amnaedra –*" the Mara's eyes closed, and the Saere crouching breathless on the ledge above knew she was picturing the face and form of a certain Amnaedra, so as to put them into the garaunt's mind – "*samanthor! Hurleena! Asarrae!*"

The garaunt lifted its head, wriggled its great stony shoulders, and nodded once. Amnaedra swallowed, backing to the end of the ledge. "*Ammathrae*" meant "hunt and capture," if she remembered the oldest books correctly, and "*samanth*" was "back," so "*samanthor*" must mean "bring back to me" ... "*hurleena*" was "hasten," and "*asarrae*" was "healthy," and so must mean a command not to harm.

If she was guessing rightly, that is. If not ...

The garaunt turned its head upwards, and Amnaedra sprang to the next ledge, knowing flight was hopeless: no human could hope to outrun a garaunt in the Stormfang, and this one already knew where she was.

So it would be at least a beating, and more weary days in the kitchens, if not worse … had Olone commanded it to dig talons into her rump? Or –

And then the stone vault Olone had been trying to unseal, its half-undone magics glowing patiently all this while, gave a curious groan – and the door burst wide.

The Starmae screamed in unison, and Olone clapped a hand to the garaunt's leg and snapped something loud and swift and desperate, keeping her eyes on what was trying to come through the door.

Peering down when she knew she should be scrambling like a storm-wind through passage after passage away from this place, Amnaedra saw something that looked like a drifting shadow – like the black gauze veils the Marae wore when a Mara died – *flow* forward out of the vault, and rise up.

It had the vague shape of a person – a head and shoulders, at least, though Amnaedra could see right through it. It moved with silent, purposeful menace, forward at Mara-Olone, and dull gems shone here and there within its gloom.

Olone shouted something Amnaedra couldn't catch – and the garaunt sprang right through the wraith, clawing and biting and … collapsing onto the floor, shuddering and writhing, convulsing with nothing at all in its jaws and talons. The gloom swirled, some of the gems within it winking more brightly – and the Mara levelled her wand at it and said coldly, "*Rethdar aummadar* droon!"

There was a flash of gem-light, a roar of flame, more screams from the wardens … and the wraith was gone, leaving behind a garaunt twisting in silent pain and a wisp of smoke rising from shattered gems in Mara-Olone's rod. The Mara stood white-faced, shaking her head slightly.

"The fault was mine, for loosing such a thing," she said, kneeling by the garaunt to touch it with her rod. She bent her head close over its stony shudderings as if listening for something. Then she nodded, her rod began to glow, and the garaunt's movements quieted.

"Bethrauma? Ilnra? Are you well?" the Mara asked, without looking in their direction.

"Aye, Lady," the wardens said in ragged unison, joining the Mara on their knees.

"W-what was that?" Bethrauma asked.

"A Gembane," Mara-Olone said bitterly. "The very reason we order garaunts to tear apart every Arcrae after death: to find any gems the dying one may have swallowed to … cheat death."

"T-that was …?"

"Once one of us, yes. The right spell-gems, and enough of them, keep the dead person alive, or at least still active – in staggering, increasingly insubstantial unlife. That Gembane must have been hiding here for a very long time."

Amnaedra whimpered despite herself – and the Mara looked up.

Their eyes met.

In a sudden whirl of terror, Amnaedra flung herself around and back into the darkness and faced along the passage, heedless of the noise she made … just wanting to get away …

The Marae told warning tales of stalking skeletons and flesh-gnawing worms and the great Thob: the many-headed, crawling guardian beast that had died a dozen times, but was kept alive by spells renewed by every Raegrele, so that it slithered yet around the lower caverns, rotting and mindless, ready to be sent against any invading force as a great devouring bulk that could block a large passage with its body – and surprise any intruding wizard who might trust in beast-commanding spells with its undead defiance …

But this was nowhere near the lower caverns, and long-forgotten vaults and coffers were the very things Amnaedra liked to peek into, to see what magics she could gain or learn!

She shivered as she sprinted down a passage and sprang up onto a ledge that let her reach a higher, hopefully-forgotten crawl-tunnel, gasping in her haste. Ilnra's curses fading behind her, Amnaedra ducked down an unfamiliar, narrow fissure – and then heard the sounds she'd been dreading: a startled squeak from Ilnra that meant the warden had been struck aside, followed by the flinty scrapings of stone on stone: the sounds of a garaunt gliding and running, scrambling and gliding again, growing closer with frightening speed.

Amnaedra burst out into a crossways cavern where two passages met – ways much larger and lower down than her fissure – and saw a dark crack on the far wall that meant her fissure continued on. She scrambled up to it and plunged through, her gasps loud in her own ears. The Stormfang was riddled with natural caves and fissures that had been sliced through by the larger, smooth-hewn chambers and halls of the Arculum ... so riddled that Amnaedra had wondered more than once why the entire mountain didn't collapse into a great stone bowl ...

No, not now, think not of such things *now* ...

Amnaedra used the glow-gem she'd successfully enchanted, letting it flash once to show her where things were in the now-utter darkness – and came to a swift halt.

Two garaunts were crouched expressionlessly right in front of her. She cringed back, expecting to feel the slices of hard, cold talons, but ... nothing. She made the gem flash again, and saw that the stoneheads were frozen.

So long frozen, in fact, that they were covered in cave-mold, the dark spiderweb patches that grew on dust and cobwebs in the dark corners of the Arculum. They were sitting side by side, nearly filling the fissure, almost as if they were guarding something – but there was room for someone slender to squeeze between them.

Someone like Amnaedra – but *not* a pursuing garaunt.

Clutching her gem securely as she let it go dark, the Saere flung herself forward, scraped painfully through the narrow gap between cold, rounded stones, and – felt the rough stone of a descending ceiling with her outflung hand. She went to her knees, flashing the gem again, and saw no waiting treasure or barrier or lurking monster, but the fissure running on as a small crawl-tunnel.

So she crawled, feeling the gentle wash of cool air on her face. This passage went somewhere larger that took air from one of the vent-fissures that wandered up to the sky, and ...

The floor fell away abruptly, and Amnaedra almost fell with it. The gem showed her a small cavern, narrowing overhead into a narrow crack that couldn't be climbed, and ... ending. She was trapped here, until thirst or hunger forced her to turn and crawl back down the lightless fissure, into the waiting talons of the garaunt that had been ordered to capture her.

And she wasn't alone. Sitting alone in the center of her newfound prison, amid much sand or dust, was another garaunt, its wings folded around it.

It looked *old*. Under a thick coating of dust and cave-mold, it was covered with so many cracks that it seemed almost to be crumbling.

Amnaedra looked at it, swallowed, and then gingerly brushed its snout clean. Laying the palm of her hand firmly on the chillingly cold stone, she took a deep breath and then told it, "*Amrael. Soloathyn. Sosoane. Alossrae Arculum tharandur!*"

Under her hand, the garaunt shuddered – and then, with the faintest of creakings, started to move.

Some of the novices were screaming. Their cries were raw, mindless, and unceasing.

Others howled, or drooled and murmured, eyes fixed on nothing … and those who remained shrank back in terror from the Marae as the black-robed women, white faces tight with distaste, raised their gem-studded rods and approached.

The wardens held rods of their own ready, the gems sparkling and glowing with risen power, in case any novice should try to strike a Mara – and solid walls of crouching garaunts at either end of the chamber prevented any of the screaming attempts to flee from being successful.

With brutal swiftness two Marae caught the arms of the next novice – this one whimpering and biting her lip rather than struggling – thrust their other hands to her head, and began the mind-ream.

No spy yet, but more than a dozen driven to screaming insanity or drooling imbecility thus far.

"This is *foolishness!*" Mara-Ylounra snapped at Mara-Daethele, whirling in a swirl of black robes. "Why look we for wolves among these rabbits, and not seek for someone here already, lurking and skulk –"

She broke off suddenly, and her eyes flashed dark fire. "Amnaedra! *Yes!* Send garaunts to seize her! *She's* who we should be mind-reaming!"

Mara-Daethele nodded and strode to the nearest garaunt. She was
not the only Lady Master to do so.

The Saere and the old garaunt stared into each other's eyes, so close
that Amnaedra's nose almost brushed the cracked grey snout – and a
taloned hand clamped down on Amnaedra's arm.

With a gasp that didn't have time to become a scream she tried to
jerk back. Too late, of course. Her arm was held immobile, as if caught
in … stone.

The other taloned hand swept up. Amnaedra tried to shriek, twist
back and turn, flinging up her free hand to protect her face from being
torn off, and –

Talons spread in a "stop!" gesture.

The garaunt waved them at her, and then repeated the "stop"
gesture, before curling all but one talon inwards into a fist. That last
talon pointed down at the cavern floor.

As Amnaedra looked to see where it was pointing, the garaunt
reached down … and started to write in the thick dust.

Fighting for breath and calmness, Amnaedra watched large, simple
letters traced in the light of her glow-gem: *Tsangara.*

Every student of the Arculum knew that name. The Founder of the
Arculum, the first woman to work gem-magic, the Mother of …

The garaunt circled that name, and with its taloned finger gave that
circle a tail, leading to its own feet, where it … made that tail into an
arrow.

Amnaedra stared at the gargoyle, and it lifted its head and stared
calmly back at her.

"*You?*" she asked in disbelief. "You're Tsangara?"

The old garaunt nodded once, slowly and deliberately. Then it
reached out and started to write again. *Bound in this shape by Raegra.
She long dead. Be my friend? Leave me uncommanded?*

The writing finger lifted to point at her.

Amnaedra nodded. "Y-yes, of course. But I'm hunted, right now,
by the Marae – garaunt-hunted! I'm – they'll find me, and –"

The Tsangara-garaunt held up its hand again for her to stop, and swiftly swiped away its words and scratched out new ones: *Show you dance to hide as bookwraith, if you free many garaunts I select. I must rule the Arculum again.*

"Rule –?"

Tsangara held up a swift finger to its snout in a frantic signal for silence and brushed away its writings, releasing Amnaedra's arm to do so. They regarded each other, nose to snout, and then the great taloned hands spread in a clear, silent question.

The garaunts were beasts, horrible flesh-eating things of stone, all fangs and talons. They were … servants to the Arcrae, silently obedient *things* that the Marae and Starmae sent unhesitatingly into danger or to do nasty or unpleasant tasks. Unruly students were punished by being turned into garaunts, and … a certain unruly Saere would very likely be the next one.

Amnaedra swallowed. Looking into those old, dark eyes so close to hers, she said carefully, voice quavering only a little, "I – I'll help you, and be your friend."

A garaunt's grin is a horrible baring of fangs, but Amnaedra looked into one unflinching, from closer than she'd ever been before in her life. Then there came a brief, insistent tug of talons on her arm.

She followed the scrambling gargoyle across the cavern, where Tsangara effortlessly plucked aside a boulder larger than Amnaedra, revealing a tall, narrow fissure – and plunged into this new way. A taloned hand beckoned the Saere to follow.

There came a sudden, furious scraping and scrabbling from behind Amnaedra. The garaunt hunting her must be trying to squeeze between the two frozen sentinels! Hastily she plunged into the crack.

Tsangara did not lead her far. The fissure ascended sharply and then ducked down and descended in a great slide, almost a plunge, to come out in … a flame-chamber!

Old and dust-covered, yet as well-equipped as any in the Arculum, with benches of brazier-stokes on one wall, and a desk stacked with ancient and crumbling tomes on the other.

The old garaunt plucked a gem from a high ledge and did something to the brazier, which burst into bright flame. Then she raced to the bench and began plucking ingredients, feeding them to the rising fire in a succession of swift leaps and bounds that left Amnaedra shrinking back out of the way.

Mother of All Gems, if garaunts could move *this* fast …

She swallowed. Aye, and who was she watching? The Mother of All Gems herself!

The brazier was blazing merrily now, and the Tsangara-garaunt clapped its hands in satisfaction and raced across the chamber to the tomes. Flipping pages in deft haste, it beckoned Amnaedra again. She came to its side and found herself looking at beautiful writing.

She read swiftly by the light of her glow-gem. The spread of pages set forth every detail of the simple dance that would enable Amnaedra to become a bookwraith whenever she felt the need.

Bookwraiths could hide *inside* books – and books were the one thing whose destruction would sicken almost any Arcrae. No Mara or Starmae would willingly damage or destroy a tome of magic.

A taloned hand waved, and Amnaedra looked up in time to see the garaunt shift its cracked and crumbling limbs in a stiff shuffling. It was trying to lead her in the dance, to help her practice!

Amnaedra gave Tsangara a grin and threw herself into the motions – and the garaunt whirled away to the bench, plucked up the tome, and came back to dance beside her, holding out the book so Amnaedra could read the words she should sing.

Tentatively, she opened her mouth and began, *feeling* for the magic …

Very soon Amnaedra felt the prickling, creeping sensation in her arms and shoulders that meant magic was taking hold of her. No gem for this dance, but only her body … and she could – could see right through her hand!

Amnaedra held up her fingers, wriggled them, and then reached for the book. Her fingers went right through the pages!

Tsangara grinned at her. Amnaedra smiled, and then held up her own hand in the "stop" gesture.

Tsangara stopped, and the spell faded.

"There's something I must know," Amnaedra said quickly. "You need me to unfreeze many garaunt, but particular ones, yes?"

The cracked old head nodded.

"Garaunt imprisoned by Mara-Ylounra, and the current Raegrele?"

Tsangara nodded again.

"So you can regain control of the Arculum," Amnaedra said, thinking aloud. "To regain your own shape, yes, but why do we not – when enough are freed – simply go together to the Raegrele and demand restoration? The Marae haven't enough spells to blast you all!"

Tsangara shook her stony head, and thrust a taloned hand into the brazier. The gem in her other hand flared, and when she stepped away from the flames and moved her fingers, letters of fire were formed in midair.

She traced them as Amnaedra watched: *The Raegrele is a spy of Dlethdrake.*

The wizard Tharammus stiffened above the chaos of rising smokes and glowing glass globes, stepped back, and cried, "Ralavoke!"

His famulus came scuttling to the door. "Master?"

"Something's happened in the Arculum," Tharammus snapped excitedly, striding past Ralavoke to fling wide the heavy tapestries of the west window and look out over the rolling hills of Dlethdrake, towards the distant Stormfang he knew he could not see. "Something's happened at last!"

"*Amrael,*" Amnaedra murmured carefully. "*Soloathyn. So-soane. Alossrae Arculum tharandur!*" The garaunt under her hand moved, a talon flashing out to rake and clutch – but before Amnaedra could even gasp, another talon moved faster.

Holding the newly-freed garaunt, Tsangara said something to it in the hissing, clicking speech of the garaunts – sounds Amnaedra had heard only a handful of times in her life, and always in such short bursts that she'd thought they were but noises made by garaunts moving on stone. The just-unfrozen garaunt turned its head sharply to regard Tsangara and then Amnaedra, and then lifted its hands in a shrug of apology.

Amnaedra gave it a smile and a nod, and scrambled on after the beckoning Tsangara, uncomfortably aware that a growing legion of garaunts that even the stupidest novice couldn't help but notice was following in her wake. And although the Founder of the Arculum had carefully led Amnaedra to outlying chamber after distant fissure, all around the Stormfang, they were now inevitably approaching the well-populated heart of the Arculum.

Where the women who'd imprisoned rivals and foes and the mis-behaving in garaunt-shape were.

What Amnaedra was doing wasn't a clear crime in the Arculum, because no one who mastered the power to awaken garaunts was ever foolish enough to do so without commanding them with clear orders. By giving them no orders but to heed her awakening, Amnaedra was granting them freedom – until, that is, they encountered a Mara or a Starmae with her rod at the ready. Whereupon a certain wayward Saere would be in very great trouble.

They were climbing a curving stair now, a tunnel that was one of a dozen ways into one of the great eyrie-caverns near the root of Garaunt Tower, where many of the garaunt were put when inactive. The scraping of talons and wings on stone behind Amnaedra had become almost a constant slithering sound – and so, as she came out into the cavern behind Tsangara, she saw the flash of talons and fangs before she heard anything amiss.

The eyrie was a great round bowl of ledges studded with clusters of motionless garaunts, ledges riven here and there by the dark mouths of passages – out of one of which hurtled a familiar-looking garaunt: the one sent hunting by Mara-Olone. It raced across the cavern, swooping right at Amnaedra.

From another, nearer passage-mouth streamed three more garaunts, and they also darted towards Amnaedra.

Tsangara clicked something hastily and snatched Amnaedra aside – and from the stair-tunnel, freed garaunts sprang out into the air to do battle.

The single garaunt crashed into the foremost of the other speeding trio, and they wrestled in midair, clawing and snapping. Gem-light crackled briefly around their limbs like errant bolts of lightning as they grappled – and the other two garaunts crashed into them, sending a stony ball of struggling limbs and clapping wings spinning across the cavern.

"*There* she is!" Ilnra snarled breathlessly from the first tunnel-mouth, and Amnaedra saw Olone's furious face behind the warden's shoulder.

"Olone?" another, colder voice snapped from across the cavern. "What're you playing at?" Mara-Ylounra stood in the passage-mouth whence the three garaunts had sped, looking every bit as angry as Mara-Olone. Her gem-studded rod was already flashing with bright-risen magic.

Tsangara tugged Amnaedra back into the stair-tunnel, keeping behind the sudden chaos of darting, circling garaunts she'd just freed, and pointed at Amnaedra's glow-gem.

Obediently the young Saere let it glow – and gasped as she saw the garaunt rake its own cracked flank until blue-black blood flowed.

With a talon dipped in her own blood, Tsangara wrote on the stone wall: "Free us all!" Then the old garaunt wiped its words into a glistening smear and was gone, hurling itself back down the tunnel and leaving Amnaedra – alone.

Gemfire flashed in the eyrie, and the cold, clipped voices of Marae rose in command, speaking unfamiliar – but long and menacing-sounding – incantations.

Amnaedra bit her lip, ran to the nearest frozen, perched garaunt, and gasped, "*Amrael! Soloathyn. So-soane. Alossrae Arculum tharandur!*"

A stony head turned to regard her, but she ducked past it to touch the next snout and repeat her words.

"*There!* Stop her!" Ylounra's shout was high with trembling rage, but Amnaedra made it through the words of unbinding and frantically crawled to the next garaunt – as the air behind her boiled with sudden shrieks of stone on stone, and the crashes of great stony bodies slamming into each other in midair.

Magic spat across the cavern like lightning, there was an almost blinding flash, and the ledge under Amnaedra trembled. Then the long, rolling crashes of shattering stone began, as stricken garaunts fell from the air. A woman screamed, and there were more thuds and more flashes ... as Amnaedra scrambled grimly on, touching snout after snout and hurriedly chanting the words. One garaunt almost hurled her off the ledge in its haste to spring past and join the battle – and right after its swoop, Amnaedra heard a raw, choked-off scream in a voice that might have belonged to Mara-Ylounra.

"She's subverted all the garaunts!" Olone cried. "We *must* capture her – alive, so we can force the spell she's using from her – or the Arculum is doomed! Bethrauma! Get all the Marae! *Now!*"

The Mara's voice rose into a shriek as Amnaedra clawed her way down to the next ledge, not daring to turn and look at the wild garaunt battle she knew was raging behind her – and gemfire flashed again, so brightly that someone else screamed, Amnaedra could see nothing but daze-dazzle – and stones started to fall from the ceiling in a thunderous roar.

Garaunts tumbled and crashed down all around her, and Amnaedra knew she was screaming, too ... as she clawed her way along the ledge of toppling, still-frozen gargoyles, and into a passage.

The Marae were coming, and garaunts were dying and crashing down all around her. She had to get away, had to flee ... they'd slay her now, sure; no beatings nor lectures, it'd be her blood they'd take, before ...

Thunder was rising behind her, and the stone around Amnaedra shook so violently that she was flung against one side of the passage – and then the other. The eyrie-cavern must be collapsing!

She had to hide. The library! A spell-brazier, and books in plenty – the only place she could do that dance and then get into hiding! All the Marae, with the wardens ... and they'd have the dancers out, too!

A garaunt dived at her along the passage, its talons spread wide – and Tsangara whirled down out of the darkness and smashed it aside. Amnaedra put her head down and ran.

"What's –"

"We're under attack! The garaunts!"

"The *garaunts?* But they can't –"

"They're being commanded! The sulky Saere – Amnaedra – and whoever she's obeying! Thannard, or some lone wizard, perhaps! We've got to get her before she –"

Olone's voice wavered as she choked on welling blood. She spat furiously, moaned in pain, spat again, and gasped, "Get her! She's headed for Old Tower!"

"Our magic!" Mara-Daethele's voice cracked like a whip. "She'll go for the gem-vaults! Garaunts, *attend me!*"

The garaunts were racing past her like a stony storm, hurtling up the passage in a spark-striking flurry of wings. Amnaedra choked down her terror and winded weariness, and scrambled the last few paces to the library door.

It wouldn't open without the right password, of course, but Amnaedra had overheard *that* on her earliest wanderings, years ago. The vaults! The Marae were sending those racing garaunts to protect the gem-vaults, with their spare rods and all … against her.

With a little crow of despairing laughter Amnaedra ran across the dimly-lit library to the brazier, scooping up what she'd need as she went. The dance was so simple …

The flames kindled, scorching her fingers. Hissing in pain, Amnaedra made sure she had clear space to dance, and then closed her eyes and started to move, concentrating on the song. It didn't have to be loud, it only had to be *right* … she had to feel it, just so …

Yes … yes …

The library burst into bright light, and there was an angry chorus of mingled cries of "There!" and her name, and the words, "Get her!"

Amnaedra opened her eyes and beheld Marae at the door, their rods aimed at her. Hastily she backed away to the bookshelves, and put a hand behind her.

"She's destroying the books!" Mara-Klathleene howled, waving her hands. "Let the garaunts past!"

Amnaedra could feel nothing behind her – emptiness. She risked a look, and saw that her hand was wrist-deep inside a musty row of books. She took a deep breath, turned, and followed her reaching hand, stepping forward. Her knee struck a bookshelf, but then somehow tumbled past it, letting her into welcoming gloom …

"She's become a bookwraith," Mara-Claere said grimly. "She's *in* the tomes. We can't strike at her without destroying them."

"How did she –?"

"She's obviously far more than a mere Saere who likes to play pranks. Sisters, form a ring about that pier of shelves. Rods ready. Put garaunts before us, in a shield-wall. Starmae-Vrauna, go you to the Reagrele, and bid her bring all the Marae and all wardens here, without delay. *This* threatens us all, and must be destroyed."

Amnaedra hung in darkness, hearing but unseeing. She could move from book to book, with a little wrenching feeling akin to misjudging a step when descending a stair and coming down a little too hard, but … that was all. Where the books ended and wooden shelves began, it was like fetching up against a solid stone wall. A real stone wall stood behind the shelves … she was trapped. There was no way out of the tomes except forward, to face all the Marae.

"How could such a spy dwell among us, for so long?"

"She had help," Mara-Claere snapped. "She was born here, not sent here as a spy, remember."

"Her mother –?"

"As is the Way, we speak not of such things," Mara-Claere snapped, "yet I know who bore her, though she does not – a kindly Starmae, long dead. I doubt many of us remember that birthing. Yet she's *someone's* favorite; no Saere who spends so much time being disobedient and doing punishments learns to command garaunts – or become a bookwraith – by herself! I –"

There was a commotion, then, and many murmured words, followed by the voice of the Raegrele: "You're certain she went into the books just there? And can't have moved to another shelf, or out by any of the doors?"

The library had only one official door, the others being secret panels of moveable bookshelves, but the Raegrele had no time for stammering over secrets when the Arculum was threatened. Various Marae were assuring her that the villainous Amnaedra must still be in the shelves, and simply – by the Mother of All Gems – could not have gone anywhere else.

"That's good," the Raegrele said simply. "Now, Mara-Themmele, take you this gem-key and approach yon shelf. It will swing towards you."

Voices murmured amazement, and the Raegrele added, "Bring me that large black book on the end, there. And my gem-key."

A moment later, Amnaedra heard the flipping of metal-cornered pages, and the Raegrele muttering brazier-stoke ingredients to someone.

"Now, Sisters," the Lady Master of the Arculum said in a loud but calm voice, "we're going to cast a very powerful spell together. It should force our traitor out of wraith-form at the spot where she entered into our books, so I'd like a double arc of garaunts around that spot. Wardens, take your rods and be ready – but strike to immobilize, not slay, until I order otherwise. We've neglected one mind-reaming for far too long."

There were shifting and shuffling sounds, murmurings, and then the Raegrele commanded, "Marae, to me. Though there's no dance, the spell is not a simple one."

Amnaedra cowered in the sightless gloom, listening helplessly as the Marae began a long, complicated chant. Several times they practised it, adding rhythm, agreeing on phrasings, and then – Mara-Themmele's distinctive singing voice could be heard – trying a tune. The Raegrele gave crisp acceptance to the result, and the casting began.

As the song rose, slow and loud and sonorous, there was a stirring all around Amnaedra, and the gloom lightened before her under the assault of gemfire. A restlessness rose in her. Power was surging through her and through the books, the gloom shifting and swirling in slow but quickening flows … and the light grew. She was being drawn forward into it, helplessly, staring wide-eyed as the gloom seemed to lessen into a thin veil, and she could see the ranks of garaunts, and the bright gemfire of the library – and the rods levelled at her, and the tense, angry faces behind them. She was being forced out …

There was a general roar as her face thrust forth, broken by sharp orders from the Raegrele to launch no magic yet, with the rest of the traitor still mingled with the books. Amnaedra stared helplessly around at all the fear and fury, welling tears making everything watery, as wraith-stuff flowed down from the bookshelves like smoke, to dwindle around ankles everywhere. It was flowing up, too, streaming out across the ceiling, curling and growing thicker, lowering like smoke to make the gems wink and sparkle like lanterns in fog.

"Pay no heed to the wrack," the Raegrele said calmly. "It will clear."

Amnaedra's shoulders were free of the shelves, now, her body trembling uncontrollably as it was forced out of wraith-form. The garaunts were only a few strides away, and the Arcrae behind them looked furious.

"M-mercy," she tried to say, the words bubbling from her lips.

Mara-Claere sneered. "Mercy, she cries! What mercy does such a one deserve?"

There would be no escape. Rods were rising behind garaunt shoulders, and brightening into full life; she would be torn apart in their first firing. It was all going to end here, not with a beating and harsh words of warning, but with her death.

"No," Amnaedra whimpered, biting her lip. "I've done nothing against the Arc –"

"Have you *not?*" Mara-Ylounra's voice snarled from the doorway behind the ring of Arcrae. "HAVE YOU NOT? How DARE you say such wor –"

There was a thump and a gasp. Heads turned to see what had befallen Ylounra, who was not loved – and the garaunt who'd plunged down out of the swirling wrack overhead to slam Old Fireroar's head against the wall launched itself at the Raegrele in a great spring that carried it right over Mara-Themmele.

Garaunts were plunging down out of the hanging smoke in a streaming storm of stony, clutching limbs, and Marae screamed. Rods spat futile fire, gems flashed, and black robes swirled in the thick of the struggle.

Amnaedra staggered helplessly forward, out of the shelves, and crouched down, not knowing what to –

"Be still! All of you, BE STILL!"

The great shout was accompanied by a burst of gemfire that sent rays of light stabbing out through the wrack, flooding the room with golden light–and the attacking garaunts froze.

Marae and Starmae all over the room turned to look, or tried to …and beheld a garaunt whose body was covered with a great web of age-cracks holding the Raegrele's throat in one tight fist, and clutching her Talking Stone in the other, the ends of its broken chain dangling.

The shout had come from the garaunt, and it now added more quietly, "You've heard the order. Hear now the consequence: 'or die.' Raegrele, call off this attack or be slain, along with all the Marae and Starmae of the Arculum. Amnaedra is *not* to be harmed."

The Raegrele glared at her captor, one hand drifting towards her sash, and the hidden chain of powerful gems there.

The garaunt shook her as if she was a toy. "Hands away from those gems, or lose them." Its snout thrust forward until its fangs were almost touching the Raegrele's nose. "All of us stoneskins, and Amnaedra, know your own secret, Mraela," the old gargoyle added, "but will keep it – forever – if you work with us."

"Who *are* you?" the Raegrele snarled fearfully.

"I am the Founder of the Arculum, the Mother of All Gems."

"Tsangara?" Several Marae spoke at once, in utter disbelief.

The garaunt nodded.

"Such nonsense!" Mara-Claere spat. "Seek not to cow us with such claims, shapeshifting wizard! Our Founder has been dead for centuries, her –"

A garaunt reached out with a talon and clamped down on her rod hand – at about the same time as another garaunt caught the fingers of the Raegrele, which had been sidling towards her sash once more.

"I feared this," the old garaunt said. "Disarm them. All gems, all chains, all rods – and if any try to give orders to any garaunt, or speak any spell, strike their mouths. Hard."

The stony strength of a garaunt can triumph over the most frantic human strainings and clawings, so it wasn't long before disheveled, hard-breathing Marae, many of them now wearing only tattered remnants of robes, stood in a ring, wrists held firmly, within a circular prison of garaunts.

"Amnaedra," the old garaunt asked, the Raegrele's chain of gems glittering in her hand, "will you do the garaunt dance? It's in the same book the Raegrele was using."

Uncomfortably aware of all the wardens and Marae watching, and the shocked scrutiny of the Raegrele herself, Amnaedra went to the large black book, and started to turn pages.

"I wrote the garaunt dance near the front," Tsangara said quietly. "About six pages in, as I recall."

"The Way expressly forbids Saeren to –" Mara-Klathleene quavered.

The old garaunt's head turned. "Yes. The Arcrae seem to have added a lot of silly, overly authoritarian rules over the years. More and more we come to resemble some corrupt king's court. Mistake upon mistake, weakness upon weakness. No Arcrae should be forbidden to do anything purely on the grounds of what colour robes she wears."

Amnaedra went to the brazier and added a handful of gem-dust, to cleanse the flames of the effects of their previous stoking. Then she carefully added new powders.

"That's not the right –" The Raegrele fell suddenly silent, as garaunt talons tightened warningly about her throat.

"The spell has changed since Raegra used it on me," Tsangara said quietly. "Now be still, and watch Amnaedra dance."

Scarcely daring to believe this wasn't all a dream, and she wasn't going to die in torment, mind-reamed by the likes of Mara-Ylounra and Mara-Claere, Amnaedra gave herself to the dance, letting the song take her. The magic was strong but simple, and left her shaking when it was done.

The wash of power had been so sharp, had felt so good ... there was a collective gasp and murmur, and Amnaedra opened her eyes and saw a tall, regal woman where the cracked old garaunt had been. Tsangara was smiling at her.

"Well danced. I declare you a Mara of the Arculum."

There was another murmur, but it ended in an instant when the Founder raised one hand for silence.

The Talking Stone in her other hand blazed up into sudden fire, brighter than it had ever been seen before, as it carried her words to every fissure and cavern of the hollow mountain.

"Mara-Amnaedra will probably be kept very busy dancing the garaunt dance in the days ahead, but I speak now to all in the Stormfang who wear wings: the choice of which shape to wear is yours, and need not be final. Back and forth as desired is fine with me – for heed me, women of flesh and blood: henceforth, all garaunt are to be treated as equals, not dumb servitors, if they join in the assembly of all – *all*; please carry those who are sick and wounded – Arcrae in the Long Hall, immediately. We have much to discuss. Mara-Amnaedra, take the Stone and free all garaunts now. You'll find the words you need on the next page of the tome, to do so without needing to touch every snout."

Amnaedra did as she was bid, trembling with excitement. She was going to live, the Arculum wasn't going to be torn apart, the –

The library was quickly emptying, as wardens, Marae, and garaunts all headed for the assembly.

When they'd gone, Tsangara let fall her hand from the throat of the Raegrele, who backed away, wincing.

"Are you going to kill me?"

Amnaedra looked from one woman to the other, fresh fears rising.

Tsangara stepped forward. "Your secret, Mraela: has Dlethdrake any hold over you, magic or otherwise?"

"No," the Raegrele replied. "I long ago turned my views away from the Arculum's downfall or joining with any realm, and gave my heart to this place and those in it … and … and I–" she swallowed visibly, and then shuddered and added in a rush, "I'll risk mind-reaming, to prove that to you."

"There's no need," Tsangara told her. "I've never lost my power to drift into dreams, and can see into your mind, if you'll let me, without doing harm."

"Then do so – and you'll see that, though Raegrele no longer, I stand for the Arculum, steadfast."

"I, too," a new voice added. From the deepest, darkest corner of the library where she'd been lurking and listening, Mara-Themmele strode forward. "I, too, renounce my spying for Dlethdrake – as I've done in truth, long ago – and stand for the Arculum … even if it cost me my black robe. Or my life."

Tsangara shook her head and smiled faintly. "I did not say that the Arcrae will stand in any new shortage of either a Mara or a Raegrele. Amnaedra, will you lead the way to the Long Hall? We've some changes to the Way to sort out, and an amusing message to prepare for the wizards of Dlethdrake."

⧡•⧡

Riverbend

by
Ruth Stuart

A licja dug her boot toes into the cracked rock face and pulled
herself to the top of the hill. Crawling forward until only her feet
dangled over the edge, she lay on her stomach, panting. The hill hadn't
looked so steep when she had begun to climb. She hadn't seen an easier
path toward the smoke she had seen rising in the clear sky. *Next time,
I'll search harder,* she thought. *If there is a next time.*

She silenced the voice in her head. With luck, she would find what
she needed here. Without it?

Sighing, Alicja raised her head. Smoke still rose before her. She
forced herself to her feet, walked across the plateau and looked down.
A village, two concentric circles of buildings, seemed to spring from
the rock of the surrounding countryside. She could see people slowly
moving through distant fields.

She searched the hillside for a way to the village below. When she
found a faint path meandering through the rocks and lichen, she let out
a slow breath and sent a wish for luck and help to the heavens. She
checked that her bags were still secure on her back and began
descending into the valley.

Alicja stared up at the carved sign bearing a goblet backed by a wreath of vines. It banged against the front of the inn, its single remaining hinge frayed and beginning to unravel.

She glanced around the village. The stable and livery stood directly across the common. Her stomach clenched at the aroma of warm bread from the bakery beside them drifting past on the wind. From visits to other villages, she knew the remaining inner circle buildings contained a meeting place for the village elders, the gaol and a bartering post. The outer ring of buildings housed the villagers.

She had no idea what this place was called, having long ago lost the map she had "borrowed" from her home village stable master. What she did know was that each successive village had appeared poorer than the last. In some ways it made sense. The land had changed from arable to rocky, the bright green of early growth giving way to dull patches as crops struggled to find a foothold.

Alicja shook her head. From the corner of her eye she noticed someone's curious gaze from the livery. *I've stood here too long*, she realized. She straightened her tunic and settled her bags firmly over her shoulder. Taking a deep breath, she opened the door and entered the inn. Tables ran the length of the room, broken by small spaces to allow the servers to move. A fireplace filled most of the wall to her left. Unlit lanterns hung from low ceiling beams.

"Ain't you a little young to be in here?"

She searched the shadowy interior until she saw the man behind the counter at the far end of the room. As she threaded her way through the tables, he added, "We're not hiring."

"I'm not looking for work." *Not with you*, she added silently. Alicja crossed to the counter and studied him. Broad shouldered and with the look of someone who had been in a number of fights, he continued wiping glasses with a tattered rag as he studied her in return.

"Can you tell me what day this is?"

He stared at her, then said, "The seventh of Stephnis."

"So late," she whispered. *Naming day is only four days away.* Traditionally on Naming Day betrothals were announced, apprentices and journeymen were granted new status, and children were presented to the village. This year it was also the day her father had set for her to find a master willing to take her on. Or else... She didn't like to think about the alternative.

"Chit," the man said.

Alicja looked at the innkeeper.

"What is it you want?"

His brusqueness surprised her. Most of the innkeepers she had met had been friendly, open to her questions about the local bard and her request to play. Those who had been more dour were in villages trying to carve farmland and crops from the rock. An inn's fortunes, and those of its keeper, were closely tied to visitors and the wealth of the village itself.

She glanced around the empty inn, taking in the battered table tops and mismatched chairs. This village appeared to be the poorest she had encountered. Small wonder the innkeeper had little patience.

"Chit," he grumbled.

She heard the warning in his voice. Abandoning her normal questions, she turned away and walked to the spot by the fireplace reserved for bards and storytellers. She had the feeling actions meant more than words to this man. Placing her travel bag on the floor, she sat on the low stool and opened the other bag. From its padded depths she worked free her grandsire's lap harp.

As the innkeeper approached, she quickly checked the tuning, took a deep breath and began to play. As her fingers plucked the harp strings, Alicja closed her eyes and let the music carry her away.

Murmurs of approval reached Alicja's ears as the final notes of *Taryl's Ride* disappeared into the muted noise of the inn. Teo, the innkeeper, smiled and placed a mug of water on a low table away from the fire. Leaning down, he whispered in her ear, "You're good for business, chit."

She returned his smile. Fingers automatically moving to the tuning peg that always came loose as she played, she looked out over the crowd. Alicja had lost track of how many inns she had visited in the months she had been searching. They all looked like this. Lamps cast a warm glow over the smoky room. Men filled most of the tables.

Some drank from rough-thrown mugs. Others talked while playing a game of cards. The oldest villagers, men and women both, sat to the left of the fireplace.

Even in her home village, it was thus. Her fingers began picking out the notes of *Riverbend*, the first song she had played in her village inn. The first song she had written that she was confident enough to share with others.

Would it be so bad to go home? She missed hearing the water when she woke in the night, missed the birds and creatures who lived in the marsh, missed the smell of the seed bread her mother baked.

Her fingers faltered, striking discordant notes until she forced herself to stop playing.

Would it be so bad? She closed her eyes and tried to imagine having those things without her music and stories. To go home in failure would mean losing what she held most dear. *I can't give up yet.*

The sound of chair legs scraping across the floor broke into her thoughts. She opened her eyes to see the men at the table before her giving their seats to another group. The way the others deferred to them told her these were village elders.

Teo caught her eye as he sent his son, Talaran, to serve the new arrivals. Gesturing to her lap harp, he nodded toward the elders. Alicja began playing *Riverbend* again, this time concentrating on the music and pushing all thoughts of her father from her mind.

Alicja sang quietly as she played and glanced around the inn. Many of the tables were still occupied, including that of the elders. It showed all the signs of being a long night and she was no closer to finding a master.

"We may as well show them our bellies. We'll not be able to make the tithing."

She turned to the elders' table as a thin man with a long dark braid over one shoulder held up his hand and leaned forward.

"Peace, Benryl," he ordered.

Benryl's gaze darted nervously around the inn. The thin man straightened and looked at Alicja.

She found herself caught by the intensity of his gaze. He studied her, head cocked to one side. She had the feeling he was trying to see inside her mind. Finally he broke their connection, shook his head and leaned in to whisper to the other elders.

Alicja blinked and dropped her gaze to her harp. Her heart pounded. *Why did he look at me that way?*

She began to play one of the riddle tunes she had learned in her travels. It fit the past and her present. A song of questions without answers. Introspection and searching.

Alicja glanced up to see the man was still watching her.

Confusion and uncertainty.

"I don't know how we are going to manage."

The worry in the man's voice reached Alicja where she stood leaning against the counter. As she sipped her water, she watched the elders, Teo among them, talking in the otherwise empty inn. She could see the concern on their faces, the tension in the lines of their bodies. As Talaran passed, she touched his arm. He rocked to a stop beside her

"Why are they so worried?" she asked, nodding toward his father and the others.

He gave her the same look her brother did when he thought she was being particularly dense. *At least Talaran doesn't roll his eyes.*

"We had a bad harvest," he said slowly. "Tithing Day is nearly at hand and what we don't have in grain must be made up in coin. Coin we don't have. It means another hard winter for all of us."

Her forehead furrowed. "I don't understand."

This time he did roll his eyes. Before he could speak, she continued. "Those villages with more help those with less. That's what Tithing Day is for."

His bark of laughter drew his father's attention. "Who would tell you such a thing?"

She crossed her arms. "My village elders as they took an extra portion of my father's harvest." She met his eyes. "Our grain goes to help villages in need."

"They lied to you."

"My elders are good men – they'd never lie," she snapped. Alicja dropped her arms to her sides, surprised to find her hands had curled into fists.

"Talaran!"

They both jumped at Teo's bellow and turned to face the tables. The elders were watching them with varied degrees of amusement. Teo glared at them. The hand of the man beside Teo stopped him from leaving his chair.

Alicja swallowed hard. It was the thin man with the single braid, the one who had studied her while she played. After a whispered conversation, Teo settled back to his chair and gestured for she and Talaran to approach.

Ignoring Talaran's mutters as they crossed the room, she wondered who this man was to have such influence with the innkeeper. When they stopped at the head of the table, Teo studied them in silence a moment. "What were you arguing about?"

"Nothing, Father."

Alicja glanced at Talaran in surprise. His eyes pleaded with her to say the same. She frowned and shook her head. He sighed and took a step away from her and his father.

"I asked why you," her gaze swept the table, "were worried. We disagreed about the reason."

"What did he tell you?" a low voice asked.

She looked at the thin man. He watched her, his dark eyes filled with curiosity.

"That your village will suffer this winter because you must pay coin on Tithing Day – that you have no grain to spare." After a pause she added, "Sir."

He smiled slightly. "Why could that not be the reason?"

"If you don't have enough grain, it must still be provided. From your neighbours, if not your own fields! In my village, on Tithing Day the elders took an extra portion of my father's harvest." She noticed all eyes had turned to her. Taking a deep breath, she continued. "They told us that portion is to help make up the shortfall from less prosperous villages, like yours, so all will have enough for winter and spring planting."

Mutters from some at the table were halted when the thin man raised his hand. "You know this for truth?"

She found herself captured again by his gaze. Licking suddenly dry lips, Alicja shook her head. "All I know for certain is the extra grain from all farms in our village was taken in a separate wagon. I believe the elders didn't lie to me. And as I journeyed, I saw and heard wagon trains traveling through the night."

"When did your elders tell you this?"

Surprised by the anger in the questioner's voice, she drew herself up and looked toward the far end of the table. She wasn't certain which of them had spoken but she found herself watching a broad-shouldered man as she replied. "When I asked them. They didn't volunteer to tell me."

"Lies," snapped the man. He wore a dark green cloak, his sharp featured face clouded like a sky before a late summer storm. "The girl's a fool."

Alicja's heart began to pound. *What is happening here?* Instinctively she turned toward the man beside Teo. He smiled reassuringly at her before looking down the table. She followed his gaze.

"Be at ease, Cal. It is not our young friend's fault."

"Alberin."

He shook his head. "Not her fault," he repeated.

Cal glanced at her before nodding curtly. She looked again at Alberin.

"Where are you from?"

"Riverbend, Sir." At his blank look, she continued, "It's a full day's ride from the sea. The village itself is on a bend of the Stervo. Above the flood plain, of course. Which is why our fields are so fertile."

"Of course," he agreed with a smile. "You are a long way from home. Why have you come to Stoneweld?"

Alicja began to answer then stopped. She glanced at the men around the table. As in her village, the elders also worked in the fields and businesses. Would they understand her need to create and perform?

Something of her thinking must have shown on her face. Alberin cleared his throat. When she looked at him, he said, "Be at ease, child. You don't have to tell us."

Nodding gratefully, she thought, *If I have a chance to speak to Alberin alone, perhaps I can tell him.* Despite his earlier attention and her uncertainty, he seemed more open than the others and might know if there was someone she could approach about an apprenticeship.

Alberin turned back to the others. "We seem to have confirmation of the rumours," he said. "We can proceed with more confidence now. If we are still agreed?"

The others exchanged glances, each nodding in turn as they faced Alberin again.

"Who will?" one of them began.

Cal broke in. "I will go."

Alberin raised his hand to quell the others. "Are you certain, Cal?"

Alicja watched as he nodded. She could see the determination in his bearing.

"I can hold my tongue when I need to," he replied. Some looked less than convinced until he continued. "We'll need a strong voice to be heard."

Alberin smiled. "I trust you, my friend."

Cal's answering smile faded as he jerked his head toward Alicja. "What about her?"

She took a step away from the table. "Me?" she squeaked.

Alberin did not look toward her as he answered Cal. "When will you leave?"

"I can be ready at first light."

Alberin nodded. "I will know by then."

Alicja tried to take another step away from the table and bumped into Talaran.

"Don't be afraid of Elder Alberin," he whispered.

She glanced over her shoulder. Something in his face made her turn to him. He hesitated, then rested a hand on her arm. "He's a fair man. He'll just ask you some questions. Nothing to fear."

Alicja felt slightly nauseous. When a village elder wished to question you, it wasn't always a good thing. The sound of movement drew her attention to the elders. All save Teo and Alberin were standing. Cal stopped for a quick word with Alberin before following the others to the door. He glanced back at her before exiting into the night.

Alberin whispered to Teo who nodded, stood and, taking his son by the elbow, led him to the counter. Talaran gave her a smile over his shoulder.

"Child."

She met Alberin's eyes. He gestured to the chair Teo had vacated. "Sit with me."

Alicja took a deep breath and tried to calm her suddenly racing heart before moving to perch on the edge of the chair.

"I imagine Talaran told you there was nothing to fear from me."

She followed his gaze to see the young man watching them until his father cuffed him on the shoulder and sent him behind the curtain leading to the cooking area. Smiling to herself, she replied, "Yes, Sir."

"He didn't reassure you, did he?"

She looked at him and found herself caught by eyes nearly as dark as the braid he worried through long fingers. "Not entirely," she said slowly.

His eyes softened slightly. "You've been here two days, Alicja."

"How do you know my name?" she began. She glanced at the counter, then back to Alberin. "Teo told you."

He nodded. "We have spoken." He laid his hands flat on the table. "Why have you come to Stoneweld?"

She let out a slow breath. Where to begin? "I've been searching for someone."

"Who?"

Alicja looked down. *How can I tell him I don't know who I am looking for?*

When she remained silent, one of his hands curled into a fist and bounced lightly on the wood. After a moment he asked, "The best way to find this person is at an inn?"

"It's the only place I know to look." She closed her eyes a moment, deciding to trust him to understand. Raising her eyes to his, she said, "I'm looking for someone willing to take me on as an apprentice."

He looked thoughtful. "In what discipline?"

She bit her lip as she studied him for any sign of mockery. Seeing none, she said, "As a bard."

His hands flattened again. "Oh?"

She could discern nothing from his tone. "Yes, Sir. My father has given me until Naming Day, two days from now," she added quickly, "to find a master." She fell silent, still not wanting to think about the alternative.

Alberin's fingers drummed on the table. Alicja glanced toward the counter to see Teo watching them. He half-smiled and nodded toward Alberin.

"If you don't find a master, what then?"

She closed her eyes. "My father has demanded I give up the idea of being a bard." A tear slid down her cheek. "I am to return home. Concentrate on helping run the farm." Her voice grew quiet. "I may perform during celebrations and festivals but ..." She opened her eyes and looked at the fireplace. "Never again from the bard's spot."

"Is it the attention you crave?"

Alicja met Alberin's eye. "No," she said firmly.

"Then what?"

She took a deep breath. "Bards capture events and places in their stories and songs." Laying her hands flat on the table before her, she stared at them. "The bards I have met have traveled to other villages, gathering new songs and stories from each and sharing their songs in return. They teach other traditions to those who will listen."

Alberin's voice was low. "Bards do not always travel. What would you do then?"

Alicja shrugged. "I'm good with children. I can work in the fields."

He touched a finger to the back of her hand. When she glanced up, he gave her a thoughtful look. "You don't wish to turn your back on that life?"

"No, Sir." She shifted on the chair to face him. "But I want more than just that life."

He studied her in silence as the inn door opened and closed behind someone. Alicja did not turn to see who it was, unwilling to look away from the village elder.

"Will you sing for me?"

She blinked and leaned back. Why would a village elder want to hear her sing? The performer in her took charge. "Of course, Sir."

As she rose to collect her lap harp from the counter top, he shook his head. "I'd like to hear just you."

Blinking again, she sat tall and began taking long, slow breaths to relax and centre herself. When she was ready, Alicja asked, "Is there anything special you wish to hear?"

"The music you were playing when we first arrived, does it have words?"

Heart beating a little faster, she nodded, squared her shoulders and sang.

Pale green shoots of early Spring grain
Struggle to stand against the rain
Villagers gather to watch the ice break
Hoping the waters their homes will not take

Beneath the heat of the summer sun
They work to complete what must be done
And sigh as the breeze, horizon born
Brings promise of relief before the morn

Heavy headed stands of amber grain
Await the arrival of the tithing train
Life grows slow and plans are made
For seasons beyond the sunlight's fade

Snow falls silent, steady and long
Burying all in a blanket of calm
Winter's heart will remain again
'Til Spring returns to Riverbend

Alicja closed her eyes and took a deep breath, remembering something Alberin had said as she sang. Slowly, she looked at Alberin. "I'm sorry for your loss," she murmured.

He sucked air in through his teeth, glancing quickly at the others in the inn before returning her gaze. "When did you write that?"

"Five years ago," she answered, then tilted her head. "How did you know?"

The elder smiled. "When bards sing another's words, they bring their own nuance to the song but something is missing. When we sing our own words," he raised one hand to touch his chest, "the performance comes from here."

She nodded. As his words sunk in, her heart began to pound. "When *we* sing?"

A laugh made her turn. Cal sat at the table behind them. He grinned at her as he reached out and punched the elder on the shoulder. "Tell her, Alberin."

He rubbed his shoulder and rolled his eyes. "Yes, child. When *we* sing," Alberin said as he faced her again. "Bard Alberin, at your service." He bowed to her.

She stared down at her hands. *Why didn't he tell me?* She considered the conversation they had just had. He had asked her what discipline she wished to follow. She licked suddenly dry lips. *Does he think my music is* that *bad?*

"Alicja?"

Slowly, she raised her eyes to Alberin's.

"What is wrong?"

Resting her clasped hands on the table, she tried to order her thoughts. "You seemed surprised I am trying to find a bardic master." Her voice shook as she asked, "Why?"

"I think he was surprised to find you aren't already bound to one," Teo volunteered boldly.

Alicja looked away from Alberin and met Teo's understanding gaze as he walked toward the table. He sat opposite them. "Even my ears can tell you have talent," he continued.

"Peace, Teo," Alberin said.

She brightened at the innkeeper's words but settled again as

Alberin laid a hand lightly over hers. "I must admit," he continued, "Teo is correct."

Prior disappointments refused to allow her hopes to rise too much.

"Stoneweld is a long way from your home," Alberin said. "You have found no master in your travels?"

Alicja shook her head. "Some villages had no bard. They traded information and directions for a song or two. The masters I did find could take on no other apprentices."

The longer the silence following her words stretched, the more tense she grew. She stared at their hands and forced herself to remain still. *Why doesn't he say something?*

"Alberin." Cal's voice was low. "Tell her."

She glanced back at Cal before turning her attention to Alberin. "Tell me what?"

When the bard remained silent, she looked at Cal. "Tell me what, Sir?" she repeated.

Cal leaned forward. "That Teo suggested we hold our meeting at the inn tonight so we could hear you play. Alberin wouldn't believe his story of the talented girl who happened upon his doorstep."

Alicja studied Alberin. He looked embarrassed. "Is this true?"

"I found it hard to believe," he finally replied. "Stoneweld's distance from everything does not make it a popular destination. Nor," he glanced at Teo, "do those with your talent simply drop from the sky."

Her heart beat a little faster. "With my talent?" she asked slowly.

He smiled at her. "Yes, child. With your talent." Alberin shifted to face her. "Do you understand why I asked you those questions earlier?"

She nodded. "I think so. You needed to know why I wish for this."

He leaned closer. "I also needed to know if you understand being a bard is more than performing."

"Yes, Sir. I have always known that."

Alberin's eyes narrowed slightly. "Do you? Responsibility comes with all gifts, Alicja. You were more right than you know to seek a Master to help with yours." After exchanging glances with the Elder, Cal, he asked, "What is your father's name?"

"Daravan," she replied. "Why?"

He held his hands out to her, palms up. "Alicja, daughter of

Daravan, will you accept me as your craft master? Will you promise to obey my requests and my demands until such time as I believe you have learned what you need to know?"

Alicja's eyes widened as he spoke. "Truly, Sir?"

He smiled. "Truly. You have talent. That alone would make you worthy. You have also shown a maturity and willingness to do what is needed to succeed."

She ducked her head, embarrassed by his appraisal. No one had ever called her mature.

"Alicja?"

She saw amusement in his dark eyes.

"Do you accept?"

Taking a deep breath, she rested her hands on his. "Yes, Sir. I accept you, Bard Alberin, as my craft master until you believe I am ready to move on."

"Witnessed," Cal and Teo said in unison.

Alberin's smile widened. "Good. I have your first assignment, Apprentice."

A happy warmth spread through Alicja at his use of the designation.

"You will accompany Elder Calenron to Hopewell and report what you've been told of the harvest tithing."

"Hopewell – the capital?"

Something of her sudden panic must have shown on her face. He squeezed her hands. "You came here on your own. You found me. This is only another step."

She slowly nodded, still uncertain. When he stood, she did as well.

"You should get some rest," he said gently. "First light comes early."

Without thinking, she moved away from the table and walked toward the staircase hidden behind the counter. As she crossed the room, the realization of what had just happened struck her. She stopped and turned toward the three men still at the table.

"Master Alberin?"

"Yes?"

"Thank you, Sir."

Alicja returned his smile with a grin. Turning away, she picked up her harp and bounded up the stairs.

Alicja sat on a padded window bench, staring out at the star-filled darkness. A combination of excitement and apprehension made sleep impossible. She opted instead to enjoy the quiet and the chance to reflect on what had happened to her.

She could scarcely believe it. "I am an Apprentice," she whispered. Bound and oath-sworn. *I think Father will be proud.*

Thoughts of her father drew her back from the stars. *I must let him know.*

She stood and stretched before crossing to the fireplace. Lighting a candle from the glowing embers, she carried her travel bag and the candle back to the bench. She placed the candle in the wall sconce and emptied the contents of the bag into neat piles on the bench, hunting for a piece of parchment. Each one she found was covered in fragments of lyrics, the rough beginnings of songs inspired by her travels.

Alicja sat on the bench again and stacked the parchments. She hadn't completed any of the songs. It would have been too hard to destroy or lock them away if she had failed to find a master. She smiled. She had no doubt Alberin would encourage her to finish them.

A quiet knock at the door brought her to her feet. She crossed the room and opened the door a crack. Alberin stood alone in the hallway.

"May I come in?"

"Of course, Sir." Alicja opened the door wide and closed it carefully behind him. She turned to see Alberin standing near the fireplace, courteously not looking at her things. Smiling as she walked to the bench, she quickly returned everything except the parchments to her bag. She placed the bag and parchments on the bed and said, "If you'd like to sit?"

Alberin turned and crossed to the bench, signaling her sit as well. She did, tucking her feet beneath her. He sat straight-backed at the opposite end of the bench and studied her.

"You said your father demanded you return to your farm if you could not find a master. Does he oppose you being a bard?"

"No, Sir," she replied. "He told me I could learn no more from Mishkel and needed to find another teacher."

He relaxed a little. "This Mishkel is a bard?"

Alicja shook her head. "She can play a little and sings well but she isn't a bard."

He nodded as he worried the end of his braid. She waited for him to say something. The longer he remained silent, the more nervous she became. Finally, he cleared his throat.

"What loss of mine are you sorry for?"

She straightened, startled by his question. Didn't he know what he had said? His voice had merged with her music, not enough to distract her but clear enough for her to have heard. "Your sister. Breyna. As I was singing of the snows, you said you still miss her."

He closed his eyes and took a deep breath. "*Elicevera.*"

Alicja repeated the unfamiliar word. "*Elicevera?*"

Alberin opened his eyes again. Pain lurked in their dark depths. "Earlier tonight Benryl spoke of our inability to meet the tithing," he said.

She nodded. "And you silenced him."

"For good reason. We elders knew but the people didn't. It wasn't something we were going to share until we had a solution."

"Then why did he say it?"

"Because he was forced to speak the truth." He hesitated then added, "As was I about my sister."

"By who?"

He leaned forward. "You."

She felt the blood drain from her face. Her hands began to shake. "What?"

Alberin captured her hands in his. "Many bards," he said, "have a gift. Something more than their talent for performing or creating."

"A gift?" she repeated.

He nodded. "You are *elicevera*. One whose music draws the truth from those who listen."

She looked away. *How could I not know?* She thought back to the last conversation with her father, how it was the first time he had said how talented he thought she was. How she had been playing *Taryl's Ride*. "Why has no one told me before now?"

"They didn't know. Seeing the gifts of others is my gift. I know only one other who possesses it."

Alicja looked at her master. Wounded pride made her voice harsh. "Is my *gift* the reason you accepted me as an apprentice?"

"No."

She kept her gaze locked on his face. Alberin took a deep breath.

"I told you before that you have talent," he said. "That alone would have been enough for me to accept you." He leaned back. "I won't deny your gift is one we can use. I am not sending you to Hopewell merely to share what you told us tonight. Gather all the information you can about the tithing. Rumours, fact, anything you hear. Especially as you play, when their hearts are less guarded."

"When they will tell the truth," she said quietly.

"Yes, Alicja."

She tugged her hands free and turned to look into the darkness again. Being a bard had been her goal as long as she could remember. Now, she was *elicevera* and being asked to use her gift, to be a spy.

The bench cushion shifted as Alberin stood. "Alicja. I wish I had more time to help you understand why I am asking this of you."

She looked up at him. His face was drawn, his eyes tired. "I promised to obey your requests and demands, Master," she replied quietly.

He closed his eyes a moment. "Yes, you did." He brushed her shoulder with his fingers. "Try to get some rest."

When the door closed behind Alberin, Alicja leaned against the wall and stared out the window, thinking.

The light of false dawn found Alicja still sitting by the window. "Almost time to go," she murmured.

What would it be like to travel with Calenron? Once Alberin had accepted her, the outspoken elder had been more open but Alicja suspected that was more for Alberin's sake than hers. Still, he and

Alberin were friends. They would undoubtedly see each other while she was in Stoneweld. The trip would be an opportunity to get to know more about the bard and his village.

When she heard the light knock on the inn door beneath her window, she swung her feet to the floor and collected her bags and parchments from the bed. She would have to ask Alberin if he had another piece so she could write her father.

She blew out the candle and descended the stairs. Before entering the inn, she placed her bags and the pile of parchments on the last tread.

Candles cast a warm glow over the table closest to the counter. Mugs, bowls and spoons were stacked at one end while a steaming pitcher and bowl of sugar anchored the other. Her stomach rumbled as Alicja breathed in the scent of spiced porridge and bread.

She moved toward the three men standing by the fireplace. Teo glanced back and smiled when he saw her. "Good morrow, Alicja," he said.

She smiled in return. "Good morrow, Sirs," she replied as Alberin and Cal turned at her approach.

Alberin nodded toward the counter. "Teo has readied a meal for this morning as well as food for your journey."

Alicja fell into step with him as he followed Cal and Teo to the table. She accepted a bowl of porridge from the innkeeper and sat, waiting for the others to join her.

Alberin and Cal took the chairs across from her. Teo distributed steaming mugs of cider then sat beside her. Alicja sprinkled dark sugar on her porridge before beginning to eat.

"Did you rest?" Alberin asked.

She looked up from her bowl and swallowed before saying, "Not really, Sir."

Cal glanced at her. "I won't mind if you sleep once we're on the road."

Teo snorted. "Keeps him from having to make conversation."

She started to laugh, then looked at Cal.

"Not good at chitchat," he muttered without looking up from his bowl.

Alicja concentrated on eating her porridge.

When the meal was finished, Alberin leaned back and said, "Is there anything you need, Alicja?"

She nodded and collected her things from the stair. Placing the bags on the floor, she sat and handed the parchments to her master.

"I need two things, Sir. Will you keep these for me?"

He flipped through them. "New songs?"

"Their beginnings." She laid her hands on the table. "I didn't have the heart to finish them."

Alberin's sharp eyes caught hers. "And deny others your words?"

Alicja stared at him. She hadn't thought of anything beyond her father's demand she give up her dream to be a bard.

"Peace, Alberin," Cal spoke into the silence. "Consider what you would do if faced with the same choice."

The bard closed his eyes, letting the parchments fall to the table. A few moments later he took a deep breath and opened them again. "You know me too well."

He rested a hand on the pile and looked at Alicja. "Promise you'll finish these."

"Yes, Sir."

He smiled. "You said two things. What else do you need?"

"An unused piece of parchment."

"That is all?"

She nodded. "I need to write my father but –"

"But all your parchments look like this."

"Yes, Sir."

Alberin picked up the pouch that had been hiding behind the bowls. The leather sides bulged, the ties stretched to their limits. The contents crinkled as he turned the pouch in his hands.

"When you arrive in Hopewell, Cal will tell you where to find the messenger service. This pouch contains a number of letters, including one for your father. There is also," he continued, "something for you."

Startled, she looked up. "For me?"

He opened the ties and brought forth a flat, thick rectangle. He handed it to her before closing the pouch.

The object was slightly larger than her spread hand. Hard covers opened to reveal sheets of parchment, bound at one end by leather strapping.

Alicja looked up to see Alberin watching her. "Master?"

"Use this to record anything you wish. Stories, songs, information."

She placed it carefully on the table. "It's much too fine a gift."

Alberin shook his head. "This is no gift, Apprentice. It is a tool of our trade."

Alicja nodded and slipped the book carefully into her bag along with the pouch Alberin handed to her. She stood when the others did.

Alberin looked down at her. "You have your harp? Good. I want you to play in Hopewell but heed Cal. There will be places requiring caution."

Unsaid was the reason why he wished her to play. Alicja silently nodded and slipped the bags over her shoulder.

As they left the inn and crossed to the livery, Alberin said, "We will speak more about your gift when you return."

"Yes, Sir."

Cal returned from the livery leading two horses hitched to a wagon. Alberin helped her climb up. She settled onto the front board beside Cal who took her bags, lashing them with the others in the wagon.

Alberin stretched past her, handing a small parcel to Cal. He stuffed it into his jacket pocket.

"You know what must be said?" Alberin asked.

Cal nodded. "I do."

"Be careful, my friend." Alberin took a step away from the wagon. "Safe journey to you both."

"Thank you, Sir," Alicja replied as Cal slapped the reins along the horses' backs and they began the trip to Hopewell.

A hard jolt woke Alicja. She lifted her head from the bag of sweet smelling grain and blinked in the bright sunlight. Another jolt and she pushed herself up until she sat among the bags and bundles.

Cal glanced over his shoulder. "Sorry," he said. "This road is in worse shape than last year."

"It's all right, Sir." Alicja rose and scrambled onto the seat board. She had fallen asleep moments after the elder had sent her to lie down in the back of the wagon.

When she was settled, he said, "Call me Cal."

She looked at him. "I was taught to be respectful, especially to those in authority."

"What authority do I have over you?"

Alicja grabbed the wagon side as they hit another rut in the road and looked ahead to judge when the next would come. "You are a village elder. You have authority over all who live in Stoneweld. I've been in the village only a few days but that authority must also extend to me. Master Alberin also said I was to heed your word."

He snorted a strange laugh. "Aye, you are a bard."

She turned to him.

"Alberin has the same way of stating something that leaves you no room for argument."

Alicja was still trying to decide if it was a compliment when he said, "It would be best if you didn't call me Sir while we're in Hopewell."

"Why?"

She watched as his dark face turned darker. *Anger?* She studied him, realizing she could not tell what he was thinking.

"Sir? Cal? What could happen?"

He was silent as he guided the horses to the edge of the road and halted them. Both took advantage of the slack reins, bending their heads to eat what remained of the grass.

Cal turned to face her. "You are respectful. None can deny that. You are also trusting, maybe too much so. There are those who would take advantage of that trust."

"What does that – "

He raised his hand and she stopped. "The respect you show could be misunderstood in some parts of Hopewell. And your trust could take you places you don't want to be."

Alicja nodded. She knew the cautionary tales, had heard and seen many things in her travels, knew the problems that could arise. "If I call you Cal," she said slowly, "it shows we know each other and you will … protect me if the need arises?"

He nodded in return. "Among other things, yes."

She stared up the road a moment, wondering what sorts of people and things she would find in Hopewell. Looking at Cal, she said, "I will try to remember."

"Good." He gathered the reins again and urged the horses back onto the road. When they were underway, he said, "We'll stop in Rockhaven tonight. Tomorrow, we'll arrive at Hopewell."

Alicja held onto the wagon side and watched the road. Only one more day to convince herself she could do what Alberin asked of her. Suddenly she found herself wishing she had longer.

As they entered the gates of Hopewell, a bell tolled three times.

"We made good time."

Alicja looked up at Cal, searching his face for signs he was mocking her. He smiled and touched a hand to her shoulder.

"No worries. Alberin and I thought you might have trouble rising early this morning."

Have trouble rising. An understatement, she thought. Rockhaven's inn had been warm and bright, its keeper friendly. Cal had shown her which of the small rooms was to be hers for the night. When he was gone, she had stretched out on the bed's inviting surface to rest for a few minutes. It was her last conscious thought until a cock's crow woke her at dawn.

Cal continued speaking. "Benryl left word at the livery that we are to appear before the Ruling Council the day after tomorrow. He booked rooms for us at the Hammer."

Alicja nodded. Cal had told her the other elder had ridden here after the meeting in Stoneweld to arrange their audience. They would speak during the open session before the Council and Speaker. The Council chose one of its own to serve as Speaker, the leader of their country. The current Speaker had only been in power a few years. She had played *Rest and Farewell* at the ceremony her village held to mourn the passing of his predecessor.

"What do we do now?" she asked. They had left the horses and wagon in the care of livery master and had entered the city gates on foot. She turned her gaze back to the jumble of buildings and the maze-like streets of the capital. This place was like nothing she had seen before. Cal stepped forward and she followed.

"First, we'll go to The Hammer. Then I'll show you some of the places you need to know about."

She stepped around a pile of rags. "Isn't it easy to get lost here?"

"It can be. But if you remember a few things it helps."

The narrow street widened until it became part of an open square. At its centre stood a group of small trees and benches. The surrounding space held market stalls and people. More people than she remembered seeing in one place. Cal led Alicja to the trees, found an empty bench and motioned for her to sit beside him.

"This is the centre of Hopewell," he said. "The major streets meet here, as do most of its inhabitants. If you can find this place, you will never be lost.

"It may look disorganized but there is an order." He pointed to the left. "The merchants' section is down the street with the sign of three coins."

She made note of the sign, then looked to the right. The sign there showed grapes and a triangle. "The inns?" she guessed.

"Aye and the main gate sign bears a horse head."

Alicja's attention was captured by a group of black robed men. Those in their path stepped away as far as they could. The group moved toward the street behind them. She turned to see Cal watching her. "Council members?" she guessed.

He did not answer. "Tomorrow I'll take you to the chamber. The open sessions began today."

"It would be good to know what to expect."

Cal stood and sighed. "Our experience will likely not be the same as anyone else's. Come." He walked toward the inn section. "We should get settled before we do more exploring."

Alicja tightened the final tuning peg and sighed. The wagon ride had
been harder on her harp than on her body. It had taken a long time to
re-tune the old instrument. Shifting until she was sitting cross-legged
on the low bed, she balanced the harp across her knees, took a deep
breath and began to play *Riverbend*.

A knock on the door pulled her away from the music. The door
opened a crack and Cal said, "May I come in?"

"Please do."

He closed the door behind him and sat on the chair. "I have
something for you."

Alicja laid the harp carefully to her side and slid across the bed
until her feet were on the floor. "Something for me?"

He nodded and pulled a small parcel from his pocket. "Alberin
wanted to give you this himself, but he felt it more appropriate to
happen today."

Today? Alicja thought for a moment, casting her memory back to
the day she had arrived in Stoneweld. With everything that had
happened, she had almost forgotten. "Naming Day," she said.

Cal smiled and gave her the parcel. Within the plain wrappings, she
found two metal brooches. One, half the size of her palm, bore a harp
surrounded by a ribbon of metal. The other divided into two pieces
connected by chain. One side carried a scroll and the other another
harp. Alicja studied them, looking up only when Cal leaned forward.

"These were Alberin's Apprentice badges. This one," he touched a
finger lightly to the larger brooch, "is to be worn on your tunic. The
other is a cloak clasp."

Alicja stared at him. "Master Alberin's?" she whispered.

"Alberin told me it is traditional for Masters to pass along their
badges to the Apprentice who shows the most promise." Cal took the
brooch from her slack hand and pinned it to the shoulder of her tunic.

She looked down at it, unable to accept the implied compliment.
"Aren't I his only Apprentice?"

He laughed. "Aye, but not his first."

She met his steady gaze. "I will earn them."

"You can begin tonight. If your instrument is sound and you aren't too tired."

Alicja wrinkled her nose. "I think I've slept enough today."

"Good." Cal stood and she did the same. "Bring your harp. After we eat, you can play a few tunes."

The Hammer's common room was crowded and warm. People lined the walls waiting for a seat to become available. When Alicja moved to the bard's spot, a short man filled her empty chair.

As she quickly checked the tuning, she glanced around the room. It was hard to tell visitor from resident. Most scowled over their mugs or argued with those sitting or standing closest. The only ones not arguing were the old ones sitting at the other side of the fire.

So many people. So much noise. Would they even wish to listen to her? She took a deep breath and closed her eyes. Alberin's voice filled her mind. *"Is it the attention you crave? Bards do not always travel. What would you do then?"*

She touched the brooch and opened her eyes. If only one person heard, it would be enough.

Alicja sat up straight and began to play.

"Extra tithings. Happened in my father's day, too," a quavering voice said.

Alicja continued to play quietly. The inn was nearly empty. The keeper moved among those who remained, checking on mugs and collecting coins. Once he had heard her play, he had kept her mug filled with water and made sure she rested.

Throughout the evening, she had listened as she played, trying to make sense out of the jumbled conversations. The city seemed prosperous. She had little doubt they could afford the extra tithing. Though, as in her village, some people complained.

She watched the old ones sitting to the far side of the fireplace, waiting for another to talk or question the speaker.

"What did it mean then, old Father?" someone from a nearby table finally asked.

The old man looked up from his mug. "The same as it does now." His voice was loud in the silence of the inn. "Famine. Loss. It means war."

Alicja's fingers froze on the strings. No one else in the inn reacted with surprise. She saw nods of agreement and grim looks.

Instinctively, her eyes sought out Cal. He studied her a moment, then signaled for her to return to the table.

She stood and crossed the room. "Cal?"

"Sit, Alicja."

She remained standing. "Is what he says true?"

He took her harp and placed it on the table. "Please sit."

Slowly, she lowered herself to the chair. She clenched her hands on her lap. "Cal."

He interrupted her. "What did Alberin ask you to do?"

She took a deep breath. "Gather information and rumors about the extra tithing."

He nodded "Just so."

"You won't answer my questions, will you?" Her voice came out colder than she had expected. She swallowed hard. "My apologies."

Cal touched her hand. "None needed." He kept his voice low as he continued. "I know you're confused. Remember what Alberin asked of you and make up your own mind."

She slumped and leaned back. *Make up my own mind.* She sighed. *Not something I was raised to do.*

The next evening, Alicja again sat in the Hammer's bard's spot, this time playing without paying attention to the notes her fingers drew from the harp. Her mind pondered the things she had seen and heard.

She and Cal had attended part of the afternoon's Council session. Many of those who appeared before the Hopewell Council had asked for an easement of the tithing rule. Each request was refused with no discussion or question. Alicja could not understand. In their Council,

Riverbend Elders would have asked for more information, debated the request before passing judgement. A few petitioners reported thefts and destruction of crops and their property. These men had been thanked and their names recorded, but with no mention of reimbursement or aid.

She had also seen the black-cloaked men, learning that they were assistants to the Council and, as some around her whispered, tithe collectors and spies. Small wonder people had tried not to draw their attention.

Alicja looked up from her harp as the inn door opened. Two of the men who had reported thefts at the council session entered and took seats at a table near her. She continued to play but focused on them.

When the song ended, she bent her head over the harp, pretending to fix the tuning. The men's voices had come to her as clearly as if they had been seated beside her. *"The thefts haven't been random."* *"The Council won't help."* *"What action can we take?"* *"They have been lying to us."*

Alicja looked up to see Cal watching her and closed her eyes. *Someone has been lying*, she thought. *But who?*

"Excuse me, Apprentice."

Alicja opened her eyes. The Hammer's keeper leaned in close.

"Yes, Sir?" she answered without thinking and winced.

The man smiled gently and said, "The gentlemen sitting near the fire would like to request a song."

She looked over his shoulder to see two men at the closest table, heavy cloaks tossed over the back of their chairs, watching her. Returning their nods, she met the keeper's gaze.

"Do they wish to hear something special?"

His eyes hardened. "They said," he kept his voice low, "Hopewell is too dreary. They wish to hear something festive."

"Festive," she repeated. When he nodded, Alicja sighed quietly. Looking at the men again, she forced herself to smile.

"I would be pleased to play."

The keeper touched her hand as he refilled her mug. "Be wary of such as them."

Alicja glanced at the far corner table where Cal sat. He frowned, his focus on the men. When he noticed her attention, his look conveyed the same warning as the keeper's words.

She took a deep breath. As the keeper moved away, she began to play *The Wedding Feast*.

Alicja sat cross-legged on the bed, her parchment book balanced on one knee as she wrote. She looked up as the door opened after one knock and Cal entered. He pulled the chair close to the bed and sat heavily.

"Is something wrong?" she asked.

He nodded toward the book. "What are you writing?"

She glanced down at the page. The words swam in the firelight. "Some of the things I heard tonight. Impressions of people I've seen."

Cal leaned forward. "The men who asked you to sing. What was your impression of them?"

His voice was tight. Alicja looked at him a long moment before dropping her gaze to the parchment.

"They were confident but secretive. As they talked, they looked around as if to check they weren't being overheard. They said – " She stopped and looked at Cal. He watched her in silence. "Alberin told you about my gift," she stated.

He nodded.

"One of them," she said, "is a member of the Council. He talked of how easy it has been to dupe people. About the council sessions. About the tithing."

She stood and walked to the window, staring out into the darkness. "He spoke of broken agreements. Of defending ourselves. And war." She turned and met Cal's eye. "When others have spoken, the talk of war has been possibility and maybe. When he spoke, it was." She stopped, searching for the words. Slowly, she said, "When he spoke, it was real."

Cal joined her by the window. "There is a difference between believed truth and real truth."

Alicja stared out into the darkness again. Truth and lies. There was no doubt someone was lying. Was it Riverbend's Elders? Or had they been deceived as well?

From where she stood beside Cal, Alicja could see the edge of the dais where the Council members awaited them. The chamber, colorful banners and flags hanging from dark ceiling beams, appeared larger now that she stood on its floor. Those who came to listen filled the seats opposite the dais, their voices wearing on her control.

She heard the Council brusquely dismiss another request for easement and call for the next petitioner. Clasping her hands behind her back to try to stop their shaking, she took a deep breath. She focused on the Council. The eleven men, the Speaker centermost, sat at tables covered with richly embroidered tapestries, while their assistants hovered behind them.

Sensing movement next to her, she was unsurprised when she heard Cal's whisper close to her ear. "Are you ready, Alicja?"

She shook her head.

"Just speak your truth. Remember," he added as the Council's page approached them, "Alberin has faith in your abilities. As do I."

She looked at him. He appeared tired and worried. "Thank you."

They moved forward when the page beckoned. Alicja kept her hands behind her back, her head down. As they stopped before the dais, a harsh voice demanded, "What business have you with the Council of Hopewell?"

"I am Calenron, Elder of Stoneweld. This is Alicja, formerly of Riverbend, apprentice to Bard Alberin, Elder of Stoneweld."

Alicja straightened, reminded of her role and status, and met the eyes of the Council. She watched them as Cal continued to speak. His voice held the same edge it had when he had questioned her the night Alberin accepted her as his apprentice.

"We come before the Council to speak of the tithing requirements. Stoneweld has always paid our tithe in full."

Several of the Council talked amongst themselves. Others read parchments. Alicja frowned. None paid attention to what Cal was saying.

"We are not here to request an easement, despite the strain of extra tithing."

At this, all eyes turned to them. Alicja forced herself to return their attention without flinching.

"Why then have you come?" asked the Speaker. His dark hair was pulled back, calling attention to his prominent nose and piercing eyes. The harshness in his expression suggested he would not be easily swayed.

Cal whispered, "Tell your truth" as he took a half-step back.

This was the moment she had been dreading. Breathing deeply to centre herself, she met the eye of each council member in turn. *Master Alberin believes in me*, she reminded herself.

"My home village is to the east, a day's ride from the sea. We have been fortunate to have good harvests for many years."

The council's attention was waning again. Alicja continued to speak.

"Last Tithing Day, I asked my village elders why an extra portion of my father's harvest was being taken. They told us the extra was to help those villages who could not meet their tithing."

"Come to the point, child. We don't have time for idle stories."

She locked eyes with the Speaker. "The point, Sir, is that the village of Stoneweld, which should have received some of this grain, is instead being asked itself for more. Our grain isn't going to help other villages. Does that mean my elders lied – or were they lied to? Where is our grain?"

The silence in the room was broken by muttering from behind her. She ignored the crowd. Instead she watched the Speaker.

"That is the business of this Council and not you." He raised a hand to dismiss them.

"There have been too many lies," Cal's strong voice added over the noise of the crowd. He stepped beside her again. "We have come before the Council to demand the truth be told."

"What truth is that?" The Speaker's voice was loud in the sudden silence following Cal's words.

"The truth about the extra tithing. I am an Elder of Stoneweld. Our requests for information have gone unanswered. Apprentice Alicja's people have been lied to. We demand the truth."

Alicja watched the Council, letting Cal's words wash over her. Most had blank expressions, giving no clue to their thoughts. But …

She shifted to her right, staring at the man sitting at the end of the dais. He returned her attention. Suddenly, she knew why she recognized him.

"Ask him," she blurted, pointing to the man. "Ask him about the coming war."

The chamber erupted in a cacophony of voices. Cal swore and stepped close to Alicja. "That was blunter than even I would dare."

She could barely hear him over the rush of blood in her ears. It was too late to take the words back. From the way he looked at her, it was clear the Council member now recognized her as the bard at the Hammer. Perhaps she and Cal could still accomplish what they had set out to do.

Over the sound of the Speaker trying to gain control of the chamber, she could hear the playing of a harp. Touching her apprentice brooch, Alicja took a deep breath and approached the man from the inn. Cal fell into step behind her.

The chamber grew quieter when she stopped. The Speaker raised a hand. "What would you know of war?"

Pitching her voice for the Council alone, Alicja recited: "'With Speaker Haroon dead, Tryma feels it can break our trade and friendship agreement with impunity.' 'What will that mean for us?' 'War.'"

The man blanched at hearing his words and those of his companion repeated. He shifted away when the rest of the Council turned to stare at him. The Speaker glared down at her. "Do you think to blackmail us?"

"No, Sir," she replied. "But you know the truth will be spoken by the people here and spread by the bards to the villages beyond."

The Speaker looked over her head at the crowd observing the session. When his gaze met hers, Alicja saw anger and grudging respect.

The Council stood at a signal from the Speaker. "This session is now closed," he announced and led the others from the dais and out of the chamber. As they left, those gathered broke into nervous chatter and conversation, the word war on every tongue.

Alicja closed her eyes a moment, breathed a sigh of relief that her time before the council was over, then turned to Cal.

"We should leave before the crowd," he said.

She chewed her lip, suddenly uneasy. Had she said too much, pushed the Council too far? "Cal?"

He beckoned her to follow him toward the door. When they reached a quiet place, he stopped and studied her. He placed a hand on her shoulder. "You did well," he said. "Alberin will be proud."

Alicja smiled. Together, they walked from the chamber into the afternoon sun.

Alicja passed her bags to Cal. As he lashed them into the wagon, she leaned against the rough sideboard and looked at the gates of Hopewell. So much had happened in such a short time. But even the things that had frightened her seemed right some how.

"Are you ready to leave?"

She turned and accepted his help to climb into the wagon. When the elder was settled beside her, she asked, "What do we do now?"

"Now?" Cal gathered the reins and set the horses in motion. "Now we go home. Prepare for what's coming."

"While I begin my role as an apprentice."

He smiled at her. "No. You've already begun."

Alicja grinned and began humming the harp tune she had heard in the Council chamber.

The Colors of Augustine

by
Michelle West

Michelle Sagara West

Joseph of the Westerfield Foundling Hall was old enough to work in the common garden that was hidden by its grand – and *old* – facade.

But he was only barely old enough, and the new sisters often tried to send him off with the younger children. He was not of a mind to go.

"You're an idiot," Michael whispered, when the attendent teacher had passed beyond hearing. "You *want* to do this?" He slapped the ground with the hoe; it got stuck. Michael was possibly the largest boy in Joseph's form.

"Probably not," Caroline told Michael, pausing a moment to wipe a dirty glove on what was ostensibly a clean apron. "But the Dags will have his head if he doesn't."

Joseph nodded energetically. "I tried it last month," he added, wincing. Being roomed, as they called it, for three days – Madam Dagleish called it something else – had been enough of a lesson; he didn't try it again. "Besides, I'm not a baby."

"They're not *all* babies," Caroline interjected, moving dirt with a soft grunt. "We were there, last year."

Michael snorted. He was the largest in Joseph's form partly because he was also a little slow to learn. He was probably two years older than either of his friends.

Still, if he was large and slow, he wasn't mean. It was an important distinction.

"Hey, Joey!"

A very important distinction.

Joseph bent his back over his hoe, and tried to pay attention to nothing but dirt.

"Joey, I'm talking to you!"

Red – called that because of his hair – came sauntering across the field. Joseph privately hoped that he'd trip in a hole and break his leg, and then immediately regretted it. He'd seen it happen once or twice, and he knew that wishing was vastly more satisfying than actually getting what one wished for.

"What do you want, Red?" Caroline eyed him suspiciously.

"Me? Nothing. But the Dags is looking for Joey here." He whistled. Joseph couldn't. "I don't know what you've done this time, but you'd better *move*."

"I haven't done *anything*," Joseph said, trying to keep the whine from the words, and failing.

Red shrugged. "Suit yourself. But she looks fit to kill."

"She always looks that way," Caroline said, rolling her eyes. But to Joseph, she whispered, "good luck."

In the city of Augustine, the foundling halls were not huddled on the edges of the poorer city districts; they were not crumbling old homes or hovels; they were grand and imposing buildings, with fine steps, fine gates, and very strong fences. They boasted finer grounds, stately trees, tended flowerbeds, and statuaries – gifts from those who had graduated from their family-less life into positions of power.

Because from Augustine, in the foundling halls, the men and women known as the Augustine Painters were culled. Artists of varied talent existed throughout the great stitchwork of kingdoms that formed the loose empire, but in no other city were Augustine Painters born; in no other city were the gifts that made the Augustine masters so valuable manifest.

Only in Augustine, with its great cathedrals – and its King – did the painters flourish, if that word could be so applied to the children who came to the gates of the foundling halls. It was for that reason that Augustine was valued so highly.

From Westerfield, foremost among them – or so Madam Dagleish often said in her forbidding, pinched voice – the greatest number of Painters emerged, and so, in Westerfield, the dour and grim-faced Madam Dagleish took pride in putting the orphans through their paces.

She did not offer them a life of luxury; after all, only a handful of the dozens, and sometimes hundreds, would prove themselves to be of value in that particular fashion. But if the others didn't, she was determined that they would become *useful* members of society.

She knew, of course, which of those children might eventually become the Painters for which the city was famed; the Painters for which, by royal and Imperial writ, the orphanages were so prized.

Because although some children came to her by the terrible accident of fire, and some by the floods that happened when the rivers were far too swollen; although some came by the summer diseases and some by the winter's harsh reign, there were those who came instead in baskets, or in swaddling cloth, and some in nothing at all; they appeared upon the steps beyond closed gates, or at the gates themselves, with no names, no clothing, nothing at all to mark them as children who had been born to any living woman.

Those children – those children were of interest.

Not only to the nobles who might otherwise adopt them; infants were of value to houses who had not been graced or blessed with children. It was, of course, the dream of many an orphan to find such a family, to be *wanted*. It was her duty to turn those would-be parents away, offering them instead children who had come to her halls by the ravages of untimely death.

And it was a terrible, thankless duty.

There were many who said that Madam Dagleish was a harsh and ill-tempered woman with a heart of steel. She fostered this impression with care and diligence; in some fashion it was true.

But it *had* to be true. She could not afford to let these children grow wild in her care; she could not indulge them, could not let them think that they might grow up to be children of wealth and leisure. Some might, but far more would become instead the laborers upon whose backs the city depended. And without ties of kin, without blood relatives, they would be forgiven little and judged just as harshly as she judged them, and if they did not measure up to that judgement, they would have nothing. Less than nothing. The winters were not kind, and if the foundling halls existed for children, very little existed for adults who found themselves with nothing.

She would not let the children in her care become those adults. And so she continued. But she was not a young woman. And in truth, it would have surprised the children of these strict and sparse halls to know that she herself had grown up under the care of equally grim taskmasters in a place such as this. If she had a home, it was this one.

But it was a home in which few others could stay.

Joseph was a quiet boy. A compliant child. He was just turned twelve years of age. He had shown no great ability in math, and little skill in reading, to the sorrow of Mr. Burkhold, who had a soft spot for his curiosity. The boy was not large, and would doubtless never be large; his spindly arms and legs reminded one of a faux spider. His hair was brown and his eyes so dark that the pupil seemed to meet the whites; his skin was pale in winter and a little too red in summer. He now lived alone – a privilege afforded the older children – in a room that was the size of a large closet, with a window eight feet from the ground. But he didn't seem to mind the lack of light.

Nor did he mind the tasks set him; he worked, and hard, without much complaint. He fetched water, he made beds, he swept the great hall in which the foundlings were fed, and he aided the staff in the cleaning. He had done so for six months now, although he was still considered small for the work.

The door creaked, and Madam Dagleish pleated her face in its more customary severe frown, walking away from the grand windows that formed the whole South face of her office, to take her seat behind the ironwood desk upon which nothing but an inkstand lay.

"Enter," she said, in a voice that would have been heard across the stretch of an embattled field.

Joseph pushed the doors wide – or as wide as he was, which wasn't – and let himself in. He looked nervous.

Then again, so did any child who was summoned to this room.

"Joseph," she said, when he paused a few feet from the doors. "Please step forward."

He did as bid. Tractable, cautious child.

"You have done nothing wrong," she told him, knowing that this would not put him at his ease. "But I have a few questions I wish to ask you.

"You've done well in drawing classes. Mr. Chessfeld is quite happy with your progress."

His smile was cautious, guarded. But he approached the desk behind which she sat.

"But Mrs. Belson, in painting, has approached me privately with some concern, and I wished to speak with you for that reason."

His head dropped two inches, and his shoulders bunched together. He was a small boy, and he made himself smaller without any obvious effort.

She opened a drawer with her left hand, and pulled out several pieces of cloth. They were evenly cut, and some reflected the sunlight that poured through the open windows; some absorbed it. He watched them all, and as he did, he paled.

"I want you to tell me what color this is," Madam Dagleish said. It wasn't a request. She pulled a piece of cloth up and held it out before her as if it had somehow offended her.

He gazed at it hopelessly. "Green," he said at last, in a voice so low she could barely make out the word.

She frowned, and her fingers tightened imperceptibly around the fraying edges of a deep, bright red. But she said nothing, and set the cloth aside, choosing another. "This one?"

"Blue?"

It was almost blue.

"And this?"

"Brown?" With each word, his voice dropped.

She nodded, and set the last piece of cloth aside. "Very well, Joseph, that will be all."

He was not, as he expected to be, excused from painting classes. He was half grateful for it, and half resentful; painting was a terror to him. It was in that class that he had first discovered – with complete clarity – that he did not see color the way the other children did. That red and green were the same, that brown and orange, blue and purple, also looked similar. Shades of any of these could be differentiated, with some subtle help from Caroline – but the truth was that he couldn't actually tell them apart on his own.

It might have been caught earlier, but the Westerfield foundlings wore a uniform. They had no possessions to speak of, no gifts, no clothing they valued; they dressed in the same things, handing them down to the smaller children as they outgrew them. Had he been forced to choose colors in which to dress himself, his teachers would have known the truth earlier.

But he had kept it from everyone for as long as he possibly could, because he knew that being different in *this* way was the end, for him. He was a Westerfield foundling, yes, but he could never be a Painter.

Still, he painted. Mrs. Belson chose his palette after his interview with Madam Dagleish, and he used it with care, furtively asking Caroline what things looked like to her. She helped him, as she could; she always had. She didn't have his skill with charcoal and pencil, and in truth, she didn't have his skill with the brush.

But what she painted was not a riot of inexplicable color gone mad.

Joseph grew slowly; Michael grew quickly. Caroline paced them, staying almost squarely in the middle; they were an odd group of friends. But they approached age with both pride and a growing sense of unease. Many of the Westerfield foundlings began to find homes outside of the hall when they reached the age of thirteen.

Michael was an exception, but at fifteen Madam Dagleish called him from class. He was strong and sturdy, and if the word lazy was never brought up in adult conversation, no one would know it to look at him.

He wouldn't find parents; he was too old. But he *would* find sponsors, and perhaps an apprenticeship, in the wide world beyond Westerfield.

And he'd probably find friends.

Caroline brought Joseph the good news, such as it was. Michael was given a farewell dinner. It was quiet, and somber, at least for Caroline and Joseph. Michael himself? He was itching to go.

But he promised to remember them. And to visit, if the blacksmith gave him any free time. Knowing Michael, he'd make it somehow.

But Michael's loss deprived Joseph of words for two weeks, and to his sorrow, he discovered that memory was treacherous; he could no longer accurately draw one of the two friends he had in the world. It was a bitter lesson, and he learned from it, as he could; he began to draw Caroline constantly, and he hated to let her out of his sight.

Caroline was more subtle, but no less affected. This was their first real loss, if one didn't count the deaths of parents neither of them remembered, and it brought them closer together.

Joseph was thirteen and a half by Westerfield count when it was finally decided that he had outgrown the robes that all of the orphans wore. He graduated to a suit, of sorts, and to him it seemed to be the same drab color as the robes had been; to Caroline, it was a soft rust red, and she loved it.

She wore the same color, of course, but she wore a dress. And while Joseph's hair was cropped short, hers was allowed to grow. It was white, to Joseph, the color of down. He helped her braid it, sometimes. This, of course, was strictly forbidden; the boys and the girls were separated by a length of intimidatingly patrolled hall. But Caroline was bold enough to chance those halls, and she would come and sit with him while he drew.

This, too, was forbidden, but Joseph was compelled to draw, and Caroline understood this.

It was on a night such as this that Joseph drew his first significant picture, and because he drew it at night, and it was forbidden, he showed no one but Caroline. And Caroline was to come to understand it in the days to follow.

He drew Caroline, of course.

But instead of drawing Caroline in the dress of Westerfield, he drew her in something far more sophisticated. Her hair was gathered above her neck, its straight fall impeded everywhere by combs and flowers; her neck seemed long, and her chin more pointed. Her shoulders were bare, and between the growing swell of her breasts, jewellery nestled. He didn't know what the gems were; his drawings were done in pencils and charcoals.

She should have looked happy.

But her lips were thin, and her eyes were darkened by shadows – shadows that didn't exist, even in the lamplit glow of a small, small Westerfield room. Her hands were in her lap; they seemed to be shaking, although that could have been the result of Joseph's unsteady hands, for his hands *did* shake.

Because behind Caroline, hands in white gloves, was a man that Joseph had never seen. His eyes were dark, and his hair slicked and pulled back from his prominent forehead; he might have been handsome, were it not for his expression.

Red had never had an expression so dark, and Joseph knew that Red was the worst bully in the form.

Caroline watched him draw. She had sat for him as a model before, but when she rose, he continued to work, and she made her way to the bed, curious to see what held his attention.

She said, "Is that me?"

He heard her. But her voice came from far away, and the image – the image was so close he *had* to draw it. To keep it at bay. To keep it from devouring him.

He hid the picture. He knew enough to hide it.

But Caroline had seen it.

Three days after, while they walked to the well to get water, their shoulders hampered by the line of carved wood upon which empty buckets swung, she stopped.

"Joseph," she said, quiet now, "that man."

He didn't want to talk about it. But Joseph rarely talked. He started to walk, and she caught his arm, her grip very, very tight.

He turned to meet her eyes, and he saw some of the shadows around their curved edges; he froze, as if trapped. As if she had somehow begun to transform, to walk out of the picture he had drawn.

"I saw him," she continued, softly. "He came to our embroidery class. He stood in the door."

"Alone?" Embroidery was something that only the oldest of the girls were taught; the boys were spared it. And to listen to Caroline, this was one of the few mercies that Madam Dagleish ever showed the boys who, by her own admission, were such a difficulty.

"Sister Lucia was with him."

"Why?"

She shook her head. "He's an important man, apparently. And he has a daughter. He said – he said he was looking for a servant. For his daughter."

But Caroline hadn't been dressed as a servant.

"She needs one," Caroline added. "And he thought that the Westerfield halls would produce a fine companion for his daughter's needs." She wrinkled her nose and added, "all the girls were talking about it afterwards. Celice said he was handsome."

"Was he?"

"You drew him. What do you think?" She shivered.

It wasn't because of the cold.

Two days after that, Caroline was summoned from the garden. She was summoned to the office of Madam Dagleish, and although Joseph hated the grand, sparse room, he desperately wanted to follow her. He was afraid, and instead, he dug. She didn't come back. Michael hadn't, either.

She didn't come to dinner though, and that was worse.

That night, Joseph dared what Caroline often dared, because she was the stronger of the two; he crept out of his room in the boy's wing. He could barely breathe; he was afraid that even breathing would be heard. If the sisters caught him, he'd be roomed for a *week*. Or worse. He wasn't a child anymore; he *knew* the rules. And he had to set a good example.

Which he wasn't doing.

He reached her room, although he'd had to stop to hide in the broom closet to avoid being caught, and when he did, he knocked lightly on the door.

Caroline opened it slowly, her eyes peering into the hallway. It was lit, but not well, and only when she saw his face did she open the door wider.

"Teach me," she whispered, grabbing both of his hands and dragging him into the room.

It wasn't what he expected to hear, although he wasn't certain *what* he expected.

"Teach me to draw."

"Caroline –"

"Teach me how," she said again, and this time he could hear the panic in her voice. Her voice had risen.

"I can try," he said, but they both knew that he wouldn't succeed. Not in time.

"He came back," she whispered, and then she buried her face in her hands. "He was polite, to Madam Dagleish. And polite to me. I would have liked him –" She closed her eyes. "But I kept seeing your drawing, Joseph. I kept seeing him as the man in your drawing. Help me."

"What did he –"

"He offered me a home. A position, he called it. In his house. And it's a grand house," she added bitterly. "He disapproves of gardening. It's why I haven't been out in the back the last few days. He says it's bad for my skin." She turned away from him. "He says – he wants me. For his daughter."

"It was just a drawing –"

She caught his hands, crushing them; hers were shaking. "It was a *painting*," she said.

"I can't. I can't paint. Paintings are –"

"It was."

And he knew, then, what she wanted him to do.

"When? When are you supposed to leave?"

"Next week. I don't know," she added bitterly. "I tried to tell Mrs. Dagleish that I didn't want to go, and she was angry with me."

"Did you tell her why?"

"How?" She demanded. "How could I tell her?"

And he realized that she hadn't mentioned the drawing. He was ashamed of himself; the first thing he felt was relief. That he wouldn't be caught.

She saw it, too. But she said nothing.

"I have to go."

She said nothing at all as he left.

He couldn't eat breakfast the following morning. It was heaped on a plate in front of him, runny eggs and bread; he moved them around with his fork. Wasting food was possibly the worst of the sins he could commit in the dining hall; it was just below starting a food fight, which hadn't happened for at least two years, and had *never* been started by Joseph.

Caroline couldn't eat either.

But worse, she wouldn't speak to him. She wouldn't look at him. He had never felt so alone, and he was a foundling; he was good at feeling lonely.

He went to classes, and he was reprimanded for daydreaming ten times before the lunch bells tolled. After that he found himself staring at another meal he didn't have the stomach for.

Why are you so afraid? he thought, as he crushed sandwich bread into a fine, thick dough.

Because you broke the rules, he answered. *Because you'll be roomed for a month, if the Dags finds out.*

And what about Caroline? What would happen to Caroline? He dared a glance at her, and he lost what little appetite he had, which should have been impossible.

"Joseph?"

Sister Lucia hovered just over his shoulder. She should have been with the younger children, and he had the grace to flush.

"I'm not – I'm not feeling well."

She frowned. "Eating would help."

"Yes, Sister Lucia."

But it wouldn't, and he had no way of telling her that without having to run half a lap around the school. Or more.

He compounded his sin by being late for drawing. Mr. Chessfeld, never as severe as the sisters, frowned when Joseph hastily took his seat – and missed by four inches. He went down, the chair followed, and everyone in the class turned to look at him, some of the students snapping brittle charcoal in surprise.

"Joseph?" the wiry instructor said, frowning.

And Joseph surrendered. "I forgot – I forgot my charcoal. And my pencils. In my room."

A grey brow rose. "Then don't waste more of my time," Mr. Chessfeld said. "Go and *get* them."

Joseph turned, daring only a glance at Caroline's stiff profile, and then he ran down the halls.

But he didn't go back to class. And he didn't retrieve his charcoal and his pencils; he had them with him. He almost always did. He wondered if Mr. Chessfeld knew.

Instead, he pulled his ancient mattress up by the corner – it was almost stiff as boards, and it was pretty much as comfortable – and he pulled the drawing he had done from its hiding place.

His hands trembled; he wanted to tear it into a hundred pieces.

Wanted to, and couldn't. In the meager light that fell from the window's height, it seemed more menacing than it had when he had first drawn it; the harsh light of day made things seem darker somehow.

He curled the drawing up into a thin tube, and clutched it a little too tightly as he made his way back down the halls that led from the foundling rooms to the grand hall itself.

There, having forsaken class and earned several demerits, he paused as he always did. The grand hall was covered in paintings. Some were framed by mad craftsmen, wood-workers who sculpted leaves, vines, crowns, and covered them all in gold leaf, as if the paintings themselves were somehow too plain; others were simply braced by unadorned wood. They were all beautiful, in their fashion, and they were all different.

Still life met battle; the largest painting of them all was one long spectacle, death and suffering captured in the wide strokes of a master's brush. He lingered there a moment, but not longer; he heard the heavy tread of steps as they echoed in the vaulted ceilings above, and he knew that he wouldn't make it if he was caught.

Swallowing air, because he'd had so little else that day, he made his way to Madam Dagleish's office.

There he paused, his hand hovering an inch from the white painted surface of the double doors.

He thought of Caroline. She hadn't told on him.

It's just a drawing, he thought with despair. *What if it's just a drawing? What if it means nothing? What if I'm ruining her only chance?*

But that wasn't why he was afraid.

And because it wasn't, he found the courage to knock at the door, although the tap was so slight no one should have heard it.

Madam Dagleish, however, had ears like a legendary elephant's.

"Enter," she said, and he couldn't mistake the voice for anyone else's.

He almost ran away, and that would be worse. But he couldn't quite bring himself to push the doors open; he stood there, trapped, until he heard footsteps. There was carpet in the room, and she was a thin woman – but her steps could be heard anyway, and they fell like doom.

Madam Dagleish opened the doors, and they framed her stony frown.

"Joseph?" she said. "Why aren't you in class? Did Mr. Chessfeld send you?"

He shook his head.

"Speak up, boy. I have a visitor."

He froze, then. But she was merciful; the doors were opened just enough so that he could only see her.

"I –"

"Joseph." If her voice had been harsh before, it was glacial now.

He held out a shaking hand, and in it, the picture he had drawn. Shoving it into her hands, he stepped back from the door and turned as if to flee.

But she barked his name, and if there was magic in the world, it was in her voice; he froze.

The doors clicked shut behind her; she had actually stepped *out* of her office. Oh, he was going to be in *so* much trouble.

She carefully unrolled his picture, her lips pursed in a thin edge. Her expression, made up of lines so deep they probably never changed, was unreadable. But her eyes, when they left the surface of the paper, were not.

"When did you draw this?" she said.

"Last – I don't know. Four days ago. Maybe a week."

"Where?"

He couldn't bring himself to answer.

"Why did you draw *this* image?" Her distaste was immediate and obvious.

"I don't know," he said, in a broken little voice.

"And this man?"

"I don't know," he said again. "I'm sorry. I don't know."

"Very well. You are confined to your room, Joseph. You will go there *now*, and you will talk to *no one*. Is that clear?"

He nodded; he couldn't swallow. Something had thickened in his throat.

She curled the picture back into its half-crushed fold, and turned her back on him. As she opened the door, she said, "Your pardon, Count Thermann, but there is a difficulty with which I must deal."

He didn't see the Count, and he was very, very grateful, because when he heard the name, he knew what the man looked like.

Being roomed wasn't so bad, he thought, as he lay on his growling stomach. He'd lived through it before, and he'd live through it again. Maybe. He was hungry, now, and he was afraid. Of what lay outside his door. Of what he had done.

He wanted to talk to Caroline, because if he could, she'd speak to him. He missed her. He missed her more than he missed Michael, and Michael wasn't even here.

But it wasn't Caroline who came to his door, hours later; it was Madam Dagleish. She came alone.

He opened the door when he heard her knock, and then he stood there, staring up at her face.

"Please move away from the door," she said, and her tone was about as harsh as he had come to expect.

He retreated into the small room, and she followed him; once she was inside, she turned and closed the door, locking it with the small latch. Then she turned back to him. She carried his drawing like a silver dragon might have carried fool's gold.

"Joseph," she said. "Sit down."

There was one chair in the room, and one bed. He sat on the bed. She took the chair.

"Have you ever seen this man before?" she asked, unrolling the drawing. Charcoal had smudged in the creases he'd made, but the pencil hadn't.

He shook his head.

"Do you know who he is?"

He shook his head again, and then, because her gaze was like a knife, he said, "Count Thermann."

"Very good. You do know better than to lie to me."

He nodded.

"Why did you not bring this to my attention earlier?"

He shook his head and stared at his knees.

"Joseph, you will look at me while I am speaking to you."

"Yes, ma'am."

"Good. Answer my question."

He swallowed. "It's just a drawing," he said, but that sounded hollow even to him. "I thought –"

"When was it drawn? I have taken the liberty of speaking with Mr. Chessfeld, and I know that you did not draw it in his class."

He shook his head. "I drew it here," he said at last, wretched.

"Caroline was here." No question, there.

"Yes, ma'am."

"That is *strictly* forbidden, Joseph. You are aware that you are no longer a child?"

"Yes, ma'am."

"Good." She laid the picture flat upon his desk and shook her head. "You should have brought this to my attention earlier," she said again. "Because things are going to be much more difficult now."

"Caroline –"

Her gaze could have cut steel. There was nothing remotely friendly in it. But she surprised him. "No," she told him, severe and remote. "I will not send Caroline to Count Thermann's household. But had you come to me *at once*, I could have refused him with grace. Now the Westerfield Hall may well be damaged by my refusal."

He said nothing, and after a moment her frown changed. Oh, it was still a frown; she was clearly very angry. "Joseph, the foundling hall is my life. I know that I am not a friendly woman, but I am not a monster. I do not raise children in order to –" She shook her head. "How many other such pictures have you drawn?"

"Just this one."

She nodded. "Good. Dinner has been served, but Sister Lucia tells me that you ate little today. The cook will send food to your room. You are to remain here until I call you."

To Joseph's lasting surprise, Caroline came with the food. She carried it on a tray, and she stood in the hall, waiting for him to answer; it was clear that this once, lights down, she hadn't had to sneak across the length of halls.

He gaped at her, and she said, "It's heavy. Can I come in?" Her voice was soft, much quieter than he remembered. As if days of not speaking had robbed it of strength.

He turned wildly and made a lunge for his desk; the drawing still lay there, exposed. He shoved it to the side, and it landed on the floor, face up. More than that, he couldn't bring himself to do. The Caroline that he had drawn was terrified and hurt, but she was still Caroline, and she was beautiful.

She carried the tray to the now empty desk, and set it down. Then she perched in front of it, staring at the paper that lay across the floor. She closed her eyes.

"I'm sorry," she told him softly.

"It's my fault. I drew it."

"Are you sorry you did?"

He was. And he wasn't. He hovered between these two truths, almost confused by them. "No," he said at last, choosing one, and gripping it tightly. "If I hadn't –"

She shook her head, and he subsided, grateful for the interruption. "You're color-blind," she told him.

He winced. "I know."

"But you still did this."

He nodded again.

"I don't have any place to go. Here. You should eat. You didn't eat anything today."

"Neither did you." He paused. "Did you?"

She shook her head. "I couldn't. And I'm roomed for a day for wasting food," she added with a shrug.

"But you're here."

"The cook sent me. I'm allowed to be here. I'm just not allowed to be anywhere else for a day after I leave." She shuddered. "He was going to come for me tomorrow. Did you know?"

Joseph shook his head.

She smiled at him. It was strained, but it was also genuine. "Madam Dagleish called me into her office three hours ago," she whispered. "And she was really mad. She asked me about your picture. She asked me if I'd seen it."

"What did you say?"

"Nothing." Her smile was less strained when she offered it again. "But you know the Dags; she can read minds.

"I thought she'd send me anyway," she added, her voice low. "I was so afraid, Joseph. I thought I would have to go. He's a *Count*."

"She's Madam Dagleish." It was the only time in his life he had ever said those words in that tone and been grateful for them. Caroline lifted the tray, and he placed it by his side on the bed. "There's a lot of food here," he said.

She sat on the floor in front of him, accepting the invitation that he hadn't quite put into words. But he didn't have to. She knew him pretty well. They ate in silence, and they ate – as Sister Lucia would have said with disdain – like little savages. But there were no younglings here to influence, and neither of them much cared.

When they had finished, they sat together, as they so often did, in silence. Joseph got up to light a candle, but that was all. The flame flickered; the window, at a height, was open, and the breeze of the early spring was cool, but not strong enough to douse the fire.

"Could I go with you?" Caroline suddenly said.

Joseph was nonplussed.

"When you leave, could I come too? You can't tell red from green; you can't tell purple from brown. I can. I could help you."

He stared at her. After a moment, he said, "Where?"

"Where what?"

"Where am I going?"

And she laughed. "You are *so* dim," she told him, with a hint of affectionate disdain. "Don't you understand what this means?" And she picked up the drawing by its folded corner. "You're an Augustine Painter."

The words lingered in the room long after she'd left it.

In the morning, Madam Dagleish summoned him. The youngling who was sent with her message made it clear that he was to dress *properly*, and he addled his hair with a comb, trying to make himself presentable. That had meaning, in the foundling hall.

Caroline caught him on the way out of the halls proper, and straightened his clothing. Which, given that it was starched, shouldn't have taken so *much* work. His hair, on the other hand, did, and he tried not to complain as she pulled it out.

"I left you some," she said with a grin. "Now go."

"You'll get demerits."

Her smile froze, and she turned, shoving the comb into her skirt pockets. "Don't forget me," she whispered, just before she left.

He nodded. He was afraid to answer.

Madam Dagleish was waiting with a certain polished patience. This meant that she smiled when he entered the room, her eyes straying pointedly to the clock's large hand.

Polite meant, of course, that guests of note were present. Joseph turned at once and offered a stiff and formal bow to the man seated in one of two grand chairs – chairs which were normally covered by large dustclothes.

The visitor was not a young man; nor was he a friendly one. On the other hand, it was hard to look friendly when one wore an austere black suit. Or so it seemed to Joseph.

"Master Havernell," Madam Dagleish said, "this is the boy of whom I spoke."

The stranger raised a perfect brow. "This one?"

She nodded.

"He's young."

"He is small for his age; he is almost fourteen."

A brow rose. The man followed. "Well, then, let's have a look at your so-called painting."

Joseph withered. "Painting?"

Madam Dagleish actually frowned. The interview was not off to a good start. "Joseph has some difficulty remembering things," she said coldly. "Joseph?"

He backed out of the door, ran back to his room, and grabbed the drawing. As an afterthought, he grabbed his pencils too.

"Pretty girl," Master Havernell said quietly, as he looked at the drawing that lay upon Madam Dagleish's desk. "And a very good likeness of Count Thermann. Have you met the Count, boy?"

"No, sir."

"Ah." Master Havernell lifted the paper and retreated to the chair with it, as if it were a book. He was silent for a long moment. "And the girl?"

"She is a student here," Madam Dagleish said, offering Joseph a stare that pinned his lips shut.

"I see. And she?"

"She has, indeed, been introduced to the Count."

"And she is in his service?"

"Master Havernell," Madam Dagleish said, in a tone of voice that was usually reserved for foundlings who had tried her very meagre patience.

The Painter actually smiled. "*Madam* Dagleish," he replied, inclining his head. "Forgive my impertinence."

She frowned. "When one asks for forgiveness, one usually ceases to partake in behavior that requires it."

"Ah, a failing of mine. It has been many years since I have lived in Westerfield." His smile deepened. "But I remember you well, Madam Dagleish. I tease the boy." His smile vanished. "This is a simple enough drawing. How long did it take you to complete it?"

Joseph froze. The minutes vanished beneath the moving hand of the clock.

"Joseph?"

He said, "I don't know. I don't have a clock in my room. And it was dark."

Master Havernell raised a brow again. "I see. And the girl?"

"She probably has a better idea of how long it took. She —"

"She is capable of paying attention," Madam Dagleish said. "It is not, however, of the girl that you came to speak."

"No. Of course not." He rose and set the drawing aside. "I would like to see your paintings, Joseph."

Joseph lost several inches in height.

"Tell him, Joseph."

"I don't have any," he muttered.

"You don't take painting?" This seemed to be the first surprising thing that the Master Painter – for he could be nothing else – had heard so far.

"I take classes," Joseph replied, wretched.

"Moraine," Madam Dagleish snapped.

This was the first thing that Madam Dagleish had done that surprised Joseph; Master Havernell, however, was immune.

"I am not teasing the boy," he said quietly. "I am testing him."

And Joseph knew two things. That the Painter already knew about his problem, and that he had somehow failed the test. Failing, he spoke. "I don't see colors the way the others do."

"No."

The minutes passed again beneath the moving hand of clock; Joseph wanted to sit, but he knew that the floor would get him roomed for a week, and the chairs were for dignitaries, not foundlings. He stood.

"Very well, boy. You are color-blind. I wish to determine how severe that handicap is. What color is my hair?"

"Brown."

"Good. Are you guessing?"

"Yes."

"Bad. My suit?"

"Black."

"And my shirt?"

"White."

"Wrong. But close." He held out a ring. "The gem?"

"Green?"

"Red." Master Havernell turned to Madam Dagleish. "It is not a minor deficit."

But the woman who ran the Westerfield Hall said nothing.

"But you have the Painter's gift, Joseph," the Master said quietly. Something like pity touched the man's features. "It is not a kind gift, and you will be troubled by it. If I am not mistaken, you already have been. Has Count Thermann seen the drawing?"

"Of course not," Madam Dagleish said coldly. "It is a Westerfield affair, and as such, no concern of his."

"If I am not mistaken, Madam Dagleish, Count Thermann is counted among the foundling hall's many patrons."

"He is not the richest," she said with a shrug.

"You haven't changed at all, have you?"

She raised a grey brow. It looked like iron.

"That was impertinent," Master Havernell added. "Forgive me."

Her eyes narrowed. She rose. "You will have words to speak with Joseph, and I have business to attend to."

"Count Thermann."

"Moraine, you are very trying today."

"It is seldom that I am summoned back to Westerfield, Madam Dagleish, and if I am grateful for all you have done for me, I confess that my memories of the hall are not fond ones." He opened his hands, palm up, as if in surrender. "But I am as yet a young Painter, and if I am worthy of note – and I am – I have no apprentices." His expression darkened again. "Nor was it my intent to take one at this time. The season has been … difficult for the Augustine apprentices."

Her face darkened as well, but she rose. "I will leave you now," she said. And she did.

"What do you know of the Augustine Painters, Joseph?" It was the first time Master Havernell had used his name.

"They paint the future?"

"Ah. Yes, in a fashion, they do." He rose, as if the chair's confinement were unwelcome. "Sit."

Joseph did.

"If we painted *the* future, we would not be esteemed so highly," Master Havernell said. He walked to the grand windows, and paused there, staring at the grounds, and beyond them, the streets of the city. "We paint possibilities. No, more than that; we paint the future that will occur without intervention. We offer guides, guidelines, to those with more power and more responsibility."

Joseph glanced at his drawing, but as Master Havernell did not seem to expect him to speak, he said nothing.

"And we are paid well for our work. It is not without risk. Have you ever wondered why Augustine is blessed with Painters?"

Joseph nodded slowly, and then added, "yes."

"So, too, do we. We have no answers. We are part of the mystery of the city." He turned, then. "But Madam Dagleish understands the Painters well enough, and if your drawing is crude, it is indeed what we would call a Painting. Your technique is good with pencil. I fear that you will find paints a challenge – and it is in paints, in the end, that the most detail lies. You will be difficult to teach because you cannot see the tools at hand. But I am not a man to step around a challenge. I do not know why Madam Dagleish chose to summon me, but I am willing to offer you a place in my house."

Joseph was utterly still. He was afraid.

And Master Havernell understood the fear.

"The Augustine Painters have no parents," he said quietly. "Nor will they ever have children. Some handful of children are adopted from the Westerfield Halls, but as of this day, you will never be among them. I know what this means," he added softly. "When I was younger – younger than you are now – I dreamed of parents. Of family. I watched other children leave with envy. That will leave you, one day. But not soon.

"I will not withdraw my offer," he continued, "but there are a few questions I wish you to answer, and I wish you to answer them honestly."

Joseph nodded.

"Why did you not show Madam Dagleish this drawing?"

"I did."

"But you waited, and she – if she does not say it – now finds herself in a quandary. Count Thermann is respected, in Augustine. If indeed your painting is accurate, it is … something he conceals well."

Joseph felt stricken. "That's why!" He almost shouted, his voice rising. "I didn't want to show her. I – we weren't even supposed to be *together*. And I – what if it's just a drawing? What if it's *not true*?"

Master Havernell listened, impassive.

Joseph was close to tears. On the wrong side. He rubbed a starched sleeve across his face. "What if I've ruined her only chance to leave here?"

"Do you believe that you have?"

"I don't *know*."

"Ah. That is unfortunate. Is it true?"

Joseph closed his eyes. "Yes," he said. And then, much more hesitantly, "No."

"No?"

"I believe in the drawing. I believe that's what would have happened."

"Why?"

"Because Caroline believed it. She was afraid. She wanted me to bring the picture here."

"She is a smart girl, then. You must let go of your doubts. Did you feel any, when you drew?"

"I didn't feel anything when I drew it. No – I did. I felt as if I *had* to draw it. As if it would –"

"Devour you, if you kept it to yourself?"

Joseph nodded.

"Perhaps it would have. You heard me speak to Madam Dagleish. This is a difficult time for the Augustine Apprentices, and there is a reason for that. But we do not speak of it outside of our own halls," he added, "unless we are forced to do so. Madam Dagleish has grown careless."

Joseph's brows disappeared beneath his bangs.

"You will understand why, in time. It is not wise to draw portraits without guidance, Joseph. But you are young, yet, and you are not in possession of your full power. Do you draw many people?"

"I draw Caroline."

"Why?"

"She's my friend." He hesitated. "She helps me remember things. And she tells me what colors things are."

"I think I would like to meet this girl."

"Madam Dagleish said –"

He laughed. "She is hardly likely to kill you," the Master Painter said. "And she has little authority over *me*. Come. We are to speak; she did not tell us *where*."

Joseph led the Painter to Mr. Chessfeld's classroom. The door was closed. "She's in there," he whispered.

Master Havernell opened the door. "The place hasn't changed much," he said, with a critical eye to the worn desks, the sparse room.

"May I help you?" Mr. Chessfeld asked, in a tone of voice that suggested he would like to do the opposite.

"Please," Master Havernell replied, ignoring the older man's tone. "I wish to speak with Caroline."

"Madam Dagleish did not send for her."

"No. It seemed a waste of the good woman's time, when I am capable of navigating the halls on my own."

"This is Master Havernell," Joseph said quickly. "He's an Augustine Painter."

Mr. Chessfeld frowned. "He would have to be," he said at last. "Caroline?"

But Caroline had already pushed her chair back from her desk. She straightened the folds of her skirt, and bowed politely to Mr. Chessfeld, rustling like dry leaves.

"If you would be so good as to join us," Master Havernell said quietly, "I have a few questions I would like to ask you."

"Yes, sir," she replied. Dutiful, quiet, and entirely unlike herself.

"How long," Master Havernell asked Caroline, as he once again reclined in Madam Dagleish's good chair, "did it take Joseph to draw this?"

Her eyes skirted the surface of the familiar drawing. "An hour and a half," she replied promptly.

"And did you notice anything unusual about it?"

"He stopped looking at me."

"Ah. This was unusual?"

She nodded. "He draws me, sometimes. Sometimes I try to draw him. But normally he does this." Her head bobbed up and down, her hands upon imaginary pencils, imaginary boards. "That night, he didn't. He hardly noticed I was there. I watched him finish it," she added.

"He's a tolerant Painter, then. It's seldom that Painters allow observers when they work."

"It's just me," she said with a shrug. "I always watch Joseph."

"Do you?"

She hesitated. "When he works," she began, with caution.

"He knows, Caroline," Joseph told her.

The starch seemed to leave her dress. "I help him," she said at last. "I'm sort of like his eyes."

"And his memory?"

"He remembers most things."

Master Havernell raised a brow. "But not his work?"

She frowned, her forehead bunching into familiar lines. "He never forgets his –"

"I forgot to bring the drawing."

"Oh. *That*." She shrugged; it made noise. "He thinks a lot," she finally said. It sounded lame to Joseph.

"And what do you do, Caroline? Do you also draw?"

She wanted to say yes. Joseph could see the desire clearly; almost clearly enough to draw it. His fingers flexed, and he curled them into his palms.

But she exhaled at last, and said, "Not like Joseph."

"Good girl."

"That was a test?" Joseph asked the Master Painter.

"It was," he replied, serene now. "But unlike you, Joseph, she passed." He smiled at them both. "Now go, the two of you. I will wait for the dragon. She and I have much to discuss."

Madam Dagleish was just one side of apoplexy. "Moraine," she said, her hands upon the flat surface of her desk. "You have developed manners and some sophistication, but you have not otherwise changed."

He smiled. "I fear, Madam Dagleish, that you are correct. But I also believe that this is why you called *me*. I am willing to take the boy; other Painters might be less willing."

"He has the sight," she replied stiffly.

"He does. But he is hampered." Master Havernell leaned forward. "And I seek to do you a favor."

"You *do not* have free run of the foundling halls."

"No, I don't. I see little harm done, however, in fetching one girl from a class in which she shows little talent."

"What you see, or what you do not see, is not of concern to me. This is the Westerfield Hall, not the Havernell manse, and you *will* respect that while you are here."

"I have great respect for it," he replied. "It is why I am seldom here. Come," he added with a smile.

Her face did not change.

"Count Thermann is no doubt already impatient. What have you told him, I wonder?"

"That is not your concern."

"But it is," he replied. "For I am willing to take the girl off your hands."

She froze, although it was hard to tell; she was seldom generous with her movements.

"You cannot place her elsewhere in safety, and you will damage her if you leave her here. She is not old, but she has only a few years before the Westerfield Hall is no longer fit home for her. The Count has offered her a position that few here will be offered. Place her elsewhere, and it will be seen as the insult it is.

"But no one, Count, King or even the Emperor himself, could object to her placement in the halls of an Augustine Painter."

"She is *not* a Painter."

"No. She does not have the gift, nor will she, if I am not mistaken. And you already know this well enough."

Madam Dagleish sat down.

"Joseph asked this of you?"

"No. But they are friends," he replied. "And he is unusually tolerant for a child."

"Tolerant?"

"She understands him better, I think, than he understands himself. She certainly trusts him more than he trusts himself. He has allowed her to be his eyes, to be some part of his vision; he has allowed her to guide his hand, and his brush.

"It is rare. Painters have, among themselves, some fellowship; the gift moves them in similar measure. But outsiders find it difficult, at times, to accept the isolation that comes with talent."

"She is a child, Moraine."

"She is, indeed, a child. But more so, Joseph. My House is not a famous House; it is not Giavanno's. While I am considered a man of talent, I am also considered somewhat unpredictable. I have the powerful among my clients," he added, with a shrug. "And in time, there will be more.

"But I have taken no apprentices."

"Few men have, this year."

"As you say." He closed his eyes. "I have spoken with Giavanno. He has lost two students in the last three years. Master Aracos has lost three. In Augustine, perhaps eleven in total have –"

"Enough."

"Some of those were Westerfield foundlings."

"*Enough*, Moraine." Her shoulders rounded. Her head bent toward the desk, its gleaming surface like a dark mirror. She seemed old, then. Felt old.

And he knew it. "I will take the boy," he continued, "because he already shows talent. Such talent cannot in safety be nurtured here. In my home, he may be safe; his handicap may afford him some protection."

"It will hamper his ability to make a name for himself."

"It will," he agreed. "But I will not take the boy without the girl. Come," he said again, cajoling now. "If she had a choice, she would agree in an instant to anything I asked. I might ask her to clean, to cook, to mend, and she would do these things without reservation.

"I am not an ogre, Madam Dagleish. And I have little prurient interest in her. She will be safe, with me. She would not be, I think, with another." He raised a brow. "I have seen what the boy drew. Do you understand the whole of its significance?"

Madam Dagleish did not move.

"Count Thermann will find her, I think. You must have begun your research," he added.

"What do you know of him?"

"Very little. He is not among my clients," he added, "and he is cautious. But I know what I saw in his face. He *will* find her. Better, I think, that he find her in my care than anyone else's. Joseph thinks he has saved her. And Caroline thinks it as well. They are both young, and neither of them has any understanding of the powerful."

She looked up at him, then. "You were always a trial, Moraine," she told him softly.

His brows rose slightly.

"Joseph is among the most sweet-tempered of my children."

"Your children?"

"Mine," she said, with a quiet, almost desperate pride. "All of them. I hate to give him to you."

"But?"

"But you are right. I cannot be certain that he will find a home with a more reputable Painter. Very well. If you will not take one without the other, you may take both." She paused, and then added, "thank you."

He stared at her; she had surprised him and he was willing to let it show. "Time teaches us many things, Madam Dagleish."

"Does it?"

"Perhaps you have learned all you need learn. But today, I have learned much that I would never have otherwise suspected. I will protect them both, in my own fashion, and I think they will be happy."

"How can you protect Joseph?" She asked, at last, and the whole of her staid and dour composure cracked.

"I have not, myself, fallen," he replied. "And I have no other students. Between us – that girl and I – we will keep him from the enemy."

"Paint it," she whispered bleakly. "Paint it, and send me the painting, and then I will believe you."

"Paintings speak only of possibilities," he replied, but there was warmth in the words. "I will come for the children in two days; it will take that long to make the studio presentable. I am not a man who is accustomed to sharing space."

Caroline was beside herself with glee. Her hair – Joseph thought of it as white, although he knew it couldn't be – bobbed up and down because she could not keep still. The sisters were harsh with their words, but they had little spirit behind them; they were happy for her.

They were happy for Joseph.

"Where do you think he lives?" she asked.

They were sitting in the great hall. Mrs. Belson had finally had enough, and had asked them, sternly, to leave the class. She had followed them out, and then she had done something that shocked Joseph: she had hugged them both tightly.

"You take care of him," she had told Caroline fiercely. Caroline had nodded, as if she were making a solemn vow.

"I don't know. A big house, I guess. He's a Painter."

"But *how* big? Do you think he has servants? Do you think I'll be one of them? Do you think he has gardens, too? Or a fountain?"

Joseph was heartily sick of hearing the questions; she'd come up with a hundred thousand of them in two days, and she never seemed to repeat herself.

"What about a wife?"

"I don't think Augustine Painters marry," he told her.

"Oh, right. I forgot. But maybe he has? Madam Dagleish said he's different."

"Not that different."

"How do you know?"

"She let us go with him," he said with a shrug.

"She will," Madam Dagleish said, coming up behind them like a black cloud, "unless she thinks you will embarrass the Foundling Hall with your gossip."

They froze, and then turned like the guilty caught in whatever act it was that would send them to the gallows.

"M-madam D-dagleish," Joseph stammered.

Madam Dagleish frowned. "Your shirt," she said, "is *not* adequately starched."

He stood up, and she put a hand on his shoulder. "It will, however, have to do. Master Havernell is waiting, and I have no desire to keep him waiting long; he gets into trouble when he is not watched."

Caroline snickered, and Madam Dagleish frowned. "Caroline, that is hardly becoming. I am sending you to his house in good faith; I expect you to do what you can to civilize him."

"Yes, ma'am."

"I mean it."

"Yes, ma'am."

They drove in a carriage.

Caroline crowed the entire way there, and it seemed to Joseph that it was a long, long way. The motion of the wheels over the stones beneath them made him queasy, and he had to close his eyes several times. He opened them when Caroline made him look at passing things: people in fine dress, fountains, pigeons, children, market stalls – in short, everything.

He was grey when he finally stepped down.

Master Havernell shook his head in mock despair. "Joseph," he said, "you will be on the inside of a carriage for much of your life; you will have to learn to tolerate it."

Joseph, trying instead not to throw up, didn't even nod. But

Caroline was still squealing with utter delight, and it was hard not to smile at her once the worst of the nausea had passed.

There were gates. Master Havernell did, indeed, live in a large, fine manse. It was not, of course, as large as Westerfield, but it was equally fine, and if its gardens were smaller, they were miniature perfection.

The Augustine Painter seemed to enjoy Caroline's unfettered approval.

"Did you buy this all yourself?" she asked, emboldened by his indulgence.

"All of it," he replied. "Although some small debt is owed to the bank."

"But how?"

"I *am* an Augustine Painter."

She whistled. Madam Dagleish would have *died*. Joseph, on the other hand, was dutifully silent; he had never mastered the art of whistling. Or of snapping his fingers. Caroline had tried to teach him both.

"But I am, among the Painters, something of a specialist," he added, as men came to take the carriage and its horses away.

She looked up instantly. "Oh?"

"Joseph, does she ask *all* of your questions for you?"

"She talks faster."

Caroline kicked his shin.

And Master Havernell laughed. "I would learn to get out of the way, were I you."

"She'd never kick you," Joseph muttered.

He was wrong, but that would happen later.

"What specialty? What do you do?"

"I have always been drawn towards paintings that are considered unfortunate," he replied with a smile. "But come; you will see them for yourself. I am proud of them, but they are not for public display."

"Why?"

He laughed. "You would do well to learn patience from young Joseph," he replied. He walked up the steps, and before he reached the doors, they opened.

Caroline's jaw dropped.

"Yes," he said, with a smile. "It is magic. A small enchantment. You will find that it works well for either you or Joseph, and far less well for unannounced visitors. Will you see your rooms first, or will you see my gallery?"

"Rooms," Joseph said.

"Gallery," Caroline shouted.

And as so often happened, Caroline won.

The gallery occupied half of the manse's second floor. And it *was* a gallery; the walls were uninterrupted by doors. Windows let light in, but they were curtained with fine sheers, and the roof itself was somehow transparent.

"Sun," Master Havernell said.

"It's not good for colors."

"No, Caroline, it is not. Joseph?"

But Joseph had lost all ability to speak as he approached the first of the many paintings. They were colorful; he had no doubt of that. He couldn't say what the colors were. He had never been able to see them; it was a fact of his life. But it was seldom as resented as it was this day; he knew that he saw half of what was there *to* see, and he hungered for the whole.

As if she knew what he was feeling, Caroline dropped an arm around his shoulder and squeezed. She had done this ever since he could remember, and he found comfort in the familiarity of the gesture; nothing else about this place reminded him of his previous life.

Not even the paintings.

There was death here. Death by hanging. Death by drowning. Death by sword, by many swords. Captured on canvas in the greys of Joseph's filtered vision, death by poison and death by disease. Fire, he knew, was orange; orange, white, red, and there was also death by fire.

Everywhere he looked, corpses.

But there was a strange beauty to their darkness, a quality that somehow defied the fact of life's absence; it moved him. Horrified, fascinated, he began to traverse the length of the gallery, losing sight, at last, of windows, of rails, of the small steps that gave texture to the otherwise flat surface of thick carpet.

"Joseph?" Master Havernell's voice was strange. Softer than it had been, but sharper, closer somehow.

"Who is that man?" Joseph whispered, standing at last in front of a single painting.

Master Havernell said, "Good boy. That man is the King."

Dead, Joseph thought, by poison. "That man is the King, too."

"Yes, Joseph."

Dead by sword. And by quarrel. Dead by what seemed to be a long fall from the sundered rails of a staircase. There was not a living man among these odd portraits.

"Those men?"

"Lord Raleigh's armed forces," he replied.

"Lord Raleigh?"

"The King's cousin. Former cousin," the Augustine Painter added quietly. "Do you understand why these can never be openly displayed?"

Joseph nodded.

"And why you're rich?" Caroline asked, in a voice as hushed as hers ever got.

Master Havernell laughed. "Yes," he said quietly. "I have an affinity for death. Had I been your friend, and not Joseph, I fear you would now be in service to a Count." And something about his voice at that moment made Joseph turn to look at him.

But his face was shuttered; if Joseph heard anything in the voice, the Painter's expression betrayed nothing.

"There are other men," he added, after some moments had passed. "And if you do not recognize them by their colors – and I fear you will not – you must learn to recognize them by their designs and their standards. They are all men of power, and your fate will be entwined with theirs."

"I don't paint death," Joseph told the Augustine Master quietly.

"Not yet," was the equally quiet reply. "But in the end, all Painters do." He shrugged. "I think we have seen enough of the gallery for today. Let me show you to your rooms. When you have had a chance to settle in, I will take you to the Studio."

Madam Dagleish would never have approved of the arrangements. Joseph found them almost shocking. Caroline's room – her *rooms* – were across the hall from his. She had only to open her door, walk a few feet, and open his; no long jaunts with brief side-trips into broom closets, no furtive meetings here.

Caroline was beside herself. She probably made enough noise to wake the dead.

Joseph was characteristically quiet. "All of these are mine?" He asked the Painter.

Master Havernell laughed. "All two of them," he said, with a mocking smile.

They were huge. The ceilings were corniced, the floors were carpeted, and the windows were the size of several large men. He found them intimidating.

"You need windows," the Augustine Painter said quietly. "You need to see, Joseph."

"I had a window," he began defensively, but the Master lifted a hand, swatting the words away as if they were gnats.

"Learn to be like Caroline," he told the boy. "Learn to enjoy the things that you're given. There will be a cost," he added. "And because you are a Painter, you will pay it one way or the other."

"But I –"

"Not yet," the Master added. "You have only newly come into your power. But you have power," he added. "And it is not without strength. You will learn to hide it, in time, as I have; you will learn to reveal it, when the moment is right.

"You will paint death to save life, Joseph. But death will be your calling." Master Havernell looked beyond him and added, "but there is a strange beauty in death."

Joseph, quiet, wondered why he had ever wanted to be an Augustine Painter.

"What happened to your master?" he asked.

"He died," Master Havernell replied.

"How?"

But Master Havernell shook his head. "You will know, in time."

The studio occupied the other half of the second floor, and it seemed to go on forever. Not a single classroom in the whole of the Westerfield foundling Hall was its equal in size, and it appeared to house a single man.

"It is mine," Master Havernell said. "Or it was. It will be ours, now. But take care to mind your own space; I will mind mine. These cupboards, these shelves, and these drawers are for your use. These palettes are yours, and the paints there, the oils, are also yours. I have taken the liberty of choosing your brushes, but you will of course want to test them; not all brushes suit all painters."

"I don't ..." Joseph let his words trail away.

"Good boy. There are pencils and charcoal as well, and paper is in the long drawer. The three easels by the West wall are yours. You have learned to stretch canvas?"

Caroline nodded for him.

"Good. You will learn it again. The Westerfield teachers are good at what they do, but they are not Augustine Painters." He smiled. "And not all Augustine Painters paint works that speak to, or of, the future. There are some who also paint the past; it is rewarding, in its fashion, and often of value to those who will commission your work."

"How will I know the difference?"

"You will know. And if you do not know immediately, Joseph, I will know." He turned to Caroline. "You were taught some of our history in Westerfield."

"Yes."

"Good. You will learn more, now. You will study three languages, and you will have, at your disposal, the texts within my own collection." He lifted a hand as Caroline opened her mouth. "History is a guide," he said softly. "Understanding of the future is almost impossible without it."

"Joseph's drawing didn't need history."

"Ah? But it was not, in the end, Joseph's decision, Caroline. It was Madam Dagleish's choice, and her choice was informed, as it always is, by her understanding of both history and the men who make it.

"You will draw here. You will paint. I will not force you to show what you have painted to any audience save myself, unless I deem it necessary – but you must begin to work, and to work consistently. You have shown talent, Joseph, but talent is simply a glimmer; if you cannot contain it, and you cannot make it work for you, you will never truly be an Augustine Master."

Joseph nodded. "I brought my pencils," he said almost lamely.

"Good. You are comfortable with them. You will learn, in time, to be comfortable working in different media. But today, we will start with pencils."

"What do you want us to draw?"

He raised a brow at Caroline. "Whatever strikes your fancy. There are some Masters who take their students on outings; they find that visiting the city streets is one passage into the visions."

"But not you?"

"Caroline, you must learn to let Joseph ask his own questions."

"But Joseph doesn't care, and I do."

Master Havernell grimaced. "You will make me regret my decision," he said, but without any intensity. "Very well. I do not do so for a reason."

"And that?"

"I have many enemies," he replied almost grimly. "My speciality is known, and the service I provide, known as well. I am one of three men in Augustine who are regularly called upon by the King or his advisors, and one of two who have saved the King's life on more than one occasion.

"If an assassin wishes to remove the King, I would be considered an obstacle. I have spent my life in Studios, and not in swordplay, but I am an Augustine Painter; I have some means of defending myself."

"But not us."

"Not you, no, Caroline. Not yet."

"Madam Dagleish said you've never taken an apprentice," she told him; her hands inched up until they rested on her hips.

"She is correct. It did not seem wise. In truth, it does not seem wise to me now – but necessity is its own wisdom."

"You need an apprentice?"

"At the moment, Augustine needs them," he replied. "You have power, Joseph, but it is not yet great enough that you are endangered by its use. Your study of history will tell you much that you do not know about Augustine and her Kings. And your study of *our* history will tell you something of the Master Painters.

"We are reduced, in some fashion, to using children," he added bitterly, "because there is too much to see, and too much to capture; because those with great power are also those who are most easily led astray."

"I won't let him be led anywhere," Caroline told Master Havernell.

"If it were that simple, Caroline, we would not now number nearly a dozen dead in a few scant years." He shook his head. "This is too grim a topic. Come, Joseph. You will draw, and I will join you."

"What will I do?" Caroline asked. It was the first time she had done so.

"Whatever it is you are accustomed to doing," he replied evenly. He walked away from Joseph. "We will work now, while the sun is with us."

Joseph nodded. He walked over to the long drawer, and pulled it open with effort; it was heavy.

Caroline helped him pull sheets of paper from the ream that lay within. Then she found herself a stool, and took a seat, near the grand bay of the largest window. She looked down at the grounds below, and she smiled.

Joseph dragged a chair over to the window as well, and then positioned himself with unconscious care, so that he might better catch her profile in the morning light.

Without another word, he began to draw.

Master Havernell watched them quietly. He had picked up his brushes, cleaning them while he glanced at his new apprentice, his new … whatever it was the girl was. They seemed two halves of a comfortable whole, and he would become familiar with the changing faces of their stillness and movement as time passed.

For now, it was almost enough to watch them.

Almost.

But he set the brushes aside and he picked up paper and board instead, seating himself with as much care as Joseph had. They didn't seem to notice him; Caroline was in her own world, and she had dragged Joseph along with her. She had not asked Joseph if he wished her to model for him; he had not asked her to sit. Wordless, they had assumed their roles.

And he now drew them.

Not one, not the other, but both. The girl upon her chair, her expression shifting and changing, swinging between boredom and curiosity, between introspection and sudden bursts of speech, and the boy who sat, almost hunched, his hands spreading out across the flat surface of paper, starting at its centre and working out toward its edges. Joseph answered her questions without looking up, and he often looked up without speaking.

Master Havernell rarely drew from life; it was an almost novel reminder of his roots in Westerfield. But he did not draw without purpose, and he bent his gift to the simplicity of stark lines, seeking shade and shadow, seeking either past or future from the moving present.

"What are you drawing?"

Caroline had abandoned her stool. When, Master Havernell was not certain, and Joseph did not seem to notice her absence.

It was going to be difficult, he thought, to have her here. But his frown passed as he lifted the edge of his board, and what it contained, from her openly prying eyes.

"It is not a matter that concerns you," he lied.

And she knew. But she didn't argue with him. He would learn to appreciate that, in time.

If they had it.

True to his word, Master Havernell arranged for history and language classes. But he also added a new class for both of them: etiquette.

"Why?" Caroline asked him, when the stiff woman in her perfect clothing had been introduced.

"Because, Caroline, you will require these lessons."

"But why?"

"I have said that many of my patrons are men of power," he replied, meeting her eyes and holding them. "And it is likely that you will meet them. Even if we seldom venture out, my clients do visit. You will be here. I would appreciate it if you learned how to approach them without causing offence."

She shrugged, eyeing the small classroom dubiously.

But Joseph said, "We have to, Caroline," and to the Master's surprise, she complied.

She was the better student, however.

Six months passed in the home of Master Havernell. During those six months, the Master was often absent; he would set simple tasks for his students, as he called them, and he would disappear for days at a time.

His household consisted of three women and two men; the teachers that he had taken on were not given rooms within the manse. But the household staff took an instant liking to the shy boy and the bold girl who had come from the foundling halls, and as often happened, they attempted to make up for the lack of family in either of the two children's lives.

As so often happened, they succeeded. Caroline took to the kitchens to help when she wasn't with Joseph or in class, and instead of stiffening or drawing a line between their stations – if Caroline could clearly be said to have one – they let her in.

With Joseph, they were more cautious, but he didn't seem to mind.

Mostly because, as Caroline pointed out, he just never noticed. It wasn't just color that he didn't see clearly.

But she saw for him.

And because she watched, she was aware of his next true painting. It wasn't done in the Studio; it wasn't done on the paper that Master Havernell provided. It certainly wasn't done with brushes, for although the Master insisted that Joseph better learn their use, Joseph shied away from paints, seeking instead to better refine his use of pencils in varying hardnesses.

But pencils were used for many things, and one of them was lessons. Instead of the slates that the foundling hall provided, Master Havernell provided notebooks; he wanted, he said, a permanent record of their progress.

Master Travatti was speaking of history in his lovely, sonorous voice, and Caroline was taking notes. She made certain that Joseph took them too, because Master Havernell hadn't lied; he *did* check their progress. And most often disapproved of it.

As she was aware that she had no real position in his household, that she was neither servant nor apprentice, she took his disapproval to heart, and she struggled to avoid it. Joseph was Joseph; he did what she reminded him to do, and little else.

But the lesson itself was interesting enough that Caroline forgot to pay attention to anything but Master Travatti, and when she finally looked at Joseph, she noticed that the pencil movements that had, at one point, been forming letters, were now forming something else entirely.

Fascinated, she watched Joseph's hands, and then followed his arms up to his shoulders. His head was hunched over the notebook and his eyes were slightly glassy.

Master Travatti frowned, but before he could speak, Caroline shushed him forcibly. It made him raise his thick, dark brows.

"I think that Madam Faira would not approve of your method of asking for silence," he said, but with a slight smile. He was indulgent, in a fashion, and because he was smitten with Caroline's interest in his field of speciality.

She nodded absently, and when Joseph reached blindly for a different pencil, she opened his box and laid all of them out in a neat and orderly row. He looked up at her, looked through her, but he smiled; he was aware of her presence because of her simple, instinctive act.

Master Travatti had been speaking of the founding of Augustine.

And Joseph was drawing mountains. They were not distant mountains, although mountains did, indeed, form part of the city's backdrops. They were not entirely familiar. But they were surrounded by trees and grass, by flat lands. Horses appeared, hooves first, upon that grass, and through it, they cut a path that implied that many others had passed this way.

There was no city, in Joseph's drawing. There were, however, men upon those horses; the horses were not wild. They wore barding, and the men upon their heavy frames wore armor. It was not armor with which she was familiar, and she frowned.

The men were tall. All of them. Tall and forbidding. They wore helms, and the helms were down; she was grateful for it. Something about this hunting party was disturbing. It wasn't the spears, although spears were carried; it wasn't their numbers, for the paintings in the gallery often boasted a much, much larger host.

But something was just *wrong*.

Too wrong.

"Joseph," she said, speaking where she had all but forbidden Master Travatti to do so.

And Joseph said, in an almost strangled voice, "This is what was here *before*." The drawing was not yet done, but she could almost hear the thunder of hooves; the horses were in motion.

And in front of them, at last, there was a man in long robes. She was not afraid of this man, but he invoked fear anyway; she was afraid *for* him.

"*Joseph*," she hissed.

But Joseph couldn't stop.

"Master Travatti!"

The history teacher frowned.

"Please – if Master Havernell is here, get him." And she reached out as she spoke and pulled the pencil from Joseph's moving hand. It didn't come easily; she had to struggle with it, and him.

But she *had* to, and knew it, and because she did, she won.

Joseph went to bed before dinner. His eyes were dark, and his face was pinched; he looked fevered, and Caroline was afraid for him. But he was *here*, and he was listening, and that was better than he had been. She'd taken his notebook anyway.

"Promise me," she told him severely, "that you won't draw anything tonight." Her foot tapped against the floorboards.

"I can't," he told her. "You've got all my pencils."

"Promise me anyway."

He lifted his pinky, and she sighed and lifted her own, entwining them in a singularly Westerfield gesture. "You should eat something," she told him.

"I can't."

"Then you should sleep."

He nodded. She knew it would take him a long time. "I'll come," she said at last. "I'll bring a lamp."

And he smiled gratefully. He seemed so young, so much younger than she was.

Master Havernell was not in residence; he did not arrive until dinner, and when he came into the dining hall, he found Caroline alone, poring over the image that was not quite complete.

"What are you doing, Caroline? Where is Joseph?"

"He's in bed."

"Why?"

"He's not well."

"Ah. You sent him?"

She nodded. And then she pushed the notebook toward him almost guiltily. "He drew this in history," she said quietly. "I –"

But Master Havernell's brows rose as he gazed at the picture, and his eyes narrowed instantly, becoming all edge. He looked dangerous. "Joseph drew *this*?"

"Well I certainly didn't."

"He didn't finish it," he said, and she heard the relief in his voice.

"I wouldn't let him," she replied grimly.

"You?"

"I took his pencils."

He stared at her. "Do you know," he said softly, "what this is?"

"I would think," she told him, and with more hesitation, "that it's about the founding of Augustine. But that man – he's going to die."

"Oh yes," Master Havernell replied bitterly. "And he was not the only one."

"It's a Painting."

"It is," he replied. "History. You did better than you know, Caroline." His eyes narrowed. "Or perhaps not. You are not an Augustine Painter."

She knew it, but had to ask. "How do you know?"

"Because I drew your history," he said softly. "And you had one. You had parents. They lived here."

"And Joseph?"

He shook his head.

"These men –"

"They are not men," he said grimly. "And in truth, I have never seen a war party of this size. Joseph is not the only man to paint the founding. I recognize the armor. I recognize the barding. He does good work with pencil."

"What does it mean?"

"It means," he said quietly, "That Joseph of Havernell will indeed be a Master Painter in his time."

But she heard the *if* in his voice, and although it was almost her responsibility to ask questions, she found that she didn't have any she wanted answers to. They ate in silence.

It took three days for Joseph to be well enough to leave his room, and during the nights, Caroline slept little. She brought him lamplight, as she had promised, and he did not draw. But she sat by his side while he tossed and turned, and when the oil ran low in the lamp, she replenished it. Joseph had often been plagued by nightmares in Westerfield, and she had found ways to bring candles to him; the light always helped. It helped now, and because it did, she continued.

In Westerfield, she had never known for certain that she would have children of her own, and as orphans often did, she wanted them. Maybe that's why she had taken Joseph under wing. But she had kept him there because he fit. She had taken to bringing him what she could because it eased him.

And it helped here, as well. The shadows receded from his eyes, and the fever left him.

When it was gone, Master Havernell summoned them to the studio.

"What you did," he told Caroline, "was both wise and dangerous."

Joseph said little.

"Joseph, there are things that it is not yet safe for you to Paint, and you *must* begin to recognize them now. I did not think that I would have this conversation with you for years, but clearly I misjudged you.

"And Caroline, there is a danger in what you did."

"Why?"

"Because it is never wise to stop a Painter from Painting. It *can* be done. I have done it myself. But it is always costly for the Painter. Joseph was abed for three days. He might have been longer. Joseph, how do you feel?"

"Tired."

"Good. Do you feel like drawing?"

Joseph shook his head.

"Better. You have so little experience. But I must ask you now, how was this drawing different from the one that you drew of Caroline?"

He shrugged, and she batted his shoulder. He rolled his wide eyes. "I don't know," he told her, annoyed.

"Well, try to answer the question anyway."

"I just – I had to draw," he told her. "When Master Travatti was talking, I could see something. It was – I had to draw it."

"And with Caroline?"

"It ... it was different."

"How?"

"I told you – I don't know."

"Fair enough. But your life now depends upon your ability to tell the difference between the two. Painters are not always wordsmiths; I do not demand that you come up with words if you *do not* have them. But the understanding that exists beneath the surface of words must be present, Joseph, or I will forbid you to draw at all."

Joseph looked stricken and Caroline put an arm around his shoulder, shoring him up. Then she looked up at Master Havernell and said, "It was different."

He raised a brow.

"I could watch him draw *me*. I was afraid of what he drew only after he'd finished it. No," she added, "that's not true. I wasn't afraid until I saw Count Thermann."

"But you knew that he was Painting."

"I knew that he was doing something, yes. I knew that he had to finish it – he's like that."

"And the other?"

"I knew that he had to finish it," she replied starkly. "But I also knew that he mustn't."

"Why?"

"I don't know either. They frightened me," she added, after a moment's thought. "And I didn't want to see *more* of them."

"Wise, wise girl. You have earned your place here, Caroline, and if I could choose who might be among the Augustine Painters, I would give you that title. But it is not my choice. Come, both of you. There is work here that I would have you see. Touch *nothing*."

He rose, and they followed.

He led them through the gallery, but he moved swiftly. Beyond the gallery, there was a door, a small door. It was locked. He touched it with the flats of his palm. "This door," he told them both softly, "will open for no one but me. Do not attempt to open it if I am not present."

Caroline nodded. Joseph crept closer to her.

The door slid inward on its silent hinges, and Master Havernell stepped through its frame.

There were paintings in this room, but they were not framed; they were stacked almost carelessly against bare floor, and the piles themselves were covered with heavy tarpaulin.

Master Havernell lifted the heavy cloth and set it aside. "These were in my former Master's collection," he told them quietly. "And I have become their keeper."

"But you don't –"

"They are not meant to be seen. If the Augustine Painters had the choice, they would never exist at all. Come, Joseph." He lifted a stretched canvas with as much care as he might have handled a poisoned blade.

And he turned it toward them, exposing a portrait.

A man's portrait. Caroline recognized the armor immediately, but the helm that had hidden the faces of the riders now sat in the crook of an arm.

The man was *beautiful*. Beautiful and terrifying. His eyes were a bright and burnished steel, and his skin was almost golden. She looked away. Joseph did not.

"Are they all of him?" Joseph asked Master Havernell. The Master frowned.

"They are," he said evenly. "Every one. They are not all done in this style, and not a single one is done in pencil. If you asked the men and women who painted these portraits – and they could speak at all – they would probably tell you that these are their life's work, their masterpieces.

"They were certainly their life's end," he added bitterly.

"Why do you keep them?"

He shook his head. "I cannot honestly say," he said at last. "But no Painter has destroyed these paintings; they are the last paintings, each and every one, that the Painters in question made."

"What happened to the Painters?"

"They died," he said quietly. "They died, raving like madmen, in a language that not one of us understands. We believe it to be his language," he added softly, gesturing at the beautiful, armored man.

"This is our history?"

"And our future," he said grimly. "It is a future that all of Augustine works to prevent from happening."

"But …"

"Yes, Caroline – Joseph, do not touch anything!"

"But there are no deaths, are there?"

"Not in the paintings themselves."

"Then what are you trying to prevent?"

"If I could tell you that," he said, with a sudden anger, "we would lose no more Painters." He looked at Joseph.

Joseph said nothing.

It was another year before Joseph's talent once again displayed itself. He had grown taller, his hair had been cut, and he still wouldn't paint unless Master Havernell stood over his shoulder. He did not look fifteen.

Caroline had grown taller. She was also fifteen years of age, but when she desired to do so, she could pass for twenty. She had been encouraged – Master Havernell's word for ordered – to choose her own clothing. As usual, she had done so with glee, but she had also insisted she be allowed to choose clothing for Joseph. Their outfits matched, although Joseph didn't notice and didn't care. She told him anyway. Because she did.

The cook told her she looked lovely. The footman told her she made him regret his decision to remain childless. Master Havernell told her to change, and offered his staff a sour glare. They weathered it with humor, however, and a great deal of indulgence. In the august home of Havernell, none of the staff had children, and if children came after they accepted employment, they lost their positions.

Understanding came with time. It was not that Master Havernell didn't like children; it was rather the opposite. But he was a man with many enemies, most undeclared, and children were reduced in the eyes of those enemies to weapons that might be used against him.

Neither Joseph nor Caroline asked him how he had discovered this.

But he told them he had found only one certain way of protecting himself. And if any thought him callous for doing so, this served his purpose just as well.

But he could not deny himself the company of his apprentice, and Caroline came with Joseph.

With Caroline, however, came other difficulties. And Joseph, as was so often the case, saw it first.

He was painting, and he had still acquired no love of oil, no great respect for canvas; he approached both as if they might bite him. Master Havernell had tightened his jaw into a steel line, and in the end he had retreated to his half of the studio they shared, leaving Caroline as their bridge. On this particular day she chattered like a chipmunk because Master Havernell had been invited to attend a festival soirée at the King's Summer palace – with his apprentices. The Master was attempting to find an appropriate way to decline on their behalf when she had entered the room in which the offending missive had been delivered, and she had been *so* overjoyed that even Havernell could not deny her. And he *had* tried.

But he, like his staff, and very like the boy upon whom she depended, and who depended so much more obviously on her, could in the end do little but marvel; for if it was true that even the plainest of people were made beautiful by joy, it was also true that Caroline was to be anything but plain.

He wanted to paint her; to capture her radiance, as if by so doing he could somewhere hoard it against the grim future that lurked so often around time's corner. He even began, choosing his canvas and his palette while she effused. But Joseph, sullen as he ever got in his struggle to master those same tools, began first, and when he had truly embarked upon has work, Havernell lost both opportunity and desire, for Caroline fell utterly silent, and the atmosphere in the studio changed abruptly.

Havernell *felt* it. He looked up to see that the girl had abandoned her chair and with it her favored place in the light; that she had crept quietly into a space that no one – not even Havernell himself – should have been able to breach, and that she was quietly and with increasing urgency choosing Joseph's colors, depriving him of those which had no place in their consensual act of capturing reality.

Even when the subject chilled her.

Havernell let them work. Sunlight left; she left as well, but only for as long as it took to fetch a weaker light in which to work. Joseph looked up at her absence, and only then. But when she returned, he held out his hand, waiting now for the right brush, the right color. And she offered both to his gift.

Master Havernell knew then that he had been right to bring her here. But watching her face, watching the growing absence of color there, he almost felt the lie in that certainty, for what she now gave to the boy came at her own expense.

She will pay the Painter's price, he thought, almost without thinking, the knowledge was so visceral. *And it may well destroy one of them.*

But she will do it as if she had no other choice. Because she is half of Joseph's vision.

The painting was not a portrait; it was not, in the truest sense of the word, a tableau. It was rushed, frenzied, a thing composed of motion that drew the eye and scarred the heart. Caroline was at its center, but she was not alone.

And the man who was with her, his face so twisted it was almost a charicature – a style frowned on by any Painter Hall of worth – was Count Thermann.

"Caroline."

Caroline looked up from the books and pamphlets that were becoming a large part of her life's work. What Joseph could not retain, she seemed determined to absorb for him.

Master Havernell stood in her doorway. He did not speak, content to watch her struggle with language that came naturally to him.

Although Joseph often watched her, this was not the same, and without another word, she set her notes aside.

"You know why I am here."

She nodded. "You don't want me to go."

He raised a brow. "Given that I've forbidden it, that would seem an understatement."

She left her chair, her hands finding her slender hips as she adopted an increasingly familiar posture of annoyance. "You promised," she told him, frowning.

"Now is not the time for games," Havernell replied, but didn't seem surprised. "You saw what Joseph painted. What he could not have painted without you."

She nodded.

"And you are wise enough to fear it."

She nodded again.

"Then I should not need to have this discussion with you now."

"You need to."

He crossed his arms over his chest. "I am not nobility," he told her softly. It was always worse when he spoke softly.

"None of the Augustine Painters are."

"But," he continued with a frown, "I *am* an Augustine Painter. This fact affords me some protection. Joseph is my apprentice; if he is not yet acknowledged a Painter, he is still afforded some of the same respect offered his master, namely, me." He let his hands fall to the side as he studied her expression. "And you already know this."

She nodded, all of her lovely motion muted.

"Then why?"

"Because Joseph doesn't."

"I can explain it to him."

She shook her head. "He thinks you can do anything. You've saved the King's life; he believes that you'd never let anything happen to us."

"Caroline –"

"And he knows," she continued, raising a perfect chin, "that he's going to be asked to paint."

Master Havernell frowned.

"We watched you packing. You took your paints. And you took his."

"Joseph noticed this, did he?"

She had the grace to color. "He can't paint yet. He's not ready. But you've already made it clear that he has to go."

"I thought I was more subtle than that." He watched her now, his face expressionless.

"You were. And I was content with that when he thought we were going because of me."

"You are perceptive."

She shrugged. "You know what you're doing. But when you changed your mind, I wanted him to be ready. He just doesn't do well with surprises." She offered him an apologetic smile.

"He is not a child, Caroline; you forget that he's your age."

"He asked me not to go," she continued.

Master Havernell was vaguely surprised.

"And he meant it."

"But?"

"He needs me to be there."

"I will be there."

She said nothing for a moment, and then she shook her head. "Did you *really* come from Westerfield?"

He raised a brow.

"I'll take that as a yes. But it must have been a long time ago. You don't remember what it's like. We do."

"You've been part of my household for well over a year."

She nodded, her hand straying to the closed cover of her notebook. "And I love it here." Her tone was not wistful; it was bold, as if she were daring him to deny her the right.

He didn't. "But Joseph doesn't?"

"He does, but that only makes it harder for him. He knows that if he fails it will make you look bad." She held out empty hands. "And it's true. It will. I told him that I wanted to go because I'd never get another opportunity to meet the King," she added softly, "and he believes me."

"And what did he say?" It was, of course another test.

"He said he was happy." Another test to fail.

Master Havernell rolled his eyes.

"Let me go with him."

"Joseph is lucky, in you. Do you understand what he's willing to risk, because he's afraid?"

She looked away. "I don't hate his fear," she said at last. "And I wish you wouldn't. You aren't the one at risk; we are."

"I am not happy with your request," he said, ignoring her words. "But if you will not be moved by reason, I will grant it."

"I have to go," she said starkly, and with the force of utter certainty that made youth so beautiful and so vulnerable. "Because if he fails in front of the King, I don't think he'll ever succeed."

"You see too clearly, Caroline."

"I have to." She smiled wanly, then. "I promised I'd take care of him."

"And who will take care of you, Caroline Havernell?"

"He will," she answered. "When he's ready."

Master Havernell said bitterly, "Do not count on a Painter for your safety." And then, because he knew she was thinking of Joseph, he lifted a hand. Surrender. And defense.

Caroline *was* excited. That was no lie. And because she was, her companions could pretend that no part of her frenetic preparations were caused by fear. She fussed with Joseph's clothing almost as much as she fussed with her own, and she cursed his hair in a way that would have made Madam Dagleish frown that special "you're confined to your room for the rest of your natural life" frown.

She would have done the same for Master Havernell, but when he came to meet them, he was *perfect*. His attire made the difference in their respective positions utterly clear. He even seemed at home in the confines of velvet, and Caroline described the deep rich purple to Joseph in hushed tones.

The carriage was called for, and Joseph was burdened with a canvas, the three brushes he tolerated, and his palette. He seldom had cause to travel by carriage, however, and he lost the colors he couldn't differentiate as they made their way through the streets. The streets were very crowded.

"Who are the men in green?" Caroline asked, letting Joseph know, as subtly as she could, that they were significant. He raised a grey face. "The ones wearing small eagles?"

"Those ones."

Master Havernell frowned. "They are far from their home," he said softly. "And if I were to guess, they are the reason that we were extended our invitation. Caroline?"

"New Barrania?"

"Very good. Yes. But they wear war garb."

"It's the city state on our Eastern border," she told Joseph. He nodded.

"The enemy is at work here," Master Havernell said. "Would that we had the luxury of only one."

"Of them?" Caroline asked.

"Enemy," he corrected her.

The palace stood in the heart of the Western city. And if it was only the Summer palace, it was still by far the grandest of mansions that either of the Westerfield foundlings had ever seen. It moved even Caroline to awed silence, and gave Master Havernell a moment of peace in which to compose himself. The presence of the New Barranian men disturbed him, and Caroline at least was aware of this. It had been a long time since he had had to take such care to guard his expression – and he had no wish to contemplate the last time. But he was now ill at ease, and for the first time in a year, he truly regretted his impulsive decision to take her into his home.

This, however, he managed to keep to himself.

If the exterior of the Summer palace was enough to engender hushed awe, the grounds had the opposite effect. Both Caroline and Joseph whispered to one another, and Caroline had to pull Joseph's pencils from his hands because the boy so desperately wanted to draw what he saw. Havernell said nothing, remembering the first time he had seen the Summer Gardens; he had been with his Master, then, and the dream of being a Master in his own right was decades away. The memory made him smile, and he welcomed it. But only for a few moments; they were early, but it would be far too easy to lose all sense of time here, and time, where men of power waited, was its own imperative.

Still, he led them away without rancor, and with a great deal of muted regret.

"Come," he told them gently. "I fear that we have been misled; you will see the inside of a studio, and if it is grand – and it is – it will never be the equal of the Summer grounds."

To his surprise, it was Joseph who spoke. "It couldn't be," he said sadly. "There's no life in it."

But not none.

It was said that the King was never alone, and to foundlings, that seemed a dream come true. But if it was, the austere man who greeted Master Havernell seemed to take no joy from the fact. He had attendants who were as finely accoutred as the Master Painter, but they were as severe as Madam Dagleish, and from their disdainful expressions, less friendly – which both Caroline and Joseph would have sworn was impossible.

Around these intimidating men were a thicket of bristling guards, hands upon sheathed blades. Yet they seemed somehow less dangerous than the King's friends.

Behind these men, were others. An old man in fine robes, and two people who were barely older than Caroline.

"Master Havernell," the old man said, bowing formally.

"Master Giavanno," Master Havernell replied, offering the deepest bow Caroline had ever seen him offer. She knew why; Master Giavanno was the most famous of the Augustine Painters. He worked at an *Emperor's* pleasure.

"I see that rumor is in this case true," the older man added. "You have indeed taken apprentices."

Caroline stiffened.

Master Havernell placed a hand upon her shoulder. "Rumor is so seldom accurate. But yes, I have. May I introduce Caroline and Joseph?"

Master Giavanno smiled. "You must have distinguished yourselves," he told them, with a sly smile. "Moraine is known throughout Augustine for his lack of respect for apprentices."

"That, old man, is entirely too much gossip for my liking." But Master Havernell smiled as well. Turning to the young man and woman who stood silent behind their master, he added, "The Master hasn't changed much, has he? Caroline, Joseph, meet Camille and Felix. They are both on their way to becoming Painters in their own right."

The plain girl's smile changed the look of her face; she was almost beautiful. But it didn't last. She turned to her Master, and said, "Where would you like me to set up, Master Giavanno?"

"By the bay window," he replied genially, as if she were a servant. She nodded, and Felix, burdened by supplies, followed her.

Caroline felt the sting of a deep envy. She watched the strange girl, and realized that she would never be her peer. Camille was a true Augustine Painter; Caroline was a fraud. And everyone would know it soon enough; King, Councillors, and Master Painter alike.

But Joseph tugged at her sleeve, and when she turned, she saw that he was the color of fine ash. His hand was shaking. She had almost forgotten him in her bitter introspection. "I'm sorry, Joseph," she told him, meaning it. "Where are we to work?"

Master Havernell was accorded the respect of the King; Master Giavanno was likewise honored. The apprentices of either were invisible, or might as well have been. The only person who seemed to notice this was Caroline; Joseph was trying his best to crawl into his own little world, and the Giavanno apprentices seemed to be accustomed to their lack of presence.

Or so Caroline thought; she was therefore surprised when Camille came over.

"Master Havernell," Camille said quietly, "is only summoned in certain situations." Her voice was grave. "My Master might be summoned on a whim; the last time we were here, we painted portraits of the King's daughters – and the men who were being considered as their husbands." She looked over at her Master; he was in conversation with Master Havernell, the King, and the King's advisors. "But we won't be painting portraits today."

Caroline nodded. She felt the strong urge to tell Camille the truth and have done, but she remembered the heavy hand of Master Havernell as it rested on her shoulder, and said nothing, feeling very much the fraud.

"Felix isn't allowed to paint portraits," Camille added, with a soft frown. "And even painting at all is a risk, for him. It's why I'm allowed to be here."

"Oh? You're not a painter?"

"I'm not Felix's equal," Camille replied, without envy or bitterness. "But that's why I have to be here. What's it like?"

"What?"

"Sorry." Camille grinned sheepishly, and Caroline felt herself liking the girl. "Bad habit of mine. I tend to say whatever I'm thinking. Felix used to talk more, and I seem to have inherited most of his words. But I'm not as good with them. I meant apprenticing under Master Havernell."

"I'm not sure," Caroline replied cautiously. "I haven't really been with him very long."

"We were really surprised when we heard he'd taken apprentices. He's not a man who likes people, especially not young ones."

"I don't think it's confined to the young," she said, as Master Havernell's voice momentarily filled the studio. "If I had to guess, I'd say he's not all that fond of the King's advisors, and any one of them is older than he is."

Camille frowned. "Master Giavanno isn't pleased either."

"How can you tell?"

"Unlike Master Havernell, Master Giavanno only shouts at people he likes, and he's not saying a word. It's bad," she added.

"What do you think they're arguing about?"

"If I had to guess – and I'm not about to interrupt them to ask – I'd say that the advisors have just told our Masters that they're going to be observed."

Caroline was shocked. "Who tells a Master Painter that?"

"The King does," Camille replied, her frown robbing her face of its elusive beauty.

The King lifted a hand, and everyone fell silent.

"He uses his advisors," Camille said quietly. "It gives the Painters the opportunity to say anything they want without offering offense. But they've said everything they can, and now that they're finished, he'll tell them what to do. And if they want to paint in the King's studio again, they won't repeat themselves."

Caroline privately indulged in a moment of prayer. And then, leaving Master Havernell to salvage – or destroy – his own career, she turned to Joseph. To Joseph, who was white with anxiety.

"It'll be fine," she told him. "Just think of it as drawing class."

"But I'm not allowed to *draw*," he said, stricken.

"No, but we've been painting together for months now, and I'll be right here. I'll give you the colors you need."

He calmed slowly, but he did calm down. And he might have stayed that way, but the studio began to fill, and the finely attired men and women who entered the large room known as the Painter's Hall entered almost as if they owned it. Only nobility had that utter certainty of bearing; the intruders spoke a smattering of the three languages Caroline was struggling to master, and they did so without apparent effort.

She would have been fascinated. She was.

Until the moment she laid eyes upon a man she had hoped never to see again. Count Thermann.

He was instantly aware of her, but he did not appear to be surprised. Nor did he appear to be unduly interested. But he drifted slowly to where she now sat, attended by others of his class.

Master Havernell was at her side in an instant. He did not look pleased, but that could have been due to the King's unexpected and entirely unwelcome command. "Attend to Joseph," he told her grimly. "I will attend to our distinguished visitors."

He could have used the word cockroach with less vitriol. She nodded gratefully, but as she began to arrange the paints and brushes, she became aware that Count Thermann, thus attended, still watched her – and that the moment Joseph truly began, he would *know*. She was paralyzed by the knowledge, but also keenly aware that Joseph was waiting.

And she had already made her choice. To do anything else was to make a mockery of her decision – and Master Havernell's subsequent decision to allow her *to* choose.

"Master Havernell," she said, with as much gravity as she could muster, "What is the subject the King has requested?"

"War," was the curt reply. "You saw its harbingers upon the open road; he wishes us to paint them."

"But –"

Count Thermann was watching with interest.

"*Yes*, Caroline?"

"But we have no models."

"Ah." His voice lost a tiny bit of its edge. "We will not be required to work from life, today. If what we paint here merits it, we will be required to travel."

Aware of Joseph, she said, "Our history –"

"Wait but a moment. A painting is being brought as a source. It is not a Work, and it has the virtue of being singularly unimaginative, but Master Giavanno's students are likewise hampered, and the King was prepared for this. The painting will be your model."

She understood the warning he so diplomatically offered, and nodded. Then Master Havernell turned away, to continue his curt but graceful response to the nobles whose presence he so clearly resented.

But he seemed, to Caroline, to be mollified, and it took her a moment to understand why.

She did, however; she had spoken like an apprentice, and none of the observers could know that it was because she almost always asked Joseph's questions for him.

The painting brought for the use of the apprentices left something to be desired; it had as much character as a tax collector's map. But it had an unexpected benefit; it was small enough that the four apprentices were practically forced to huddle together. Caroline had learned that, when Madam Dagleish was not present, there was safety in numbers.

"I don't understand," Felix hissed, as he cast a furtive glance at nobles he clearly recognized. "Why were we invited at all? We're not going to do good work here. This – this is too damn big for us."

It was something Caroline herself had been thinking, and she didn't like the only answer that came to mind, so she didn't offer it. Besides which, Joseph was silently wondering the same thing, if for markedly different reasons, and she didn't want to add the paralysis of guilt to his near panic.

Instead, she said, "It doesn't matter. We're here, and we don't have much choice; let's just do the best we can." And saying that, she handed Joseph a brush. But she held the brush for a moment longer than necessary, so that their hands were connected by wood.

Joseph had never been so nervous. He did not want Caroline to let go of the brush because when she did he would be alone. She found it easy to talk to these strangers; he found it impossible. And it wasn't because he was a Painter; the other girl was a Painter, and she spoke as easily as Caroline did. No, he thought, bitterly. It was because he was Joseph, and he was just not capable of – of whatever it took to deserve to be here.

Felix started first, and after a few moments it became clear that he would have no trouble continuing. The girl – Camille? – started next, and if she was vastly more hesitant, she too became caught up in the act of painting; they both grew remote. But Joseph's hand shook terribly.

He stared mutely at Caroline, and after a moment she shrugged stiffly, and brought out his drawing board and his beloved pencils. If Master Havernell was present, he said nothing, and Joseph knew; he listened for the sound of no other voice.

"Come on," Caroline said. "You've never done a real painting without sketching first. This *is* the way you work, and in the end, they aren't the Painters; you are."

His hands shook as she gave him his pencils. "Caroline – " he began, meaning to confess that he was a failure.

But she shook her head fiercely. "You *are* a Painter," she said, catching his hands. "You saved me. You gave me my whole life. You can do this. Look at them," she added, lowering her voice. "They have everything they've ever needed. None of their lives depend on you." She was wrong, although neither of them knew it.

"But mine does. I think it always has. You won't fail me," she added, and she dropped an arm around his shoulders.

Another boy might have found her faith a burden; to Joseph it was an anchor because her words were always true. He had only come close to failing her once – and then, not because of incompetence, but because of fear.

He took the pencil in hand, as Felix, older by at least five years, had taken the brush, and he set it not to finely stretched canvas, but to paper. But when lead began its slow spread across the sheet, when Caroline began to sharpen other pencils, he glanced at the painting that was meant to be his model, and he surrendered to his gift.

And Caroline stood watch behind him, like the King's own guards stood watch over the King.

"Well," Count Thermann said, "this *is* unusual. An apprentice with no brushes?"

Caroline looked up, schooling her expression. Reminding herself, in the absence of her Master, that it had been her choice to come here.

And she had been right. Joseph *did* need her.

She therefore pretended not to hear the Count, and this was a mistake.

"Caroline," he said, when it became clear she would not answer. "It has been two years that you have been in Master Havernell's care. Has he put you to no better use than this?"

She almost handed Joseph the wrong pencil. Frowning, she corrected herself. She wanted Master Havernell, but she knew he was painting at the King's pleasure and the King's command. He had warned her; she had taken the risk. But the studio was *full* of people, and she knew there was safety in that. She reached for a pencil, and then frowned and brought out charcoal instead. Joseph took it without comment, and began to add broad, wild strokes to his landscape. She loved to watch him draw; it was only in this way that he was bold and definite. She did not, however, care to have him observed, and certainly not by a man like Thermann.

"Pencils?" The Count continued, oblivious to her growing resentment. "Is the House of Havernell so insignificant that it expects its students to labor with inferior materials?"

She handed Joseph the hardest and thinnest of his coals. Then, frowning, she handed him the softest of his pencils as captured vision began to emerge. It was not that she felt no fear of the Count; she couldn't help but fear him. But she had always found Joseph's work compelling, and today was no exception. He didn't need her to filter color; there wasn't any. But he did need her; she was not about to disappoint him.

She flinched when Count Thermann's hand touched her shoulder. "Madam Dagleish did you a disservice," he said softly, his lips by her ears. "You are wasted here, little better than a common servant."

"Better that than a whore," Caroline said, before she could stop herself. His hand tightened.

"So," he said softly. Just that.

Oh, she regretted the words. But she could not take them back; could not withdraw them.

"You forget yourself," he told her softly, "and that is unwise, for it is clear to me now that you are, as I thought, no Painter."

Joseph looked up at her; his pencil had stilled.

"She *is*," he said, with a ferocity she had never seen from him outside of the act of Painting. "And only a Painter would understand how."

The Count's brow rose; Caroline was afraid for Joseph.

But Joseph looked through him, and said, "I've painted you, Count Thermann, and if you want, I can do so again." He reached for a clean sheet of paper.

"Are you threatening me, boy?"

"No. I'm offering you the gift of an Augustine Painter."

The Count's gaze burned. But he let go of Caroline's shoulder.

Only Caroline knew what the gesture had cost Joseph; he had forsaken a true work to make it. And he had done it for her, when she had been almost certain that he could no longer hear her. She fumbled with his pencils, and found the right one instantly, taking the blank sheet of paper from his nerveless hands.

"Joseph," she whispered, seeking to comfort him.

But he seemed almost a stranger to her; he took nothing but the pencil, and seemed to require nothing else. But he needed that, and in the end it was Caroline who took momentary comfort from the fact.

Count Thermann vanished. He was angry, Caroline thought; angry and afraid. Master Havernell had been wrong.

There were no portraits painted. She knew there wouldn't be because she could see what Joseph drew. His drawing, much faster than painting, even the broad strokes that Felix seemed to favor, was clearly of a large body of men, and they were all in motion.

They reminded her inexplicably of the drawing he had begun in History class, although she couldn't say why. No, she thought, watching as the drawing emerged. They reminded her of Lord Raleigh's men, the men who adorned both grave and Havernell gallery. She handed Joseph fine pencils, and she continued to mark his progress by their dwindling length.

But she must have been caught up in the work, because when

interruption came, it came in the crimson of sunset. The studio was almost empty, the nobles who had come to satisfy their curiosity, gone.

"It is a good foundation," an unfamiliar voice said, and she looked up to meet the eyes of Master Giavanno. "It lacks fine detail, but it is better by far than the pencil work produced by most houses." He looked at her for a moment, and her stomach responded before she could. She should have died of embarrassment. But she didn't; there was something about this man that seemed safe.

"You don't paint," he said, but the words were not an accusation.

"No."

"But you are sensitive, for one who doesn't. I finished a half hour ago –"

"You *finished* a painting?"

He frowned. "I finished for the day. Most work is not done in one sitting; the compulsion eases as the light passes." He raised a brow. "But judging by your companion, perhaps you are not aware of this. What was I saying?

"Oh yes, I remember now. I watched you and young Joseph while you worked, and I will say this; you worked almost as one man. Or woman," he added. "It is most unusual, but I expect that from Moraine. Master Havernell," he added. "The boy is nervous, but he is gifted, and it is not a weak gift; I see almost nothing of the master in the student."

As if, Caroline thought, that were a good thing.

"And if this is unorthodox, perhaps there is value in your approach – the boy's rough work is almost done, and I think I can see why we're here." His gaze was thoughtful, but the thoughts clearly troubled him. "Come," Master Giavanno added. "If you can attract the attention of your companion, we are to be fed for our work here, and there is no kitchen finer than the royal kitchen."

Master Havernell joined them before Joseph was finished.

"Should I stop him?" she asked, still handling pencils that had visibly shortened over the length of the day.

"He should stop soon."

She hesitated, and then said, "Joseph painted the first picture at night."

"You see, Havernell?"

Master Havernell frowned.

"The boy has a powerful talent."

"Perhaps he had incentive, even if he did not recognize it himself at the time," Master Havernell replied. "Yes," he added, finally answering Caroline's question. "Interrupt him if you can; he must eat."

Very quietly Caroline started to put his pencils and charcoal away. But she was aware, as she did, that Master Giavanno's eyes did not leave her.

Dinner was a fine, even gaudy affair, and Caroline would have loved it were it not for two things. The fact that she was hideously underdressed – unsuited to be even a servant in the grand and endless halls – and the fact that Count Thermann was present. He appeared to be with his wife, but Caroline saw no safety there; she saw instead the bright, beautiful shroud of a deadly Winter. No joy warmed it; no life sustained it.

She found herself pitying the Countess, although she didn't understand why; she would never have done so had they met in Westerfield. Of the daughter for whom her service had in theory been intended, there was no sign.

The food was better than good, but even with the help of over a year of etiquette lessons, she found the utensils daunting, and ate little. Joseph, she noted wryly, ate well; if he picked up the wrong fork, the wrong spoon, or the wrong knife, he didn't seem to care, and she hadn't the heart to draw attention to his lapse.

There was talk in the long hall. Since she didn't eat much, she listened to some of it – but it was muted and distant. What she knew, for certain, was that she had the furtive attention of many of the men and women present; all of the apprentice painters did.

Felix was quiet; Camille was less so. But they ate as carefully as Caroline did, which is to say, hardly at all.

It was Camille who finally asked. "You don't paint, do you?"

But she asked it of Joseph.

Joseph looked up, and spoke around a mouthful of food. "I don't like paints," he mumbled.

"I wondered. But your pencils are very fine. And you finished something; neither of us did." She hesitated, and then added, "Do you know what it is that you drew?"

He shrugged. "Armies," he told her. As if it were natural.

Felix turned to Caroline. "You don't paint either." It was a different question.

Caroline froze, and forced herself to unfreeze. "No," she said, almost guiltily. "I can't."

"But you watched them, didn't you?" Camille asked Felix. Felix played with his food. Nodded. She turned back to Caroline. "You knew what he needed."

Caroline hesitated, and then said, "I've always helped him."

"Why?"

"I – I don't know." She smiled almost fondly as she said it. "In Westerfield, he was one of two friends. The other left almost a year before we did."

Camille brightened. "I came from Westerfield!"

"You did?"

She nodded. "Is Madam Dagleish still there?"

"She'll *always* be there," Joseph told her, frowning.

"How did you meet Master Havernell?"

The silence was awkward and profound.

"Never mind. I shouldn't have asked."

"Camille always says that. *After* she asks," Felix said, with a kind smile. "It doesn't matter. Master Havernell must have thought highly of both of you. He hasn't taken an apprentice before."

"Do you know why?"

Silence again, awkward in a different way. Camille glanced at Felix, and Felix glanced at dinner. Then they both looked up to the end of the table to see the two Master Painters engrossed in conversation. "Yeah," Felix said at last. "But it's only gossip."

"Gossip is better than nothing," Caroline said, a little too quickly.

"Gossip is bad," Joseph said, at the same time. They glared at each other.

Camille laughed. "I guess you *are* friends," she told them. "Master Havernell was an apprentice in Giavanno's House for five years."

"But he –"

"He was taken on by Master Evardos, after that."

"Master Giavanno kicked him out?"

"Moraine Havernell was a very, very talented painter. But his vision was always dark. Giavanno likes to take walks in the park; he likes to draw from life. We often go to the fountain in the city square, near the markets; we've done a lot of drawing there." They exchanged a glance that made of the words something private, something they were willing to share, but only barely.

"Moraine was a foundling – I guess you know we all are. Foundlings either make friends or they refuse to trust anyone."

"He didn't trust anyone."

"He did," Camille said, the soft lines of her mouth tightening a moment, as if in remembered pain. "A girl. Her name was Allaine. She came from Hovenshall Hall. He came from Westerfield. She was three years younger than he was, and he terrified her because he was so quick to anger."

"You were there?"

"No. We were both too young."

"Then how do you know –"

"There are paintings," she said quietly. "In Giavanno. Allaine's paintings. And many of them are of Moraine Havernell. His own, he took with him when he left – but the paintings he made of her, he destroyed."

Joseph's eyes rounded; it was almost shocking. No; it *was* shocking.

"What – what happened?"

"She died," Camille said quietly. "She was trying – we think she was – to paint a picture of Moraine. A portrait. And she was a little too old, a little too close to her power."

They did not speak of what she had painted in its place. They didn't have to.

But after the knowledge had taken root, Caroline said, "Master Havernell must have felt terrible."

"I don't know. He left shortly afterward. But I think –" She shook her head. "He hated his gift, for a while. He hated the painting. I think he thought it had failed him."

"He can save powerful men," Felix added softly. "He's saved the King's life many times. But he can't see … other things as clearly."

They were all very quiet, then.

But it was Joseph who spoke first. "Saving the King saves a lot of other lives," he said firmly. "I believe in him."

"Good," Camille told him, meaning it. "I think he needs it."

"He doesn't need anything."

But she stared up at the head table, lost a moment in thought. "I saw Allaine's paintings," she said at last. "I think she loved him. He frightened her, but he was kind to her, and they were friends, in the end; he protected her, and he told her how the world worked."

Like me, Caroline thought. *Like me and Joseph*. And she reached over and caught Joseph's hand in hers.

After dinner, they were shown to their rooms. "We don't get to go home?" Joseph asked quietly.

Master Havernell smiled, but it was a guarded smile. "We have the privilege of being the King's guests," he replied. "And the rooms here are very fine."

"Where are yours?"

"Mine are connected to both of yours. It is the custom, with Painters and their apprentices, when they are called upon by royalty."

Caroline felt herself relaxing. And Master Havernell noticed this. "Yes," he said quietly. "I saw the Count."

"Joseph –"

Joseph had squared his shoulders. "I offered to paint him," he said quietly, with no fear at all. He wasn't tall, would never be tall, but he had gained a few inches, and Caroline was aware of them then in a way that she had never been. "I told him that I had already painted him once."

"He must have been speaking with Caroline," Master Havernell said quietly. "You did well, Joseph, but you were very bold. He will know, now, why Caroline was not ceded to his household, and he will know, as well, that *you* know why. Be careful."

Joseph nodded. "Did you see my drawing?"

"Both Master Giavanno and I have studied it," Master Havernell said quietly. "And we both feel that it lacks color."

Joseph's height vanished.

"But in detail it is sound; the men you drew are the armies of Lalonde. They are prepared for war, and they are numerous. They have not gathered in haste." He paused, and then said, "We do not mean to be unkind, Joseph, but it may be that your drawing will be the most accurate Painting we produce, in the next few days.

"And if that is the case, you must *paint*."

"He'll paint," Caroline said, speaking where Joseph seemed to have forgotten how. "I'll be with him."

In the morning, they were fed breakfast in their rooms, and then they were led back to the studio. This time, the room was empty; the silence was both comfortable and daunting.

"The King will come with his advisors later in the day," Master Havernell told them. "Until then, we are free to work." He paused, and the look he gave Joseph made his meaning clear.

Joseph withered. If he'd slept at all, it didn't show; there were dark circles under his eyes, and his skin was sallow. Caroline put an arm around his shoulders; she hadn't slept either. Every step in the distant hall made her start, and every dream that she had when she did manage to doze off always ended with Count Thermann. The Count and his cold, cold wife.

Arm around his shoulder, Caroline led Joseph back to his easel. Felix and Camille were already there, seated in front of the static painting that had served as Joseph's guide. But they looked at his drawing, not the painting, and they whispered quietly, their heads pressed together to stop their words from traveling.

They started as Joseph approached, and Camille actually blushed and looked away.

But Joseph didn't seem to mind. In fact, true to form, he didn't seem to notice. He sat in front of the drawing, and Caroline began to prepare his palette; she looked at the unfinished work of the Giavanno apprentices for guidance. Greens, she saw; blues. Muted, russet red. She shook her head. "We'll have to mix," she told Joseph.

He nodded.

"We thought," Camille said, as Felix cleared his throat. They looked at each other again, and Felix smiled. "We thought," she began anew, and this time Felix waited, "that we would concentrate on those men, the ones you drew there."

"Why?"

"Because they seem to be at the centre of your drawing, and they're probably important. We don't know what this is about," she added. "And Master Giavanno doesn't want to influence us. Much."

"You want to use my drawing as a model?" Joseph asked, almost incredulous.

"It's a helluvalot better than the one we were given," Felix replied, with some heat.

Caroline smiled, although she had a lapful of oils that threatened to get very messy very quickly. She knew that Joseph would be pleased by Felix's rough praise; she was.

"Sure," Joseph told them. "If you want. I have to –" He looked awkwardly at Caroline.

And Caroline made a decision. "Joseph is color blind," she told them both quietly.

Camille's brow's rose; Felix's face became impassive.

But Joseph trusted Caroline; although he flinched when she said the words, he didn't add any of his own.

"So while you use *his* drawing as a model, I'm using your rough colors as a guide."

Camille nodded thoughtfully. "What do you paint, when she's not helping you?"

"Nothing," Joseph said.

"You should try," she replied, still thoughtful. "Just pick and choose the colors as *you* see them. It would make a really interesting painting."

"Camille," Felix began, but she shook her head.

"I'll shut up now."

"She won't," Felix said, as he began to blend his own colors.

They began to work, falling silent; Camille did talk, but mostly to herself.

Joseph waited for Caroline, and when Caroline handed him his palette, he began to paint. His hands shook; his brows folded; the movement of the brush was stiff. Were it up to Caroline, she would have given him nothing but pencils.

But she knew they couldn't fail Master Havernell.

"Joseph," she told him softly. He looked up and met her eyes, lifting the brush as he did. She took the brush from his hand for a moment, and she very carefully, very delicately, made the first stroke. He frowned at it, as if it were a blot, and took the brush back, his brows almost comical in their rise.

She hid her smile, and hid the pang that lay beneath it, watching as he worked to correct the minimal damage she had done. He held out a hand for the finer brush; she gave it to him, and once again began to choose color, to see the whole emerging from the scattered traces.

They painted, caught up in the rhythm of brush stroke, the smell of oil, the blending of color. When the brush that Joseph worked with needed cleaning, he set it aside, and she offered him a finer one; when he needed a different color, she pointed to the one he should use, telling him, almost wordlessly, what it was, and why it suited the growing shape of his work.

Then the chimes sounded and the doors opened. The King had arrived.

Felix and Camille did not work on the same canvas. But they worked far more quickly with paint than Joseph did; they worked, Caroline thought, as if driven.

She watched them in the lull that the King's presence made, and then turned back to Joseph to see that she was mistaken; he was painting *quickly* now. It was almost as if he failed to notice the King at all. But where Camille and Felix had chosen to centre their work and attention upon the heart of Joseph's pencil sketch, Joseph himself was drawn to its outer edge; to the farthest left corner in the upper quadrant. There, he painted trees, or the stumps of trees, their fallen branches left to be trampled; there he painted a horse, two horses, riderless and panicked.

There, she thought, he began to paint something that looked familiar. The colors that she offered him changed, although she didn't realize it herself at first; they darkened. Shade, she had thought. But she was wrong, and when she saw what began to emerge, she knew it.

She caught the brush he held and yanked it from his hand; it left oil in his palm, but his hand still moved, as if the loss of the brush did not deprive him of subject, of the ability to capture what now inspired him.

He reached out and grabbed a larger brush, one ill-suited to detail work, and he dipped a corner, no more, into something that was mottled grey-green.

"Master Havernell!" She shouted, unmindful now of courtiers, of King, of men with swords. "*Master Havernell!*"

She did not dare rise; instead, she took the brush he held. In fact, she took *all* of his brushes, dumping them unceremoniously in the folds of the skirts she had chosen with such care. She had ruined the dress, and part of her knew it – but most of her didn't care. What did it matter, after all, if Joseph – If Joseph –

Footsteps sounded against marble. Heavy, unfamiliar steps. But they were fast; they came at a run.

Master Giavanno grabbed her shoulder and almost shoved her aside. But he did not ask her why she had shouted; he did not doubt the urgency of her plea.

"Moraine!" he shouted, enjoining his voice to hers.

Master Havernell came next, his hands still clutching a wet brush, his face still adorned by the peculiar grace of deadly vision. It was slow to leave him; she realized than that he had not actually heard her shout.

But Master Giavanno had. That was enough.

"Joseph," the older Painter said, catching the boy by the shoulders. "*Joseph*, look at me!"

Joseph shuddered and tried to pull himself free of the old man's hands. His fingers – his fingers were as smeared as Caroline's skirts; he was trying to paint with his hand. Was, Caroline realized, succeeding.

Master Havernell swore.

"Caroline," he said, voice urgent. "Help us."

"What can I –"

"Make him stop," Master Havernell told her. As if she could. As if only she could.

And when he said it, she realized what Joseph was painting. She took the palette from him, then, and when he reached for it, she slapped his hand. She had not done that for more than six years; the Westerfield Halls had done much to gentle her.

But that gesture did what Master Giavanno's rough hold could not; Joseph looked *at* her, and froze. His expression folded slowly into lines of pain. "Caroline?" he said, bewildered. "Why did you hit me?"

"Sorry," she muttered, as she had done so many times in the Westerfield Hall. "I lost my temper. It wasn't your fault."

"But what did I do?"

"You drifted off," she said, as if they were both young again. "You were – you were sleeping." She paused, and then added, "And the King is here."

His eyes rounded in panic. Familiar panic. Madam Dagleish had had the same effect on him, and it almost made Caroline smile. Or wince. "You did well," she added softly. "Really well. But you *have* to stop now. It's dangerous to do any more."

"Very dangerous," Master Giavanno said softly. "Moraine?"

Master Havernell looked at Joseph's partial painting. Most of the canvas was empty. But the corner that wasn't was detailed enough that a man could be clearly seen, standing above the ruined remains of a dark tree. The uniform he wore was unfamiliar – or rather, it was the same as the uniforms worn by the men in Joseph's sketch. But she recognized him anyway, by his cold and perfect beauty. He was gazing toward the heart of the white, empty canvas, and his lips were turned up in a predator's smile.

"So," Master Havernell said, with a bitter anger that the word itself could not contain.

"The enemy," Master Giavanno added. "Your majesty?"

The King had come to stand some ten feet away from his Painters, and when Caroline turned to look at him, he was the color of milk.

"Camille. Felix." Master Giavanno's voice was a piercing bark; Caroline was surprised that such a sound could come from the gentle old man.

Both of his apprentices, however, looked up immediately, and she knew that the tone was a familiar one, to them.

"Master Giavanno?"

"You have finished for the day. We will do no more work in the studio for the moment. Your Majesty?"

The King nodded, grim now. "My apologies," he said quietly. "I had not realized –"

"No more did we. But perhaps we should have."

Joseph began to tremble. Caroline, seeing this, eased the brushes from their wet, messy place in her lap, and set them to one side. They had to be cleaned, she thought, but she left them anyway; left them to go to Joseph. She put an arm around his shoulder, shoring him up. He was shaking uncontrollably.

"Master Havernell," she said, a different urgency informing her words.

He nodded. "With your permission, Your Majesty, I will see my apprentices to their rooms. Joseph will need some time to recover."

Joseph made it half-way down the long hall before his knees collapsed. Master Havernell, however, seemed to be expecting this; he was behind Joseph when Joseph began to crumple, and he caught him quickly, lifting his weight as if were insubstantial. Maybe it was, to the Master Painter; Joseph was small.

Caroline led the way, pushing the door open. When she entered the room she all but ran to the windows and yanked the curtains shut. "I need different light," she told him. "I need lamps or candles. Can you get them?"

Master Havernell nodded. He smoothed Joseph's hair from his forehead; her eyes adjusted slowly to the sudden change in light, and by the time they had, the Master's face was impassive. But she thought she had seen something else in it, for a moment, and her throat was suddenly too tight for words.

"Thank you, Caroline," he said. He carried Joseph to the bed, and she ran over to pull the counterpane back. To smooth the sheets, to make them somehow safer for the burden they would enfold.

"It was him, wasn't it?" She asked, as she fluffed pillows, avoiding Master Havernell's gaze.

"Yes. And you saw it, where neither the Master Giavanno or I would have done. You saw it in time," he added.

"Maybe –" She fell silent.

"Yes?"

"Maybe you *all* need someone. Like me. Someone without talent."

But Master Havernell shook his head. "You undervalue yourself," he told her gently. "I told you, when we first met, that Joseph was unusually tolerant; it was the truth. I cannot think of another painter of any age who would allow *anyone* to choose their palette, to choose their brushes, to direct their work. There are many," he added, "who might try, if they understood the events of today. But there are not, in my opinion, many at all who would succeed. We are driven by what we see, and it is what *we* see that moves us. We cannot give control of that to any other hand."

"But Joseph does. And you take no more than you should, and give a great deal more than I expected." He pulled the blankets up over Joseph, and watched as their creases changed; Joseph was shuddering now.

"But –"

"I must return to the King," he said softly, but he lingered, waiting.

"You do it. After Joseph is finished. He lets you paint over his work; he lets you correct him."

"Ah, but that is not the same," he said softly. "The vision – if it is there in strength at all – has passed, and he seeks, at that point, to learn. It is the difference between art and craft, and while there must be a blending of the two, it is the art in the end that defines us."

She nodded, although she didn't really understand, and he left her by Joseph's side, closing the door gently upon them.

The King was grim; Master Giavanno was grimmer. Felix and Camille were standing behind him, almost clutching the fine velvet of his outer robe. No one spoke, but they all looked up as Moraine Havernell entered the studio.

"Will the boy recover?" the King asked.

The Master Painter hesitated. "I believe he will," he said at last. "He does not rave; he does not speak in tongues. He has not asked for paint or canvas, and he does not seek to leave the side of his – of my other apprentice." He put out the words like a challenge.

No one chose to take it.

"The boy has a gift," Master Giavanno said, with some regret. He disentangled himself from Felix and said, almost gently, "it is time for you to leave." Felix nodded; he had his back turned to Joseph's unfinished painting, and he did not once attempt to look at it.

So, Master Havernell thought. The rumors were true. "Felix?"

Felix looked away. He, too, was trembling.

"Felix is also talented," Master Giavanno said. "But he has survived it. Come, Camille – take him elsewhere. The King's gardens are open to you; go draw the fountains."

"Yes, Master Giavanno."

"But take pencils; take no paints."

"Yes, Master Giavanno."

Three grim men stood alone; Courtiers and guards had moved to a respectful distance. If the King had anything to fear from the Augustine Painters, he was already a dead man.

"The boy painted him," the King said softly.

"He did not finish."

"No – but he came close. It is a striking likeness."

"Coupled with our paintings," Master Giavanno said quietly, "it is also not a portrait in the true sense. It is, in my opinion, a painting – an Augustine Painting. The enemy was not aware of the boy."

"Are you so certain?"

"As certain as I can be, where the enemy is concerned. It has happened before," he added softly. "No; the enemy's hand is in this war. As we suspected."

"Can you – can either of you – finish what you have begun here?"

The two Master Painters exchanged a glance. It said much.

But Master Havernell nodded grimly. "I can," he said quietly.

"Will you take that risk, Moraine?" Master Giavanno asked, without much hope.

"If not me," he said quietly, "than who? This is my art," he added, with a bitter smile. "It speaks of death, of the dying."

Master Giavanno nodded after a moment. "We will need a different canvas," he said at last, and Master Havernell stopped in sudden surprise. "Yes," the older man replied almost serenely, "I will witness. It has already been proved that there is a danger."

The painting took four days; Joseph was on his feet at the end of three. Caroline looked almost as haggard as he did, but that vanished when they were invited to return to the hall on the morning of the fourth day. Because she could see, as she was granted entry by the King's guards, that Master Havernell had been Painting; that he still did. Although she was most familiar with Joseph's face, she had come to see the similarities that existed between the two Painters of House Havernell.

It was an entirely different work from the one that Joseph had begun; it was very like the work that adorned the Havernell gallery. The colors were both bright and dark, the bodies of the dead, and the dying, aground like so much refuse. Their faces were indistinct, but she saw that one man's was not.

The King lay upon a dirty stretcher, surrounded by his soldiers. An arrow jutted at an awkward angle from his broad chest. He was in great pain, but it would pass; death did that.

For the first time, Caroline wondered at the strength of the King. He was neither kind nor friendly, but perhaps he couldn't afford to be. Caroline knew, as she turned to study his impassive profile, that she could never have stood as he now stood, bearing witness, every time Master Havernell came to paint, to his own death.

The thought made her tremble.

But Joseph was suddenly beside her. He reached out very awkwardly and put an arm around her shoulder, as if he understood why she needed comfort.

She looked at him, feeling very strange. He *looked* the same as he always did, but he was almost a stranger. It was her job to offer comfort, not to need it. But she didn't remove his arm. Instead, she looked at the painting.

"He'll finish today," Master Giavanno told them. "He wanted you both to be here. I didn't," he added gruffly. "It will cause me trouble with my own apprentices – I've forbidden them the studio."

"Don't be angry with him," she said.

Master Giavanno smiled. "I find it difficult to be angry," he told her, as if confessing to a grave crime. "And I shouldn't. He puts you both at risk."

"He trusts us," she told him.

"I trust my apprentices too. But they are young enough to seem like children to me, and I hate to force children to play an adult game when the consequences of failure are so profound." He reached out and put a hand upon her shoulder. "You must survive, Caroline. And you must watch both of your Painters."

"Master Havernell isn't mine."

"But he is," Master Giavanno replied. "And it is the first time he has taken such a risk."

"You mean taken apprentices," she said.

"Do I? Ah, he has finished, for the morning. Join him."

Master Havernell was happy to see them both, although he didn't say so in so many words. He, too, wore the days poorly. He had not shaved, and his hands bore the traces of oil. He talked little, ate more. She served him wine and water.

But when he rose, she rose with him, Joseph by her side, and she felt blessed.

Master Havernall was not happy with the painting. Caroline realized this when he took his chair, and she came to stand at a respectful distance by his side.

"What's wrong?"

"I cannot see," he told her, "where the arrow came from."

She frowned. "In the painting with the poison cup, you couldn't see who'd poisoned him either."

"You didn't study the painting," he told her, a hint of disapproval in his words. "The cup was distinctive; the wine, distinctive as well. The light in the hall told the time of day, and the King's attire, the season. He lacked guards, a sign that he was with someone he trusted."

"He can't, can he?" she said quietly.

"Trust? Not safely, no."

"Poor man."

Master Havernell frowned. "Speak carefully, Caroline. Remember where you are."

She nodded.

"This is not like the painting of Lord Raleigh," he added, forestalling her. "In that, it was enough to see the standard of the Baron. The King could then move against his cousin before the army so depicted could be full gathered.

"But we have no such easy recourse with foreign nobility. These men are already gathered. The only certain safety for His Majesty lies in absence, and it is not a safety he can afford. No," he added, clearly frustrated, "there is an answer here, but I have not captured it." He picked up his brush. "Tell the old man that I am ready to resume my work."

It took her a moment to realize that the old man he spoke of was Master Giavanno. Her raised brows made Master Havernell laugh out loud. "Years you've been in my house, and you still react like one of Madam Dagleish's students." He shook his head. "Go get Master Giavanno."

Red-faced, she did.

Master Havernell painted into the late afternoon, and he might have continued were it not for Joseph. The boy came running into the studio, and bounced off the armor of two unexpected guards. Unexpected, at least, by Joseph.

Master Havernell heard the sound at a distance; the gift was upon him, and its grip was not gentle. But he heard panic contained by familiar syllables, and his brush froze as he tore himself free. Frowning, he rose; Master Giavanno was already making excuses for Joseph's inappropriate conduct. Or so it seemed, because it made sense. But as Moraine approached the parting men, he realized that he was mistaken.

"Where, Joseph? Where did you last see Caroline?"

"By the fountain," he said miserably. "She was by the fountain. I went to get my pencils. She offered, but she was tired because of me, and she was just so happy to be outside –" He turned as he saw Master Havernell approach.

And Master Havernell said a single word. "Thermann."

But the Count was summoned by a wary King; he was still upon the grounds for the festival that Joseph had been entirely unaware of. He was cool, but cooperative, and he offered the King his aid in locating the missing servant.

"She is no servant," Master Havernell said coldly. "She is my apprentice."

"Then perhaps you should have taken greater care of her, Master

Havernell. You have many enemies, and it is likely that not all of them relish the prospect of additional Havernell Painters."

Master Havernell took a step forward, but Joseph intercepted him. He stared at the Count without blinking. "Your Majesty," he said, voice low, "I beg a boon."

He did not look at the King as he spoke, because his nerve would have failed him.

"Ask," he heard the King say.

"I wish to paint a portrait of the Count."

The silence was endless, and Joseph knew before it came what the answer would be.

"If the Count so desires it," the King said, "Although I do not judge it wise."

"The Count does not desire it," Count Thermann replied coldly.

Joseph turned away.

He returned to the studio where Master Giavanno was waiting. One look at the old man's face told the Master Painter all that Joseph knew.

"Where is Master Havernell?"

"With the King," Joseph replied bitterly. "The King who wouldn't order the Count to sit for a portrait."

"You asked *that*?"

Joseph nodded.

"You are Havernell's," the Painter replied. "But the King must have judged you worthy," he added. "If he let you return here after such a public display."

"It *had* to be Thermann."

"Joseph, I do not doubt you. But he *is* a Count, and it is unlikely that Caroline would have willingly gone with him. If she was taken from the gardens, she did not leave with Thermann. He would never publicly risk that much – not when the King now depends upon Master Havernell."

"Then how?"

"Think, boy. If I wanted her cooperation, I could have easily obtained it. I would send someone in the King's livery, with an urgent summons. Given the state of the painting, and the hours she's been keeping, she would have left immediately."

"Then where is she?"

"That, I cannot say. But I think it unlikely that she has left the grounds."

"Could she be in the Count's quarters?"

"He would know that he would be a suspect in her disappearance. I think it unlikely. Ah. Moraine."

Joseph turned to see Master Havernell enter the studio.

Their eyes met. Joseph froze. "Master Havernell?"

The Master Painter said nothing for a long moment. And then he looked at Joseph and said a single word. "Paint."

He had never painted without Caroline. He could no longer remember a time when he had drawn without her.

"Joseph," Master Havernell added, when he saw Joseph's hesitation, "I would do it, but it is not within me; it has never been my gift. If I paint her, we will see how she dies."

How. Not if.

"And if I thought that information could be used to save her in time, I would do it. But I fear that if she is not found upon the grounds, we will never save her." He donned his smock as if it were armor.

"There is a risk," Master Havernell added. "You should not be asked to paint so soon after you –"

Joseph grabbed his own smock.

Master Giavanno did not speak at all. But Joseph knew what he would have said and he appreciated the Painter's silence.

The lone apprentice in the King's studio sat in front of a blank canvas; it didn't occur to him to wonder where it had come from. But it hadn't been there when he'd left. Master Havernell handed him his hated brushes, his terrifying palette.

"Paint," he said again, but this time, the word wasn't a command. It was a plea.

Joseph had never chosen his own brushes before. Caroline had done it. But he could cope with that. It was the paint itself that terrified him.

"I could draw –"

Master Havernell shook his head. "Detail," he said. "Perhaps if you had been taught to work in draftsmen's inks – but you weren't, and we have no time. Even if you're the only one who can interpret the colors you choose, we need fine details." Unspoken, another truth: So did she. Joseph took up the brush in shaking hand, wondering if he could do it. He was only half a Painter; Caroline was the other half. But if he couldn't do this without her, he would never be whole again.

Hands stiff with the effort to still their movement, he began, choosing the colors that he couldn't see. No, he thought grimly. He was choosing the colors that *only* he could see, with no certainty at all that they would work in his favor.

He looked up, as he often did; his field of vision was empty. The window was wrong. Caroline's seat, even empty, should be part of it. He stood with purpose, setting his brush aside. Master Havernell watched, bitter and wordless. Joseph wanted to say *trust me*. But he couldn't. What was one of his earliest lessons? Trust was earned.

He took Caroline's empty stool and placed it with care in the spot from which the greater part of the external world could be seen. She would have chosen it herself, had she felt bold enough within the King's studio to do so.

Thus positioned, the stool stood in want of its occupant. But it often did at home as well; she was Caroline; she couldn't be caged.

She was proud of her ability to sit for hours on end; neither Joseph nor Master Havernell had ever had the heart to tell her that she, in fact, did no such thing. Instead, she would perch until she needed to fly, and then she would circle the room until her bright, restless curiosity was satisfied. Having surveyed her nest, she would return. In between those quick forays, Joseph would catch a glimpse of her, capturing some essential quirk of her nature with coal and pencil. But in truth he knew her well enough to do without; those brief glimpses had more to do with comfort than information.

He began to paint Caroline. He didn't have the comfort of knowing that *this* painting would be an Augustine work, and in the end, that became his greatest fear. Greater even than the fear of painting alone; greater than the fear of public humiliation that the colors were certain to bring.

He chose her hair first; chose next the color of her Summer skin, so different from that of Winter. He chose the color of her eyes, the pale hue of unadorned lips, the white of teeth.

He moved on from the things he knew best, losing at last the marked hesitance of making those choices. The shadows at his side dwindled; the quality of their silence changing as he worked. Only once was he aware that he was not alone, and he lifted his face instinctively to glance at Caroline. She wasn't there, of course. Master Giavanno was; his lips were parted, his hand raised.

Joseph frowned and returned to his painting, to the silver sheen of armor. Armor. His grip tightened, the movement of the brush stilling. But the armor was not the ornate work of the nameless enemy. It was, as Master Giavanno had so wisely suggested, the familiar armor of the royal guard.

"Continue, Joseph. Forgive my interruption," the Master Painter said.

Joseph had already begun. He didn't fear the enemy, although he believed that Painters had died in the attempt to capture him. He didn't fear death; not his own.

He won't kill her, he thought desperately. *It's not her death he wants.* But he couldn't force himself to believe it, no matter how much he wanted to. Because the Count that his master had once called careful had chosen to do something that could well expose him – and if safety lay in Caroline's death, he would kill her.

He would kill her after.

Master Havernell and Master Giavanno stood watch in the distance. They had half hoped that Joseph, tolerant boy, would either ask for or accept their aid, but were not surprised when this didn't happen.

It was not the apprentice who was unique; it was the pairing.

Still, they took what they could from their observation. Caroline, he had drawn. But her hair was a tangle, her skin marked by bruises. It was difficult to interpret them cleanly, for the colors were a jumble, almost a cacophony. Her dress was wrong, but not only in its base state; the shading clashed as well.

Yet it was, without question, a work, an Augustine painting, and they watched it unfold with the same dread and fascination that the King must have felt watching Moraine Havernell at work.

Where is she, Joseph? Master Havernell thought, his hands clenched tight in useless fists. But he did not speak; there was no point. Joseph, true to his beginnings, painted figures first; the background, if it came at all, would come later.

But later loomed like thunder, like doom.

Do not make me paint, boy.

Moraine chose to give in to helpless rage; it eased his fear.

Caroline was silent, still, shorn of the joy that was her strength. Her hands were bound before her, and her gaze fell to her lap. The men, both of them, cast short shadows across her slightly bowed head – but again, it was hard to tell.

Translating the vision of a color blind boy into the vision of men who made color their life's work was almost impossible.

But were it not for the circumstances in which they made the attempt, it would have been rewarding as well, for it was seldom that either man was called upon to dissect the visual language by which they made their living.

"There," Master Giavanno said suddenly.

Master Havernell frowned. "Where?"

"They are not in the barracks. They are not in the palace proper."

"How can you tell?"

"The flooring," Master Giavanno replied, speaking softly, lest his voice travel and somehow break the subtle spell that bound the apprentice painter. "It is the same color he's chosen for the darker shade of her hair."

"I see it," Master Havernell replied, frustrated that he had not seen it sooner. "Where are they, then?"

Master Giavanno shook his head. "I cannot say, Moraine. I have been a Master Painter for the whole of the current King's reign, and Master Painters, as you are well aware, are treated as honored guests. It is not a room that I think honored guests see often, if ever. But that tells us something."

Master Havernell nodded. Bitterly he added, "Not enough."

"No. But the men in armor might tell us more, if possible. Think: How easy could it be for strangers to gain the armor of the Royal Guard?"

"He had days – at least – to plan."

"He had days," Master Giavanno said, correcting his former student. "He could not know for certain that Caroline was not an Augustine Painter. And had she been, with war waiting on our borders, not even he would dare the King's wrath with such impunity."

Because he wanted to believe it, Moraine Havernell nodded.

"Remain here," Master Giavanno told him.

"Where are you going?"

"I am going to fetch my lazy apprentices," he replied with gravity.

"I think young Camille would cry foul should she hear herself so described."

"Oh certainly. But while I did deny them the studio, I did not give them permission to do nothing. They should properly feel ashamed of themselves, and I intend to make them work to make up for it."

"Oh?"

"They can visit the King's quartermaster."

Joseph painted. Lunch passed him by. It avoided Master Havernell as well.

But Master Giavanno returned shortly with crusty bread and cold water. "Eat," he told Moraine, in a tone reserved for wilful apprentices.

"When Joseph is finished, he will be weakened. And that will serve neither of you well."

Master Havernell took the bread. "Your apprentices?"

"They understand the urgency."

Silence.

After a moment it was broken by the sound of resentful chewing.

"Moraine, may I ask a question?"

"I've never been able to stop you before."

"True. You did, however, try."

Moraine swallowed. "What is your question?"

"You were not surprised that Caroline disappeared. Upset, yes, but not surprised. Why?"

"The first of Joseph's paintings."

"Done in Westerfield?"

Master Havernell nodded.

"Ah. Madam Dagleish summoned you, then."

He nodded again. "She had already all but ceded the girl to the Count."

"But instead she gave them both to you."

"I told her I would not take one without the other."

"Ah. Would you have taken the boy had his first painting been of another subject?" It was a shrewd question.

"You talk too much," Master Havernell said, but without rancor. He hesitated, and then said, softly, "No. I knew what it would cost to leave the girl. Both to Westerfield, and to Joseph. It was the first time since I established my own House, that the risk of refusing the application seemed the greater danger. But I will not forgive you if you repeat this."

Master Giavanno nodded. He might have spoken further, but Camille burst through the closed doors. In the absence of the King, there was nothing to slow her progress, not even Felix.

"Master!" she shouted, as if there was only one in the room.

"You have news?"

"I have better." Her words were informed by a fierce smile. "I have the quartermaster." She turned, stopped, and added, "well, Felix does."

It was true. Felix led the quartermaster into the cavernous studio. The quartermaster was not young, and he was definitely not small. He dwarfed them all.

But he was aware that he stood, not in the presence of nobility, but in the presence of people who actually served a purpose, and he halved his height by offering the two Master Painters a deep bow.

To Felix, he added as he rose, "My apologies for doubting you, boy."

Felix, still aware of their obvious difference in size, simply nodded.

The quartermaster turned to Master Giavanno. "I've come at the request of the young lady."

"I am Master Giavanno. This is Master Havernell. What news do you bring us?"

"They wanted to know if I'd misplaced two suits of armor." His momentary frown made his face distinctly less friendly. "I haven't."

"Would you recognize the men you outfit?" Master Havernell asked quietly.

"Probably." The answer was guarded.

The two Painters exchanged a glance. "Understand," Master Havernell said quietly, "that the men of whom we speak have performed a service, in uniform, for a Count – without the King's knowledge or consent."

The quartermaster's face shut down; no expression escaped it. But he did not accuse them of lying.

Instead he stepped forward, as both Masters again shared a glance.

Joseph's painting lay exposed. It was not yet complete, but the figures, with their oddly colored skin, their correct armor, were finished.

"The boy is talented," Master Giavanno said softly, "but he sees color askew. Can you recognize either of these men?"

The quartermaster nodded, staring first at Joseph, and then at the painting. "Who is the girl?"

"She is my other apprentice," Master Havernell said gravely.

They watched the quartermaster. The quartermaster watched Joseph. And after a moment he said, "The boy's crying."

It was finished. He could see it clearly now; could see the terror in Caroline's mute expression. The men were bored. And the room they stood in was almost featureless. He wasn't certain it had windows.

He'd finished, but all he knew was that she was captive somewhere, and it didn't take a painting to tell him that.

He dragged a sleeve across his face.

"Joseph," Master Havernell said quietly, "you've done enough."

"I haven't done anything!" he shouted, unable to contain himself. "Look at her – she needs us, and I can't tell where she is!"

"Easy, boy, easy," a stranger said.

Not even a stranger's presence was enough to stem his tears.

Not his presence, no. But his words?

"Aye, I know them both. And I know where they probably are."

"Can you see it?" Joseph asked, because he couldn't quite let himself believe the man's words. "Can you see it, in what I painted?"

"I can see that she's very important to you – to all of you," the giant replied gently. "And yes, I can see enough. I'll take you there," he added. "Just let me go and get a couple of things first."

A couple of things, in the quartermaster's estimation, were half a dozen armed men and a crossbow. The men wore no armor and no obvious insignia.

"Quartermaster?" Master Giavanno said, with some hesitation.

"They're friends," the quartermaster said firmly.

"Off duty friends," one of the men said, with the bare hint of a smile. It left his face when the man beside him barked a succinct command.

"Understand," The quartermaster said softly, "that we're not in the King's employ at the moment. It seems," he added, "to suit the situation, since the men in your boy's painting aren't either.

"It would look bad," he added, and this time, threat laced the words, "for the Royal Guard, otherwise."

"Understood." Master Havernell said coolly.

"Good."

"We only want the apprentice back," he added.

The man who had barked, barked again. The words were both loud and near unintelligible. "Follow at a distance," the quartermaster told them. And then, his voice inexplicably softening, he said to Joseph, "You can come with me. Don't say a word until it's safe," he added.

But Joseph appeared to have run out of words entirely.

Caroline was afraid.

The men were muttering to each other, and if the words didn't quite reach her ears, their tone did. Something had gone wrong, and they hadn't yet decided what to do about it – but she knew that a decision might be worse. For her.

They had approached her while she sat by the fountain, her hands cupping a thin trickle of cold water. Since she knew she wasn't supposed to be playing in that water, she had been embarrased and nervous. They had told her that something had gone wrong in the Painters' Hall, and she had believed them.

Had believed them until she realized they were leading her in the wrong direction.

She had tried to make noise, and one of the two had almost broken her jaw. The other had drawn his sword. After that she had done nothing that would anger them; she had barely allowed herself to breathe.

They had brought her to an outbuilding used by the gardeners in the Autumn; it was empty now, although some tools hung on the far wall.

She knew why she was here.

She knew that Count Thermann would eventually retrieve her, if not here, then later, at a more convenient location. That much, she had gleaned by listening to them talk.

But it appeared that the Count had failed to send word at the agreed upon time, and the men were now nervous. They had to report for duty soon.

And it was clear that they didn't wish to leave her here.

They were still arguing when a knock came at the door. She stiffened, but she made no noise; her jaw still ached from the last time she'd tried, and that was all it had gained her.

The two men relaxed, and one even spared her an unwelcome smile. The other answered the door – and froze there.

He backed away slowly.

His companion frowned.

Caroline rose. Her hands were tied in front of her, and she had no weapon but hope.

"Grab the girl!" the man at the door shouted.

The girl leapt awkwardly out of the way as the guard at the door fell back. Everything happened suddenly.

The second man seemed to understand what was happening as well; he drew his sword and lunged for her arm.

Had he done them in the reverse order, he might have succeeded. Instinct was sometimes treacherous.

Men with drawn swords entered.

One of them used his weapon. He was followed quickly by a second, and then a third man; Caroline closed her eyes.

Blood splattered her pale face like warm rain.

She bit her lip, as afraid of these strangers as she had been of her captors.

Someone touched her shoulder, and Caroline screamed.

And then she heard a familiar voice. "It's all right, Caroline. They won't hurt you. You're safe. We're here."

She opened her eyes to Joseph's face. Only then did she begin to cry.

The King was waiting for them when they returned to the studio. The men who had so quickly dispatched two of their own didn't make it that far; they said their goodbyes – such as they were, at the edge of the garden.

But Joseph, timid Joseph, had left her for just a moment in Master Havernell's care and he had run to catch up with the vanishing men.

"Quartermaster," he said, for the man had never introduced himself, "I count myself in your debt."

"Don't," the man replied, blunt and short with his words. "You pointed out a problem – but it was our problem. We fixed it," he added with a shrug.

"Without you, we wouldn't have found her."

"Aye, well take better care of her next time," the large man said with a smile.

"I'm from House Havernell," Joseph continued doggedly. "And if there's ever anything I can do –"

"You can," the quartermaster said, grim now as he signalled and the rest of his friends dispersed. "You can tell that Master of yours to finish his painting."

And Joseph knew for certain then that they were Royal Guards, because no other men-at-arms knew of the painting. He nodded.

Joseph faced the King.

"I see that you found your lost apprentice," the King said quietly. He was flanked by men in now familiar armor. And it came to Joseph, before words did, that the King knew full well what had happened. And that this was as much of a public acknowledgment as he would ever offer.

Mindful of his debt, Joseph nodded solemnly. "We did, Your Majesty."

"Good. Then perhaps I can now avail upon Master Havernell to finish what he began?"

"Your Majesty," The Master Painter replied, folding gracefully at the middle.

Joseph wondered what Master Havernell had said to the King after he'd left them alone in the audience chamber.

But Caroline's eyes widened.

She knew. Her eyes were red; the side of her face, dark, and not with shadow. "Master Havernell, you – for me –"

The rest of her words bunched together; she swallowed them as

Master Havernell gave a curt, swift shake of the head. "No man would be foolish enough to commit treason in time of war," he said gravely, "no matter what the circumstance."

He walked to the unfinished painting that adorned the large easel, and took a seat. His brushes had been cleaned. Caroline realized that someone else had been given her duties in her absence. She stiffened, uncertain of who to thank.

But a glance at Joseph made clear that he hadn't even noticed; he probably thought brushes magically cleaned themselves. Either that or he just didn't care; he hated brushes anyway.

"How did you find me?" She asked softly, as Master Havernell began to blend his oils.

Joseph hesitated for a moment, and then he shrunk a little. "Here," he told her, as if he were ashamed of something. He didn't take her hand, but he walked slowly, constantly turning to make certain she was still there. At any other time, she would have laughed at him, but for now, she was grateful.

He stopped in front of a painting. "There," he told her, stepping aside.

She covered her bruised lips with a hand, and then walked forward until she stood in front of Joseph's canvas.

"Is that me?" She asked solemnly.

He winced, and she realized instantly that she'd asked the wrong question. "No, that's not what I mean – it's just that she looks so –"

"That's not what you really look like," he told her firmly. "It's not even how I see you. But ..."

She touched the back of his hand. "You did this by yourself."

"It's obvious, isn't it?"

She looked at her dress, and then back at the painting. "Yes," she whispered. "It is. We have to keep this," she added.

"Why?"

"For the gallery."

"I don't want it there!"

"I suggest," a familiar older voice added, "That you save this discussion for later."

They started guiltily, and fell instantly silent as Master Giavanno's tone made clear that if the discussion continued, there might not be a later.

"Come," he told them both, offering a smile that belied the severity of his tone. "The King honors your Master's skill. Let us now do the same." He took them both by the shoulder, and led them between the King's guards.

Caroline began to fold at the knees, but the King simply shook his head; it was not only Master Havernell that he chose to honor.

Together they watched Master Havernell paint what he painted best: death.

Afternoon vanished. Early evening filled the studio with an unusual depth of pink and pale blue, altering the landscape that unfolded beneath the moving strokes of a Havernell brush.

Master Giavanno frowned.

Caroline looked at the older man. "You can't tell, can you?"

He did her the grace of understanding her awkward question. "No," he said grimly.

"Maybe the archer isn't in the picture."

Master Giavanno frowned. "Caroline, your Master is many things, but if you have been two years in his care, and you can ask that question, one of those things is not a competent teacher."

She smiled bitterly. "I'm not an Augustine Painter," she told him. It was her way of excusing Master Havernell's shortcomings.

But Joseph touched her shoulder and said, quietly, "The information is in the painting. If it's a true work, the information is always there. Sometimes we just can't see it clearly."

They needed to.

Master Giavanno nodded grimly. "Joseph is correct."

Joseph was also frowning.

He mumbled something under his breath, and left to fetch his pencils.

Caroline watched him go. "He would have asked me to do that, before."

Master Giavanno looked at her profile, and he shook his head.

"Give him time," he told her gently.

She didn't understand why.

Didn't have the time to try. Joseph came back, shouldering his way between guards whose attention was rivetted on the painting itself.

On this depiction of their utter failure.

Joseph seated himself on the floor, and Caroline left to find him a stool. He took it, pencils already making their way across crumpled paper. He was not painting; he wasn't attempting to. There was no narrative flow to the shapes he drew, but she recognized them, shorn of color: He was drawing breastplates.

Master Giavanno raised a brow. "Joseph?"

"I think," he said, his hands continuing to move, "That we should summon the quartermaster."

The quartermaster looked bemused as he was once again led into the studio by Felix and Camille. But his expression changed instantly when he saw that the King was present.

The King favored him with a sharp smile. "It appears that you are in demand everywhere, Paolo."

"Your Majesty."

"Oh, I assure you that I did not summon you; that was the wish of the young Havernell apprentice, and you may thank him for it at your leisure." But the King turned to Joseph. "He is at your disposal."

Joseph nodded gravely. "I'm sorry to bother you again," he said, clearly meaning it. "But I wanted you to look at these."

Master Havernell was removing his smock. He looked weary. "Joseph?" he asked, as he became aware of the quartermaster.

But Joseph didn't hear him. Nor, it seemed, did the quartermaster.

The large man was frowning. "No," he said at last. "You're right, boy."

Joseph turned to his Master.

"Look," he said, handing his rough sketches to the quartermaster. He walked over to the painting, and pointed carefully at one of the King's men.

Master Havernell frowned. "Yes?"

"The shape of his armor is wrong."

The King's men became suddenly more alert.

"The ... shape of the armor?"

Joseph nodded. "It's not ... It looks to me like he's wearing the same colors as the rest, and the surcoat is right – but the shape of the breastplate is different."

"The boy is right. Look at the shoulders," the quartermaster added. "We haven't worn armor like that for over fifty years now – but you can see it on display in the Royal Museum." He shook his head. "That's quite an eye from detail you have, boy."

"I can't see colors clearly," Joseph told them, aware that he had the attention of everyone in the room. "So I notice things like shapes."

"That's it, then," one of the armored guards said, with relief.

The King even smiled. "Once again, we are in the debt of House Havernell. I will retain the painting until we have no further use for it. And now, if you will forgive me, I have a reply to tender the ambassador."

He turned and swept out of the room.

"He'll see to the Count," the quartermaster said softly, when the grand, peaked doors swung shut. "Not publicly, and I'm sorry for it, but he won't let the matter lie."

"He can't, can he?" Joseph asked, staring at the closed doors. "And not for our sake. Not even for justice."

The quartermaster seemed to deflate. "You're older than you look, boy. No, he'll do it because even nobles have to understand that there's a price demanded of those who would interfere with the guard."

Joseph nodded. He was beginning to learn.

They returned to House Havernell late that evening. The King had extended his invitation, but the three invitees had had enough of the palace to last them for some time, and they tendered their gracious regrets.

Joseph still found the carriage uncomfortable, however, and when he stumbled out of its small doors, Master Havernell sent him straight to bed.

"Well, Caroline," the Master said, when they were alone in the gallery.

She looked at him.

"You had a very close call. It's natural that you would be somewhat subdued, given events. Still, I cannot help but feel that your silence is not due to the actions of the Count. Please correct me if I'm mistaken. I will admit that, where the young are concerned, I am not so infallible as Master Giavanno."

She glanced up at him, and then away.

"I'm not wrong."

"It's just that – " she shrugged almost helplessly. "I've spent most of my life watching out for Joseph. It's why you brought me here," she added bitterly. "But you saw what he did. With the painting of me. With your painting."

Master Havernell nodded.

"It's – what am I good for, now?"

The dim lights gentled the bruises around her eye, but added soft shadows.

"There is a difference between necessity and choice," Master Havernell told her.

She shook her head again, and looked away. "I should be proud of him. He'd be happy for me if our positions were reversed. But I'm only worried about myself. I guess I'm not as good a friend as I thought I was."

"You're a Westerfield foundling, Caroline. It's natural that you fear to lose the only family you have. I feared it," he added.

She looked at him then, remembering what Camille and Felix had told them.

"But Joseph feared it no less. Don't let fear define your life. Learn," he added, without bitterness, "from mine." He smiled. "Joseph is more than half a Painter, but without you, he will always be less than whole. Accept that he will grow, and grow with him." He bowed to her and began to walk away.

But he stopped at the head of the stairs. "Had he not painted you, had the Count not interfered, Joseph would not have been so well acquainted with the shape of the armor the Royal Guards wear. I would never willingly sacrifice any of mine in such a fashion," he added darkly, "But you were right; he needed you. We all did."

And then he took the stairs and left her alone.

In the morning Master Havernell was absent from breakfast.

"You shouldn't be here either," Caroline told Joseph. "You look like you should sleep for days."

"I want to," he said, crumbs escaping his open mouth along with the words. "But I can't."

"Why not?"

"Because I wasn't sure that we'd ever come home again, and I want to really feel like I'm here." He swallowed, and added cheerfully, "You look worse than I do."

She kicked him under the table, and he jumped up, scraping the floor with the feet of his chair. "Come on," he said.

She joined him without damaging the floor. "Where?"

"The studio."

She nodded and followed him. "Why?"

"Because I want to paint."

If her jaw weren't attached, she would have lost it. "You want to what?"

He frowned. "Paint."

"I heard what you said – and now I'm *really* sure you should have stayed in bed."

Master Havernell looked at the first drawing he had done of Caroline. He had never showed it to her; he never would. It was, after all, of death

– the death of her parents. Even in matters of history, his gift was not gentle.

He set it aside, wondering.

After a while, he stood and made his way to the studio. Not so fine or large a room as the palace boasted, it nonetheless had the distinct advantage of freedom: the freedom to simply paint for the sake of painting.

But the studio wasn't empty; he saw this, and stopped a moment in the doorway.

Caroline was perched on a familiar stool, but even as he paused to watch her, she got down to inspect Joseph's canvas.

The Augustine Painter raised a brow in silence as she sorted through Joseph's brushes, and at last selected one.

"I've run out of the red," he told her apologetically.

"It's green," she replied. "I'll mix some more."

The boy waited, content, and Master Havernell smiled to himself and shut the door slowly.

❧ • ❧

White Shadow

by
Marie Brennan

The fire of your heart. The rhythm of your breath.

She sat in the center of a ring of flames. There was water at her side; the scorching air burned it out of her as quickly as she drank it down. Her body grew hollow and light; the pulse of the drums resonated in her head and down her bones until she was nothing but the flames and the beat.

The fire of your heart. The rhythm of your breath.

The words formed a counterpoint to the measured cadences of drummed prayer. The fire of her heart. The rhythm of her breath. These were the keys she sought. They would lead her to what she lacked. They would lead her to the Other, to a name and an otherform. The keys were in her; she must go out and find them.

The fires blazed higher. The drums intensified. They built up in a crescendo that made her body tense, preparing –

A gap appeared in the ring of flames.

She rose and sprinted into the empty blackness of night.

Autumn had come early to the isles, bringing chill winds and rain. She didn't feel them; the flames were still with her, burning inside her skin, driving her on. For the first night she ran blind, finding her footing by instinct, or by the grace of Ika and Ise. Trees and sharp boulders flashed by, unseen, but sensed through her sweat-covered skin. There was not even a moon or starlight to guide her. Sometimes she did not know if her eyes were open or shut.

But the perfect blackness could not last; eventually it began to lighten to grey, and her surroundings took on more definite form. Exhaustion caught up with her then. When dawn came in full, she found shelter under the low branches of a tree, and there she slept for several hours.

She awoke feeling more real than she had since the ceremony began. The flame was still inside her, and so was the beat, but they were muted. She felt her body, now, in all of its damp stiffness. A light rain had begun to fall, and for a short while she merely sat, cross-legged on the leaves, watching it come down. There was a rhythm there, too. The fire of her heart; the rhythm of her breath. She had to find them, in order for the Other to find her, in order to become fully Kagi. She could sit under this tree if she chose, or she could move onward, seeking her answers in the wild lands of the isles.

She chose to move.

Her mind began to wander. One part of it remained on the ground ahead, searching for the smoothest path, or whichever direction drew her the most. Another part sank inward, living in the beat of her pounding feet, the counterpoint of her breath and her heart. The rest was free to study the world around her.

The animal life drew her attention. It called to mind her childhood lessons. She watched it all, from the dragonfly hovering ahead, to the salmon leaping in a stream to her left, to the squirrel that darted away at her approach but paused on a tree branch to observe her progress. Those were the first three to catch her eye, and she considered them a good omen. One creature of the sky, one of the water, and one of the earth. A proper balance. None of the three drew her gaze, though, and she did not try to focus on any of them. She must not consciously reach for anything, except the fire and the rhythm. Those who reached could end up with nothing.

She stopped at a stream to drink the icy water and stayed there for some time, looking at the creatures which lived beneath the surface. Stubborn salmon, that would swim upstream against the fast current. Bottom-dwelling fangfish, whose greatest virtue lay in subtlety and surprise attacks. Limpets, clinging to the rock. She almost dismissed them as insignificant, but caution stopped her. Sometimes people came back from their quests with nothing. Was it arrogance that made them fail? She didn't know, but she couldn't take the chance. The limpets, then: good at defense, with their hard shells, tenacious grips, and coloring that blended with their surroundings. She could learn from the limpets. She could learn from everything.

Then she sat with her back to a tree and let the array of land animals pass by. Mountain deer, stocky and tough, ever wary of the world around them. She knew some people like that, but did not think she was one of them. Rock-wolves, feeding on the deer; that might be closer to the truth. But she must not reach for anything; the Other would come to *her*, not the other way around. She moved only because she felt like it, not because it was necessary. What else was there to observe? The squirrels she had seen before, cocky and playful. Granite snakes; they reminded her of the fangfish in the river. Right before she rose she spotted a lynx, wary of her presence but confident in his own speed and agility. Maybe that would be right.

She dismissed the thought from her mind and ran on.

As the afternoon ripened she climbed to the top of a rocky crag and sat there, letting the wind whip her skin numb, watching the sky. Hawks and eagles, proud kings of the air. Vultures, disliked but necessary all the same. Endless varieties of insect, some feeding on plants, others on blood. Very different creatures, those, with different lessons to teach. Night descended and she remained where she was, watching the population change; day-flying birds departed to be replaced by those of the night. Bats, seeing with more senses than sight. Owls both large and small, silent as ghosts on the wind, but often deadly. She climbed down at last, cold and stiff, to find herself shelter for the night.

A full day gone, with nothing to show for it. She swallowed her fear. Maybe fear was what made people fail. But she wouldn't be one of them; she wouldn't let herself count the time. She just hadn't found the right keys yet – the fire of her heart and the rhythm of her breath. She needed to focus on that, and not look for the Other. He would come when she was ready.

So she would make herself ready. She wouldn't go home with nothing, to become one of the Unformed, outcast and alone. She wouldn't.

She slept with the lessons of the day whirling endlessly in her head, dancing to the beat of the drums.

Feet, pounding one after the other on the ground, slowing over uneven parts, pausing when she leapt to the top of a rock. Breath, shifting in and out like waves on the beach, rapid but regular; her body was in good condition, and she was proud of it. She took pleasure in testing it in the wilds of the isles. Heartbeat, also fast, but strong and even. Her body felt that pulse the most strongly; she sank into the beat.

Heat of the flames, heat of her body, like the fire Ise made with His dance when He created the world. Fire and air. Blood and breath. A rhythm in each, like the drumming of Ika, when She made the rhythm for Ise. They were the keys she sought. She could feel them in her. They weren't far away. The fire of her heart, and the rhythm of her breath.

"What is your name?"

She jerked to a halt as though she had slammed into a wall. Her first instinct was to look around; she clamped down on herself before she could move and stared straight ahead. The ground there dropped away in a fall of rock; perhaps she would not have to climb down it, now that a voice had come. The Other. She had found the keys in her heart and her breath, and Ika and Ise had sent someone to her.

"I have no name," she said, trying to slow her breathing so she wouldn't gasp the words out. "I have come in search of a name and a form."

"I know of a path which might lead you to such things. Will you follow it?"

She hadn't believed them when they told her she would be afraid. Now, however, she understood; there was ice in her gut, and trembling in her body that had nothing to do with the exertion of running. Sometimes people didn't come back. Sometimes they came back, but empty, lost. Meeting the Other was no guarantee of success. This was a test, not a stroll in the wild. She could still fail.

She wouldn't fail.

She swallowed her fear and clenched her hands into fists. Fear wouldn't stop her. "I will."

A whirlwind took her away.

In fifteen years of life she had seen nothing to match it.

The world spread out below her, colorful and alive, looking nothing like the flat maps she had seen. The Kagesedo Isles were tiny next to the vast bulk of the rest of the Nine Lands; she had never realized how small her home was.

Her eyes devoured the view. She had grown up on the hard, rocky isles of the northern archipelago; now she had her first sight of thick jungles and flat grasslands, hard desert and the hunched shoulders of snow-capped mountains. She could feel it all, as though she were in every place at once: the heat and the cold, the rain and the dry, searing wind. It was nothing like she had ever imagined. Her mind could never have created something so awe-inspiring.

The voice spoke again from the air around her. "How does this make you feel?"

"I want to see it all," she whispered. "With my own eyes – not in pictures. I want to travel, to ride from one end of the land to the other. I want to see the forests of Tir Diamh, and the great docking caverns of Stahlend, and the fountain-gardens of Aishuddha. Cities and markets and rivers and mountains – *all* of it. I want to see it all." Her eyes closed against the sight, and to keep tears in. "But I can't, can I? Not safely. Because there are too many people who ... don't like us." Why couch it in gentle terms? The Other was a servant of Ika and Ise; he knew the truth. "They fear us. Or hate us. Because of what we are. Because of the gift Ika and Ise give to us."

"And you feel … "

"Bitter," she admitted. "Angry. It's not right, that they should keep us penned up in the Isles, just because we have otherforms and they don't! Why does that scare them so much? Maybe if we could travel more freely they would know us better, and wouldn't be so afraid of us. But it's dangerous, going out there, with them watching you at every turn, waiting for a chance to lock you up – or to kill you." Frustration made her press her lips together. She *wouldn't* cry. "I love my home. But I also want to see the world."

"So you desire freedom."

She looked at the vivid spread of the world below her. It called to her soul. "Yes."

The whirlwind took her away again.

She threw herself to one side and slammed into the smooth dirt. The impact knocked the wind out of her, but she forced herself to roll and come to her feet before her attacker could advance again.

There was a knife in her hand.

She dodged and wove, ducking the blows of the man who pursued her. Each came closer. She couldn't defend herself; she didn't know how to fight!

But she couldn't lie down and let him kill her, either.

There was a knife in her hand.

She looked for escape. The featureless dirt stretched as far as she could see in every direction. No walls, no doors. Nothing to hide behind. She was fast; she could try to run.

He lunged at her. She sidestepped, and in that moment saw her opportunity. Her hand moved, and the knife she held plunged into his chest.

The man fell.

There was someone else right behind him.

She leapt back, bloodstained knife held at the ready. The second man held a sword unsheathed in his hand. But he did not move to attack.

They both stayed where they were, crouched and wary. The man had his blade up, but he did nothing with it. Hate shone in his eyes, but he did not move.

Then he was gone.

"Why did you kill him?"

The knife had vanished; so had the body on the ground. She wrapped her arms around herself and tried not to feel sick. She had expected tests, but not like *this*. "He would have killed me."

"You could have fled."

"And then he might have gotten me from behind. I had an opening; I took it, rather than run and maybe die." Some part of her mind had made that calculation instinctively.

"But what of the second man?"

The memory of those hate-filled eyes made her shiver. "I ... I didn't have an opening."

"Was that all?"

The voice continued to sound impassive; still, she couldn't help but read a slightly knowing tone into it. She had to answer his question; not cooperating could be another trap, another road to failure. "No. I ..." Why *hadn't* she killed the second man? The look in his eyes had made his attitude clear. "He hadn't attacked. Which meant he wasn't an immediate threat."

"So you kill only when it is expedient."

It sounded so harsh, when phrased that way. She couldn't disagree with the voice's conclusions, though. Some part of her mind had weighed the situation and made its decisions based on the results. She knew that her behavior here was not natural; she'd never been in a fight, and should *not* have been that calm. She should have been panicking.

But at the same time, it *was* natural. It was her, and the way she thought. Or the way she *would* think, if she were experienced with situations of this kind.

Did that mean she was destined to be that sort of person – one who fought and killed?

No. This wasn't prophecy; it wasn't anything of the future. It was *her*. What was in her heart and her soul. Her true nature.

If her true nature was to be expedient about death, fighting it wouldn't accomplish anything.

She had not answered the voice yet. He seemed to have endless patience. She squared her shoulders and nodded. "Yes."

The whirlwind came once more.

A black leather cord lay in her hands. She stared at it mutely.

At first her mind refused to acknowledge what the cord was. The feel of it in her hands could not be denied, though. It was a *keishoni*. She'd seen people wear them, wrapped around their arms, mostly at the festivals that celebrated the creation of the world. The women who drummed and the men who danced; they wore the *keishoni*, for their actions echoed those of Ika and Ise. The role of a god; that was what the *keishoni* signified.

"I can't wear this," she whispered.

It had nothing to do with being fifteen. She'd *never* be worthy of wearing the *keishoni*. It was an honor and a burden; she didn't deserve the former and didn't want the responsibility of the latter. More than that, even; she *shouldn't* have it. She wasn't right for it.

The *keishoni* lay in her hands, waiting for her to put it on.

"I can't," she repeated, and clenched her fists around the cord. Her heart pounded in her chest, not a steady rhythm but an irregular beat that made her hands shake. No one really knew what happened to those who came back without an otherform, what they had done to fail. Maybe this was it. The *keishoni* was a gift. Rejecting it – her heart thudded painfully. Rejecting it might be an unforgivable crime.

She knew why she had the *keishoni*. If she put it on, she could go forth and change things. She could move against the prejudice that kept the Kagi trapped in the Isles. She could help her people. Good things would come about for the Kagi if she put the *keishoni* on, for with it she would have the backing of Ika and Ise. With it, she could start a crusade that would shake the world.

Wasn't that what she wanted?

"Yes," she admitted out loud, trying to explain. "I *do* want it. But – not like this. We ... we should do it ourselves. We should convince other people to change their ways, instead of just killing them. And we should do it without needing Ika and Ise to hold our hands. It would be different if the situation were worse, maybe, but right now it's just prejudice and stalemate. We don't have to have the help of the gods. We can stand on our own two feet – and we *should*."

Slowly, one hair's-breadth at a time, she opened her fingers. The *keishoni* was still there – but she wouldn't wear it. Not unless there was no other choice.

"We still have a choice," she said softly.

The *keishoni* disappeared, and the whirlwind caught her up and swept her away.

Flames leapt about her, hot and fierce. They reminded her of the flames that had surrounded her at the beginning of her quest. They would still be burning, tended until her return.

Assuming she returned.

She stood in the fire and wondered why the voice had not spoken to her about the *keishoni*. Had she failed? Made the wrong choice? Spurning Ika and Ise – that wasn't what she'd meant by her refusal, but perhaps it had been interpreted that way, despite her explanation. She wanted to speak, to apologize, before the Other could condemn her and send her home empty. But the flames began to whirl in front of her, forming a vortex that drew her eyes and would not let go.

The flames entranced her, and in them she could hear the memory of drumbeats. Her heart pounded with them.

The fire of your heart. The rhythm of your breath.

She had found them within her, and the Other had come. She had been tested, in order that she might become an adult, with a name and an otherform. All of the keys were in her possession.

She closed her eyes, and gathered it all within.

A burst of heat opened her eyes again. The vortex grew in

brightness until she had to shield her face; then it subsided. And where it had been –

A white raven.

Not albino; the raven was pure white, but with the black eyes normal for his kind. He spread his wings to a not-inconsiderable width, then folded them again, flicking them so the feathers would align.

She stared at him for a long moment before finding her voice again. When she spoke she had no idea what she would say, but the words came of their own accord. "Freedom. And death, but not for its own sake. And –"

"Contradiction," the raven said, speaking with the voice of the Other, the voice she had heard throughout her tests. "You do not do what is expected."

She thought about the *keishoni*, the temptation she'd felt. But she hadn't taken it, even though logically she ought to have. She had followed her own path, however surprising it was.

"White feathers," she said. A bird for freedom, a raven for death, and white that should be black for contradiction.

The Other cocked his head to one side, studying her with a bright black eye that reflected the surrounding flames. "This is what I saw in you, Shikari."

Shikari. *Shika*, meaning "shadow." *Ri*, meaning "white."

"Contradiction," the raven repeated. "White Shadow. With the form of the white raven. This is what your path led to. Do you accept the name and the form?"

It was not what she had expected. The lynx had felt more likely. But she'd come out here to find herself, her true self, and even if it wasn't what she'd thought, could she refuse it? She might not get a second chance. Refusal might leave her Unformed, not fully Kagi.

Refusal would separate her from this Other, who had led her along the path. It would be a slap in his face, and a dagger in her own heart.

"I accept," Shikari said.

The rains which had been falling steadily all afternoon finally stopped, leaving the trees and boulders slick with a sheen of water. The clouds cleared away, bathing the islands in fading autumn light.

In the shadow of the stones, a bright light flashed.

Then a white raven spread her wings and leapt into the sky to find her way home.

Offering of Trust

by
Jana Paniccia

Jana Paniccia

And so it came to pass in the sixth year following their initial attack on Tor Shalar, that the red dragons were lured back into Tariyadin, one of the two realms of magic, and locked away from our world forever. The Redback War was ended. Peace swept across the land as the survivors left their mountain havens and took up the task of rebuilding. The challenges were manifold. With years of restoration ahead, rampant famine and threat of plague, the future of mankind remained ambiguous. Considering the struggle for survival paramount, few wondered at the powers wielded in humanity's defence. With the gates sealed, all that remained of the magic rested on golden wings and in the imaginations of those who couldn't forget...

"History of the Redback War" by Nylar Kendrake

☙•❧

D ragons.

Only two months past the end of the Redback War, with the reality of their ferocity and relentless power still numbing the minds of every human in the realm, Shen dreamed not of war but of golden dragons.

Only once in his life had he seen them up close – felt their powerful magic running through his body. On the cusp of dying, the golds' arrival through a gate from Kariyadin, twin to the realm of the redbacks, had offered Shen the relief he had needed to survive. Their very presence had offered peace, drawing pain away and wrapping him in a blanket of soothing light long enough for his father to find a healer. They had saved his life – and that had only been one of their lesser powers.

From what Shen had heard, the golds could also perceive and shape the energies linking the three worlds together, sensing even the smallest of changes occurring within and between the worlds. This talent lay at the heart of their power, a power they dedicated to helping others. Even as the redbacks were destroyers, the golds were Protectors and Healers.

Laying flat on an outcrop of granite, his legs lined and red from the bite of edged rock, Shen could easily imagine winging through the sky atop a golden dragon on a day as clear as this. Sunlight gleamed through the veil of mountain mist, reflecting off the quartz-encrusted granite cliffs, and casting a luminescent spider's web over the castle being erected in the valley below. Laughter echoed up from the builders, reaching Shen's ears on a wisp of wind teeming with joy and exuberance. Yellow and blue cloaks flickered between the cedars as bands of berry pickers harvested the summer's bounty. Fendior was reborn, and everyone able to be abroad found a reason to walk in the sunshine – secure in the open air for the first time in six years.

Eight weeks now since the train of Fendior's knights had brought word to the mountains: the Tariyadin gate – the final remaining gate between this world and the magic realms – had been sealed. Eight weeks of clear, smoke-free skies. No fears. No death. No dragons.

Dragons.

Shen studied the cobalt blue above the mountains with a fierce determination, sure if he kept focused he would uncover a glint of burnished gold or perceive the faint trill of almost silent wingbeats. His eyes watered as he forgot to blink. His arm lay outstretched over the edge of the cliff as if willing the shadows to reunite into the creatures his heart could only yearn for.

A raspy voice wafted up from the foot of the cliff. "Shen, are you up there?" At the sound of his father's voice, Shen came out of his reverie. While climbing offered a respite from his inadequacies, he knew he needed to get back to the things he could do. Everyone was working hard to get the outer walls up before the first snows – and he would do no less.

With a soft sigh, he rose to his feet and dusted away the remnants of his rocky perch from his skin and pale green work tunic. With one last faint look of longing towards the empty expanse of blue, Shen turned and carefully started the climb back down the rock face. Compensating for his lost arm was always harder on the descent. At least going up, he could see where he wanted to place his hand before he moved. This time, he had no trouble, pausing only once to regain his precarious balance.

Shen's father, Athered Faltair, stood at a makeshift table thrown up beneath a leafless birch as a base of operations for the engineers rushing the construction of Fendior Castle. His gaze flicked constantly around the valley, keeping an eye on the scattered work crews. The older man's grey streaked, rust-red hair was tied back in a tail, and his face, though lined from years of fear and worry, appeared less careworn than in the weeks past. The pale patch of burn scar on his father's cheek sent a chill through Shen, an echo of that fateful day, six years past, when the dragons had fired their home.

Home. As Shen drew closer to his father, he tried to push the vision of Tor Shalar from his mind. A bustling seaport on the edge of the sea, Tor Shalar had been the centre of the world's trading industry. Hundreds of ships would anchor at her docks each day, bearing brilliant flags of all five nations and dozens of city-states. People of all cultures gathered in her markets to exchange goods, from the exceedingly rare Trianti diamonds to curry powder made in the Eastern Desert. Until the first gate had opened between the human world and the magical realm of Tariyadin, bringing the first of the redback dragons.

A burnt face rose in his mind's eye, and Shen turned his thoughts away from his mother. Nothing could bring her back. Not her, and not the thousands of others caught entirely unprepared for an attack. Shen drew his hand up to his face, clearing away new tears.

But those were the redbacks. The gold dragons are Healers – Protectors. He remembered.

Only nine when Tor Shalar burned, Shen nevertheless remembered the gold dragons appearing the night after the initial attack, stemming the tide of disaster. For days, dragon had fought dragon above Tor Shalar's flame-engulfed city, sowing further destruction in their wake as the battle extended out over the Everglen Forest. Only by collapsing the redbacks' first gate had the golds forced the attackers away, granting time for the survivors to flee for the mountains.

With the closing of the gate in Tor Shalar, the course of the war had taken a new twist. Redbacks sought to seal the golds' entry points into Fendior, even as the golds worked to do the same in reverse. When the redbacks destroyed the golds' last gate to Kariyadin, stranding them in the human world, they must have thought they had won. After all, how could the redbacks imagine the golds would destroy the sole remaining access to the magic realms?

But they had, in order to seal the redbacks away – forever.

If not for golds, Shen would have died from the burns suffered when a coil of flame had set their house alight. But with their intervention, his father had managed to carry Shen out of the city and find him a healer. He knew how lucky he was to only lose an arm and not his life. But now, with the war over, Shen longed to know more about his saviours, the ones willing to give up their own world by sealing the gates – and all for the survival of another race.

Not that anyone else shared his dreams – most were glad enough to be rid of all the winged ones, and if that included the good with the evil, it did not concern most people enough to question. For the remnants of the war would be visible across the continent for years to come. Once fertile forests wasted by fire offered only finger-high saplings among the burnt out trunks, leaving no promise of sustenance for the thousands left unsheltered. Food scarcity offered dire motivation to the homeless as they migrated to the unpopulated mountains in the north and west, where trees still offered fruit, and mountains could be mined for both castle rock and iron ore. Even here, where Fendior Castle was being raised more than a thousand miles from its original home on the Ironwood Plain, the outlook of long-term survival remained ominous. As the chances for survival dwindled, the humans forced to rebuild five countries from nothing cast their blame across the entire race of nonworlders, not only those who had caused the ruin.

The possibility of ruin shadowed the leafy green eyes of the elder Faltair, even as he struggled to halt the descent into chaos. This project would rebuild Fendior, or it would sanction the beginning of the final days. Athered's hands rested flat against the unvarnished tabletop whose surface had collected piles of drawings and sketches of the work in progress. Around his feet lay a scattering of metal pipework bought at a ransom's price from the south.

"Where have you been?" Athered Faltair asked as Shen stepped up to the table.

Shen grimaced, knowing how much his father hated his climbing. "I was up on the cliff watching the skies."

Athered shook his head resignedly. "They're gone. There's no need to be watching for them anymore – we're safe now." He came around the table and rubbed Shen's shoulders. "They are really gone – I promise."

"But, I wasn't..." Shen stopped, finishing his thought silently instead.

...*waiting for an attack.*

"Everyone is – but we have to get over it. The war is over, and the dragons are gone."

"I know Father – I'm sorry," Shen said.

"I understand, Shen. Come on now, Petram could use your help with marking the boundaries of the inner bailey. He's already over there –" Athered pointed across the building site to where a tall man was pacing out land and pounding stakes into the earth.

Shen nodded. Pacing was one of the few things he could do to be of help. They certainly couldn't use a one-armed teen on one of the splitter teams, or even in hauling the rock to the walls.

Athered waved to a bundle of stakes laying under a nearby oak with a mass of wrinkled bark that reminded Shen of the scar tissue under his shirt. "Can you manage to bring those over with you? I can help if you need ..."

"No worries, I have them." Shen reached down and pulled the bundle up, balancing it between his knee and the tree until he had a firm grip. He started across the clearing, leaving his father muttering softly over one of the diagrams on the table.

As noon passed, the day turned warmer, and Shen worked hard at all the tasks he could find himself. After pacing out the walls, he ran errands to the splitter team leads, so they could begin cutting out the appropriate sized slabs of granite. Several teams sheared the rock apart from the mountain face using long iron wedges and hammers, while others carted the rock to the edge of the building site using horse-drawn sledges. Shen went before the carters, clearing paths, and directing traffic as best he could.

As the sun moved higher in the sky, the day grew even hotter and Shen busied himself bringing a water bucket around to the sweating laborers. Many of the men greeted him fondly, giving him pitying looks when they thought he could not see. At least once the castle was up – he'd be able to do more. Although he was not entirely sure his father's plan of an apprenticeship with the Lord Marshall was really what he wanted. While he *was* good with numbers, the thought of being closed in with account books for the rest of his life did nothing to inspire his mind. Between carrying the water and thinking on the future, tiredness set in and his mind drifted away from his makework projects and turned towards more inviting thoughts.

They'll return. They have to. After all, where else could they go?

The gates were closed – the golds were stranded here. They had paid a huge price for the safety of Fendior.

A loud clanging brought Shen up short as a deep voice roared through the valley.

"DRAGONS!"

Shen shivered with each knell of the emergency bell. Around the valley, people ran for safety. Screams rent the air and echoed through the mountain peaks as women grabbed their children and headed into the trees. In front of him, a young girl in a pale yellow sundress was swept up in the arms of a woman with russet brown hair already carrying two wailing babies. In denial, a row of cliff breakers turned their iron wedge away from the rock and held it menacingly toward the eastern sky.

"Dragons," Shen whispered, frozen to the ground while the world tilted and whirled on its axis. His eyes, long accustomed to searching the sky, were immediately drawn to the dark shadows stretching closer with each passing moment. A glint of gold scale just as he had always imagined captured the sun and sprawled thin rays of its light outward in glistening star patterns that bedazzled the eyes.

As they drew closer with each breath, Shen began to count their visitors, fear never entering his mind. These were the gold-winged dragons of Kariyadin, the sworn protectors and guardians of the world. These – these were beings of magic. He shivered in anticipation. Only once had he seen them up close – on that first journey north after the death of his mother and disfigurement of his father.

Most of the dragons flew in a large cluster, gold and cream wings beating against each other as they worked to keep steady a package dangling from ropes attached to their hind legs. An outer ring of a dozen free dragons flew protectively around the burden.

Whatever it is, they consider it valuable. Dragon treasure?

"Come on boy!" A strong hand clasped Shen's shoulder and pulled him away from the clearing and into the trees. Athered muttered curses at the looming front of dragons as he dragged Shen behind a small stand of pines no better for hiding than a castle would be for a giant.

A large gust of wind preceded the arrival of their unexplained visitors as a flurry of winged bodies made to set down. The immense

burden came down gently in the centre of the castle plot, followed by
the landfall of its carriers. Dragons – on the ground, their size dwarfed
all Shen could imagine; one creature alone stood larger than his former
house in Tor Shalar.

Beneath the noises of wings and settling, Shen was amazed to find
silence. No dragon had voiced a sound – unlike in battle, where loud
cracking screams had ripped the air with roaring thunder.

::We come for your help.:: At first Shen thought the words in his
head were directed at him. His eyes widened perceptibly, and his slight
frame rocked with the wonder of mind speech. A glance at his father
revealed the older man had heard the words too. Athered's grip on
Shen's shoulder held him firmly in place.

"Stay here," he ordered. "Without the king here, I may have to face
them, but you'll stay where it's safe. Don't move."

Shen wilted, wanting to follow as Athered Faltair, Chief Builder
and King's Voice, straightened and walked out from behind the pine.

"What do you want here?"

*::One of our kind is passing beyond the veil. She has no strength to
go farther, and must rest. We cannot carry her through a gate to
Kariyadin.::*

Shen could hardly see the dragon who spoke, though he could
sense it was the one standing to the left of the bundle. Its scales rippled
in the light, accenting its orange-gold color. As the dragon turned its
head toward Athered, Shen saw it clearly for the first time and was
immobilized with awe. A ring of sharp bones thrust upward from its
forehead towards its back. Eyes of bright green emerald lay inset
between scaled ridges that offered slight protection. A jagged – closed
– line marked the dragon's mouth, several of its teeth poking outward
in sharp lines bigger than Shen. As the dragon spoke, the mouth did not
move. The teeth remained still.

Desire for a closer view overcoming his initial awe, Shen ducked
out from behind the trees and took a few steps towards the dragons.

"Who are you?" Athered demanded.

::I am Mendraganam, and this–:: The dragon's head nodded
toward the burden, *::–is Koradethkalion. She was injured whilst
closing the Tariyadin gate. She has bought peace with her lifegift.::*

The burden was a dragon? That lopsided package Shen had mistook for dragon treasure? Without thinking, he ran towards his father and the gold-orange dragon, eyes locked on the oilcloth wrapped bundle. Stepping around piles of granite, it took no more than a moment to come directly in front of the package.

A single glittering brown eye watched him approach. Even while his father tried to reach him, an arm outstretched to pull him back, Shen was caught up in the pain carried by that single eye. A swath of blood soaked cloth covered most of the injured dragon's body, hiding the worst of the damage. A twisted forefoot and the jagged edges of a torn wing peeked from beneath the covering, offering a taste of the devastation beneath. Only the eye remained – the last bastion of perfection – and full of solemn lucidity and understanding.

Tears slid down Shen's face in sympathy, leaving muddy tracks through his dirt-stained cheeks. Fingers clasped into a fist at the truth staring him in the face. A circle closed. His mother – her burned body a mass of broken bones and charred skin – had died on that first day – in that sooty, smoke-filled city by the sea, as he had watched on – helpless. Now, again – this dragon stared at him with the same resignation of impending death. And he could do nothing.

::Your presence is comforting.:: This time the mind voice was only for him: a feather light touch almost imperceptible. A knowing glimmer of understanding shone in her eye.

"I'll stay, Koradethkalion," Shen offered gently, recalling the alien name the other had spoken. He raised his hand out in reassurance, remembering his own mother speaking to him.

"Don't ever lose your caring," she had whispered with her final breath as he had hovered nearby, hand grasping her burned one without fear.

A sharp claw snaked around his stomach and grasped him backwards. Shen screamed as something sharp lifted him into the air. Legs and arm dangled helplessly as he looked down upon the gaping mouth of an angered dragon. Almost-white scales rippled down the dragon's chest as his wings waved open. This close, the pinkish tendons and lines of muscle stood out candidly against the thin layer of skin sheathing the underside of the wings.

"Shen!" His father's desperate voice stung in Shen's ears. Far below, Athered Faltair struggled against the hold of the first dragon, Mendraganam.

"Let him go – we'll help you – but please, let my son go! He's been hurt bad enough," Athered begged.

::Tiamberdarian, let the boy go. You aren't a killer.:: It was the orange-gold Mendraganam who spoke so calmly.

::It was them. They killed her.::

::Brother, the Banished Ones killed her. These mortals – their lives are in our trust. Your loved one maintained her duty.::

::Duty. What is duty amidst a forever of loneliness? I want no hand in Duty.::

With a violent thrust, the dragon dropped Shen to the ground on the outside of the foot high castle walls closest to the mountains. Curls of mist swirled before his eyes, multiplying as needles of agony stabbed through his chest and head.

::Stay away from her.:: The order burned into Shen's mind, refusing his denial. *Stay away. Stay away. Stay away.* Stumbling to his feet, vision still clouded by pain, Shen took one terrified glance at the white and gold-scaled dragon arching menacingly over his head, then ran.

Where to go when being chased by a thought – an irrational order to move he could not countermand?

A cliff appeared before his eyes, the edge of the rocky outlook overshadowing the valley where he had spent the morning dreaming of dragons. Moving faster than he thought himself capable of, Shen grasped for a handhold and pulled himself upward, climbing heedless of caution in his desire to reach his safe haven.

Away. Away. Away.

Not far enough, he stepped onto the dusty cliff edge, colored by weeds poking out from between cracks, and wanted to move farther. He continued climbing up the side of the mountain, desperate to outrun the demand on his mind. Never before had he climbed so high, for fear of falling. Loose rock offered a treacherous grip and he found himself scrambling to keep control of the ascent. Sharp edges broke his fingernails and tore skin as his hand ached. Two hundred feet up, the cliff face tapered off into the crest of the mountain – more a foothill of the Icecaps range.

Forced to pause, Shen came out of a daze as the burning desire to get away receded. His palm, shredded from the jagged rocks, dripped blood. Fingers curled inward protectively. Wild grass sprouted up in clumps around the rock at his feet. Looking down into the valley, a wash of vertigo ran through his mind.

"I climbed that?" he whispered, amazed at his ability and caught off guard. He had climbed all the way up with only one hand. His father would die when he heard! Beneath the ledge, a sheer face tore downward into the valley, offering a flawless view of the unfinished castle and the dragons.

Dragons.

As he watched, he could see the two big ones, the orange-gold Mendraganam and the white-gold Tiamberdarian, talking to his father. Even from up here, he could tell things had calmed down. People were starting to come in from between the pines and cedar, forming semicircles on the outside of the farthest row of dragons. Cookfires lit up around the valley, brightening the sky as the builders settled in to wait for the dragons' next move. Shen's father turned toward the fires, leaving the two dragons alone with the injured one.

Now what? Shen wondered.

Even as he thought the words, the wings of Mendraganam stretched outward, and beat in a flurry of power. Created currents of air allowed the being to take to the air, and he flew high into the darkening sky. As Shen watched from his desolate perch, the large dragon turned on a wingtip and flew out into the mountains. Utter wonder at the dragon's grace caused Shen to forget the demand to get away. His wobbly knees toppled him to the ground. Sight darkened for a moment, and then came clear, as a large blanket shape appeared mere feet above his head. Orange and gold.

The dragon settled beside him, taking up the entire top of the hill, wrapping his spiked tail around Shen in an almost protective manner.

Wings folded neatly onto his back, Mendraganam's large head sunk down to the ground, his eyes steady and focused.

Shivering nervously, it took a few moments before the heat emanating from the dragon's tail soaked into Shen's skin, calming the overwhelming shaking. A few deep breaths were enough to harness the courage to look up.

Understanding.

Dragon and human sat in silence as the light of dusk faded to black, taking comfort in each other's eyes. As stars began to flicker into luminescent being, Shen knew peace for the first time since before his injury – since before his mother's death.

::*Koradethkalion knows no peace. Tiamberdarian knows no peace.*::

Shen's head rose to study the dragon's eyes, unsurprised at their intensity. "Why?" he found himself asking.

::*They are bondmates. Protectors live forever in Kariyadin. Even when bodies no longer live, because of the magic of our land, their souls live on. Caught here, her spirit will dissolve and die. Tiamberdarian will no longer have his companion. Koradethkalion will be no more.*::

Since his first sight of one of the Protectors, not long after the burning of Tor Shalar, when the survivors had thought this other race of dragons from Kariyadin was bringing the end, Shen had thought of dragons as timeless. Stuck in the back of a wagon, feverish from the pain of burning and amputation, Shen had watched them force the Banished Ones away for a time, and protect the train of people moving up into the mountains. Always graceful. Shining with the light of unknown power. Magic: a child's daydream until the war, it burned in these creatures so brightly.

Timeless.

No more. Tears stung in Shen's eyes, burning with sudden grief at the realization that even these creatures could not conquer death. Their magic did not save them from his mother's end – only increased their pain.

What now, for me? Shen wondered. Always he had thought that no matter what he did, no matter what happened in the world – the

Protectors at least would remember. They would hold firm to their destiny, even as mankind's time ended. They had been safe to love.

Nothing is safe now. No one is safe. The inevitability of it all crashed down on him, as he recognised that everything he loved would forever be at risk.

Unless there was a way to protect them.

"I need to speak with them." Shen hardened his tone to match the granite he rested on, sure in his desire.

Mendraganam seemed to sense it – and perhaps he did. After all, the limits of the Protectors' magic had never been deduced.

::*Use my foreleg and climb up between the ridges above my wings.*:: Shen awkwardly did as he was asked, finding a perfect inset between the dragon's wings that would keep him from shifting or falling.

::*Take care – This will be a sudden drop,*:: Mendraganam announced.

Gripping the scale ridge tightly with his hand, Shen locked his knees tight against the warm scales. Fear and excitement knotted his stomach. He shut his eyes. His stomach gave a sudden lurch upwards as the dragon dove off the cliff. Grass and ground rushed up to meet them creating a tumultuous vertigo that threatened to overwhelm his stomach. Still-bloody knuckles turned white as he tightened his grip, thankful for the protruding spines holding him in place. Thoughts of death rushed through his head even as Mendraganam levelled out and circled the castle site.

Opening his eyes, Shen gasped at the brilliance of the land below. The just-started walls of the castle shimmered in the starlight, almost ghostly in their surreal beauty. Rings of people and dragons kept vigil outside the boundaries. Cook fires burned patterns of rainbow brilliance against reflective scales. Only Tiamberdarian remained within the confines of the castle design, his body laced around the injured one's protectively.

A hint of fear prickled at Shen's back as he worried about Tiamberdarian's state of mind. Would his overtures be completely rebuffed?

Will he kill me?

Not enough time to guess the response. Mendraganam landed into the clearing with a soft touch, and bent to allow Shen to dismount.

From somewhere, he heard his father calling, relief apparent in Athered's thankful tone.

Without thinking about it, Shen offered a quick wave in the direction of the voice and slid off the dragon's back. With a deep breath to calm his nerves, he turned to face the three sets of larger-than-human eyes studying him intently – two filled with fear and hatred, and one with overwhelming relief and understanding.

"I want to help," Shen said.

::*Find yourself another place to go then. I do not want you here, nor do I need your help.*::

"You do need me." Shen recognised Tiamberdarian's defensiveness as his own from after his mother had died. Alone before his father had come, he had resented the intrusion of another life after the abrupt end he had witnessed. "Perhaps there's a way to save her."

::*If we cannot bring her through to Kariyadin, how do you think you can, mortal one?*::

"Does she have to go through for her spirit to be saved?" he asked simply.

Tiamberdarian fell back onto his haunches, struck dumb with incomprehension. His wings twitched.

::No.:: It was Koradethkalion who answered. Exhausted and weakening, she dredged up the energy to form coherent thoughts. *::Can imbue anything living here.::*

"Take me then." Shen offered his own death willingly, knowing that with her life the dragon could protect his father and the entire human race. He had never decided what he wanted to do after the war. The thought of being a bookkeeper as his father had suggested never held any draw. Maybe this was it – what he was meant to do – give himself up for the safety of others. "I doubt missing an arm would stop you from your work. It's better this way."

::NO:: Tiamberdarian's scream rang through Shen's head, echoing within the confines of his thin mortal skull and almost sending him to his knees. Koradethkalion's broken forearm halted his dissent and propped him up. Her single eye shone with bright new hope, even through the pain of moving to save him.

::*Yes. Yes. We can do this. Give this boy a part of my soul – keep me alive. Let my power go toward helping them rebuild – after all, it was our brethren who destroyed their world.*:: Hope brought a surge of energy into her mindvoice.

::*And the rest?*:: Mendraganam asked, not allowing his own response to taint the conversation.

::*Others. Large land. Give to others. Let them protect. Hold it for them, Mendraganam. Hold it in trust.*::

::*But you'll be gone –* :: Grief threatened to overwhelm Tiamberdarian. He brought his head down to rest upon his bondmate's.

::*Not gone. I would have been gone. Now – I'll be in them. I'll be there for you.*::

Tiamberdarian's nostrils oozed steam in resignation. His eyes fell shut, blocking away his agony. ::*If you want this, I won't stop you.*::

::*Boy?*:: Her voice lightened again, and Shen knew she wouldn't last much longer. The flare of power along her skin was fading. The final darkness loomed over her head.

::*Certain?*:: An influx of pictures filled his head: warm hands holding him safely in a lap, shoulders offering a seat to see him through to the end of a beach, his mother's gentle spirit – bidding him to never stop caring.

Caring. I will always care. That is what my life is for. Caring for others.

Trying to turn his thoughts into words, Shen stalled. What words offered death for life, life for safety? With a faint cry, he thrust his thoughts of love and safety, certainty and promise outward.

The dragon accepted it. Claws pulled him tight towards her, bringing his face into contact with the broken scales beneath her perfect eye.

::*Take it.*::

A gentle hum. Music, soft and insistent, rang inside and outside his body at the same time. It seeped into his skin on a wave of luminescent light that brought his eyes out of focus with the world. He knew he was smiling.

Light filled the clearing, brilliant and powerful and promising. It spoke of possibility. Magic. Without turning, Shen knew each of the dragons resonated with its responsibility, its thirst for usage not for gain but for guardianship. It was what made them Protectors. Even now, their brethren lived because killing was abhorrent. The Redback War was not war in these eyes. It was a breaking of trust. That breaking had forced the banishment – the locking of the gate. For all peoples to live in peace and safety and promise, the Protectors had worked their magic. Now, that magic worked in Shen.

::Peace, Protector.:: Last words. Final words. Koradethkalion breathed her last.

Magic erupted behind his eyes, casting Shen into a world of myriad colors and feelings. Passing out was an instant relief.

"Shen?"

A voice interrupted the pleasant darkness by forcing remembrance. Shen opened his eyes to meet the worried gaze of his father. With the movement, the older man grasped his shoulders, pulling him into a tight embrace.

"Father?" Shen said the word uncertainly. He was still here. Alive. One glance was all it took to see that Tiamberdarian and the body of Koradethkalion were gone. As were the other dragons, except for an orange-gold one, whose heat Shen could feel pressing against his back.

Shen turned toward Mendraganam, filled with remorse. "It didn't work, did it?"

A ticking sensation played down his back as if the dragon's laughter could seep into his skin. As a laugh burst out of his own mouth, Shen realised that maybe it could. Not a word had been spoken, yet he *knew* his large companion was pleased.

::It worked, younger brother. It might take a few years for you to realise what you have, but it worked.::

"But I'm alive!"

::A Protector could not take someone else's life – but can only give up his or her own. Selflessly, you offered to take on a part of Koradethkalion's soul, and she granted it unto you. She has gifted you with the magic to become the first of the human Protectors.::

"Protector," Shen tried out the word, still unsure. He had been ready to give up his life so she could continue to be a Protector – but could he do as she had done? His failure could break the three worlds apart.

"My son!" The relief in his father's voice reminded Shen of another plan.

Feeling slightly guilty, Shen turned to his father. "It's not what you wanted for me," he said.

Athered smiled. "Son, all I have wanted for you is for you to be happy – to be able to do what you want to do, without the limits this –" he touched Shen's shoulder gently, where the mound of scar tissue still ached in the cold. "Gives you. If this dragon thinks you can take on their job, who am I not to let you go? You can do anything you set your mind to. Just do me and your mother, and Fendior, proud."

"She would be, wouldn't she?"

His father nodded solemnly. "She would."

Brushing a tear from the corner of eye, Shen glanced back at the dragon, "What now?"

::While you have been gifted with a part of Koradethkalion's soul, I yet hold the remainder in trust for others. As you recovered, we decided that since there are five human kingdoms, it is appropriate that there now be five human Protectors. We must find others who would share your burden.:: Mendraganam let his mouth open wide to let out a verbal hiss. Shen recognised it as laughter. The smooth top of the dragon's nose pressed him from behind and into his father's arms. *::We can wait for tomorrow before we start the search. You have time to say goodbye.::*

Away from the dragon, Shen stumbled into a mist of glowing colors. Swirls of green and brown shifted before his eyes, coloring his father's skin and tinting the very ground around them. His stomach threatened to revolt as he struggled to maintain an awareness of his surroundings. Sounds saturated his being as voices rang not in his ears, but in the caverns of his mind. And over it all, like a shroud of purest light, a gauzy haze of gold wafted up from his body, a mesh of luminescent rope drawing him outward into somewhere unknown.

::Not yet.:: With Mendraganam's thoughts, a wall of almost glass cut through the swirling turbulence of light and sound and grounded

Shen back into reality. Still partially sensing the flows moving around, he found their brilliance no longer clouded his vision.

"What is it?" Shen asked, rubbing at the back of his neck as the prickles of power tingled against his skin.

::The center of our magic. It will take you years to grow accustomed to it. For now, when you are near I can shelter you from most of it.::

Shen shivered in remembrance of the overwhelming sensations that had encompassed him totally for a moment. He swallowed nervously, leery of the power he had been granted. Already he couldn't imagine not feeling that sensation against his skin – the link that he almost wanted to swallow him whole. Already he was being changed.

::Go now. Your father is afraid for you.::

The thought of such a strong man worried made Shen fiercely protective.

Reaching out, Shen hugged his father close. "You've taught me well what duty is – you know. You never stopped pushing me forward. Always trusted me. Trust me to live by your lessons. I will do Fendior proud."

"I know." Athered smiled.

A Protector, Shen thought, while walking with his father around the foot-high castle walls. Together they passed by the cliff where he had just that morning been dreaming of dragons. Always dreaming. Now, he would be going with them. Sharing their burden. Sharing their trust. The task of learning to control Koradethkalion's gift daunted him – it promised a long struggle and years of uncertainty. Yet, his spirit burned with the opportunity the future presented. Looking at the unfinished walls of the castle, he saw their promise. Soon, pennants would fly atop shining towers, offering a beacon of hope in a new world – a new world in which he now had a real place.

With the faces of his mother and Koradethkalion both burning brightly in his mind, Shen knew he had made the right choice.

⮞ ● ⮜

A Prayer of Salt and Sand

by
Karina Sumner-Smith

Karina Sumner-Smith

Morning approached, brightening the sky over the ocean with the palest wash of blue. Asha saw the light and was afraid.

Reaching into the bowls that lay at her sides, she took up fistfuls of salt and sand from her dwindling supply. The sand was the fine, silvery sand of Sacrifice Beach; it clung to her sweaty palms and caught beneath her fingernails. The salt was coarse and white as sun-bleached bone. Sand in one hand, salt in the other, she continued her pattern.

When Asha had first gone to her knees in prayer at dawn the day before, the wide flat stone that lay embedded in the ground at the edge of the cliff had been a naked expanse of black. Now, as dawn again approached, little of the stone's dark surface remained. Patterns – the thin lines, tight curves, and unending waves that formed the symbols of her goddess' worship – covered it from edge to edge.

Asha opened her fingers and the sand began to flow in a thin, steady stream. She drew one horizontal line, then another, and another: the symbol for the flood, the water rising. In salt she drew an upward curve: a hand in supplication.

Her mouth was dry as the sand, her tongue heavy and thick, but still she chanted. She didn't know how long she'd been speaking, nor what words her lips shaped, only that she could not stop the flow of her prayer, not while she still had breath.

Please, she begged of her goddess. *Please speak to me.*

There was no sound except that of her own whispering, the sand falling on the flat rock, and the waves crashing far below her; no vision but that of the sun brightening the sky.

Time slipped away as quickly as the sand. She had not finished her last pattern, but the salt fell through her fingers and was gone. There was no time for another handful, no last breath of prayer, for the sun had broken the horizon and Asha knew that she had failed. Again.

For a long moment Asha stayed where she was, kneeling on the flat, black prayer stone with her eyes closed. Her damp fingers, coated with sand and salt, lay still against her thighs. She could feel the warmth of the sun on the top of her bowed head, see its pale light through the veil of her eyelids, and felt no joy. There was only a great, heavy emptiness inside her chest, the hollow beating that was her heart.

Many did not find the goddess the first time that they called. But she was not the youngest to have called, and now, at fourteen, the other young initiates had long left her behind. This was her fifth year, her fifth vigil and calling that had gone unanswered.

"Why, Narelle?" she whispered to her silent goddess. "Why?"

She had thought that this year would be different. Instead of praying in the temple or on the common prayer stones as she had in years past, she had come to Sacrifice Point. It was here, on the same piece of ground where Asha now knelt, that the goddess Narelle had stood in her last moments of life as a woman. Then the waters of the ocean had raged, drowning the islands as the water steadily rose. Already it had swallowed the wide, flat island of Drift, taking with it all the knowledge from the old land and many lives besides; the islands of Rise and Wake would soon follow. It was here that Narelle had gathered her will and her strength, knowing that she might have the power to stop the flood but that it would take her blood and her life, willingly given, to complete this magic. Narelle stood on the edge of the cliff of the place that was to become Peak of the Ocean, and made her final sacrifice: she leapt and fell and died – and the water stopped rising.

It seemed that not even coming to this sacred spot was enough to make the goddess send her even the smallest of visions.

Asha opened her eyes, and brushed away the tears that clung to her lashes. Someone was coming. Already the sun was over the horizon, and the ocean before her sparkled and danced. After rubbing her hands together to clean them, Asha forced herself to stand, ignoring the numbness of her legs as she struggled to her feet. She turned.

"Té'ahn-Narelle," Asha said to the woman behind her, bowing her head in a gesture of respect. The high priestess nodded in return.

"Té-Narelle," she replied, using the formal term for a follower of the goddess Narelle. "Your fifth vigil has come to an end. Has the goddess sent you word or vision?"

"No, Té'ahn," Asha said quietly. "Neither. My prayers have not been heard."

The Té'ahn nodded once in acknowledgement, her face grave. Then her pale eyes softened in sorrow, and she was no longer Neryanté Té'ahn-Narelle, but simply the woman that Asha had known as mother for as long as she could remember.

"Oh, child," Nerya said, opening her arms to embrace her adopted daughter. "I am so sorry." But Asha jerked back, shaking her head. Her eyes stung with unshed tears and she wanted nothing more than to run into her mother's arms, but she stopped herself. How could the high priestess understand the pain of a failed initiate? The Té'ahn, she who carried the burden of Narelle's sacrifice and dreamed the goddess' will waking and in sleep – she could not know the pain of this rejection, and Asha did not need her pity.

Nerya hesitated, then nodded again. "There is fresh water waiting for you in a pitcher in the kitchens, Asha Té-Narelle," the Té'ahn said. "Drink soon. Your body needs the water."

She turned to go. "Don't be too long, Asha," she said softly, and walked towards the temple without waiting for an answer.

Asha's stomach ached with emptiness, and now that her prayer was ended she was aware of the ringing in her ears and the faintness in her head from dehydration. She thought of walking back to the temple of Peak of the Ocean, the long walk through the kitchen, communal rooms, and the courtyard until she could at last escape to the security of her room, and shook her head. She could not face it. Not yet.

Kneeling gingerly, she began to clean her wooden prayer bowls, emptying out the last traces of sand and salt onto the ground.

Worthless, now. She stared for a long moment at the prayer stone, looking for some flaw in her patterns. She studied their forms, the precise lines of pale and white. Yet even those that covered the farthest edge of the stone, a day old and partially scattered by the warm ocean wind, seemed perfect. Salt and sand and stone on the edge above the ocean: her prayer was beautiful.

Without a word, Asha swept her hand across the flat surface of the stone, obliterating the patterns that had taken a full day and night to form. She removed all sense and meaning with wild, angry sweeps of her arm until there was nothing left but shapeless piles of mixed salt and sand. She gathered some of this mess in her hands, clenching her fists tightly.

She walked to the edge of the precipice and gazed down the vertical plunge of the cliffs to the ribbon of beach just emerging from the water as the tide receded. Waves rose and fell, washing up the rocks and falling back in the slow and constant breath of the ocean.

Asha opened her hands and scattered the remnants of her useless prayers to the wind.

Asha woke the next morning to the sound of singing. It was Renewal, she knew, one of Narelle's holy days. Women's voices young and old sang united in a clear harmony, the sound echoing through the temple and then flowing out, rising and falling across the rocky slopes of Rise like a spring storm.

The Té of Narelle sang of the man that Narelle had loved in life, Aeyen. But though she had lost him when she sacrificed herself to save the islands, Narelle did not forget him. Shortly after her sacrifice, Aeyen was struck by a powerful vision. Without knowing who he was looking for or where he was going, he searched through the survivors of the great flood and found Trellan, the woman who would become Trellanté Té'ahn-Narelle, the new goddess Narelle's first follower and high priestess.

All those who had been called by the goddess now sang the song of Aeyen's sorrow as he fell at Trellanté's feet, knowing that she would be closer to the woman he loved than he could ever be again. Realizing that though she lived on, Narelle was forever lost to him.

Hearing the singing, Asha felt as if she had to struggle for breath, for all that she pulled air easily into her lungs. She knew this song. She knew these words. It would be so easy to just let herself relax into the music; her lips would begin shaping the lyrics and the tune would rise unbidden from her throat. She knew it, and yet knew just as clearly that she had no right to sing it.

It was not that an unbound Té could not sing the Renewal songs of remembrance, nor that she would be unwelcome with those she had always thought of as her sisters, aunts, and cousins, bound and unbound priestesses alike. She was not the first to have her prayers gone unanswered, nor would she be the last. Even if she could play no formal role in the Renewal ceremony at sunset, she could still sing, and refill the prayer bowls with salt and sand, and bring cool water for the others to drink. She could still pray.

Except that in the moment the sun had risen the morning before, it was as if something had broken deep inside of her. At the time, weakened by long hours of fasting, she had only been able to feel anger and hurt at her goddess' betrayal. Yet now it was as if the weight of the ocean pressed down on her, and she had not the strength to push it away, nor the will to rise.

Asha had always thought she was special. No, more than thought – she had known with every inch of her body that the goddess had chosen her. That there was a plan for her, a path that Narelle had set her upon and all that was required of her was that she be strong enough, courageous enough to walk that path and face the trials along the way. She had never thought to question her destiny, and all had believed that she would become Té'ahn when her mother at last set aside the heavy burden. Was she not the blessed child, the girl saved from the disaster at Lee? Of the houses swept from the rocky cliffside of the village of Lee, she alone had lived; the young Asha, barely more than an infant, had been found safe and unhurt on the shore when all her family and neighbors had drowned and been swept away by the vicious current.

And though she'd never been given visions when she prayed throughout her childhood, she'd had dreams. They were vivid, powerful dreams; dreams of prophecy, some said, or dreams of divine will. Their images returned to her night after night as she grew: the streets of a drowned town, the houses choked with seaweed and the waterlogged wood crumbling; a great wave, hanging motionless in the sky; the feel of water entering and leaving her lungs in slow breaths, and a sensation of absolute calm.

Still she dreamed. The night before her vigil she had again had a sleeping vision of a wall of water that stretched as far as she could see in every direction. In the dream, she had her hands outstretched before her, fingers splayed, and all her muscles trembled with fatigue and strain as she fought to hold back the water of the entire ocean with her bare hands alone. She had thought it was a sign sent to encourage her, and woke glad, despite her fear, believing that this time she would succeed. Knowing that for all her struggling, Narelle would not desert her.

Even now she could not say that these were just dreams, but no longer had the will or presumption to interpret the images. Only one thing was clear to her: that for a fifth time she had opened herself to the goddess, laid her spirit bare, and been found wanting. Beneath the words of her prayer and all the symbols that she sketched in salt and sand, there had been but one thought, one prayer and one plea: *Hear me.*

She didn't have the strength to try – or to be rejected – again.

Which left her with … what? She looked around the small room from her grass-stuffed mattress on the floor. If the goddess had no need of her, what right did she have to live in this place? The stone walls around her and the thatched roof above her, the temple and living complex belonged to those who served the goddess Narelle, not for the adopted daughter of the Té'ahn, whose spirit the goddess had found wanting. She had little else to call her own. A few sets of clothing, all cut in the various styles of the Té. A wide-toothed comb made from shell. A bracelet of gray stone beads.

Who was she if she was not Asha Té-Narelle? She did not know how to begin to answer. The uncertainty trembled in her chest.

There was only one thing that she could say for certain anymore: wherever she belonged, it was not here.

Rising from her bed, Asha began to dress. She pulled on a pair of thin, loose pants and pulled the drawstring tight about her hips, and then took a wide band of soft blue fabric and wound it around and around her upper torso so that it covered her from just above her bellybutton to just below her collarbone, pulling her small breasts comfortably close to her chest. The ends she secured in the back with fingers deft from long practice.

In the kitchens she found stacks of covered honeycakes, still warm from the pan, waiting until the evening when the Té could at last break their fasts. She took a goatskin bottle from a peg on the far wall and filled it from the bucket of well water that sat on the wide stone table. Slinging the bottle over her shoulder, Asha hurried from the room. She would have to go quickly if she was to leave Peak of the Ocean before the Té had finished the morning's songs and prayers.

Walking with a firm, decisive stride to hide her fear, Asha made her way uphill towards Sacrifice Point, not letting herself slow or look behind her. There was only that great rocky peak of land, covered with hardy grasses and the flat black rectangles of the prayer stones. Past that there was only the ocean, wide and blue and flat for as far as she could see and beyond.

When at last she stood at the cliff's edge, she looked down to the thin curve of beach far below. Many times she had stood here and wondered how long it had taken Narelle to fall. She'd close her eyes and imagine the long seconds: one breath, two breaths, three. The cliff was so high, its peak countless body lengths from the beach and restless waves.

Asha sat on the edge of the cliff, allowing herself to savor the familiar fear. She inched closer, clinging to handfuls of the stiff yellow grass, and allowed her bare feet to hang over the edge into the empty air. She pushed herself farther still, grinning fiercely to belie the way her heart pounded. She felt herself begin to fall and *twisted* –

There. Her callused feet hit something cold and hard, then settled themselves on the first metal rung. She grinned again in excitement and relief, and started climbing down. No matter how many times she made this descent, she was always half certain that this time she would fall.

There were eighty-seven iron rungs bolted into the rock of the cliff face. Not even the Té'ahn knew who had put them there or why, only that it had been centuries ago when metal had been plentiful enough to waste on things like ladders. The rungs were coated with rust now, but only those at the bottom that endured the waves and the tide showed any signs of weakness. Beneath Asha's hands and feet, the thick, orange-spotted metal felt cool and heavy, as immovable as the cliff itself. She made her way carefully down.

At last she reached the bottom and brushed the rusty residue from her palms. The tide was out, exposing almost twelve feet of fine silvery sand, and the water, protected by the slight curve of the cliffs, was calm. A few feet from the base of the ladder was a dark gray rock veined with lines of quartz and faint ribbons of red. Altar Rock it was called, and it marked the place where Narelle's body was found after the magic of her sacrifice stopped the flood.

Asha reached for its sun-warmed surface, but stopped herself before her fingers could brush the stone. She let her hand fall to her side and turned away, choking on the need to cry as she walked down the beach. Soon, the pale sand beneath her feet became rocky, dotted with iridescent shards of shell that shone in the morning light in tones of turquoise and peach. There, in a shallow protected by a large out-cropping of rock, she'd hidden her boat.

It was a small boat, little more than a raft, but it had a real wooden mast and a white canvas sail. The ropes she had woven with her own hands. Quickly she scooped the accumulated sand from the inside of the boat, retrieved the sail from a small crevice and, climbing aboard, cast off.

By the time the morning songs and prayers had finished and the Té'ahn began to wonder why her daughter had not yet appeared, Asha was no more than a white dot amidst a great ocean of blue.

For a time, it was easy to lose herself in the motion of her boat across the ocean. The deep, clear water did not ask questions; the beating sun passed no judgment. The boat did not care what one goddess thought of her; it just listened to the ropes and the great force of the wind that filled the sail and pushed. There was only the rhythm of the waves and the pull of her hands on the ropes, the spray in her face and the sunlight that flickered across the water like fire.

After a while, Asha let the sail fall and allowed her boat to drift in the current. The island of Rise seemed small, no larger than her hand held at arm's length, and the green hills of Wake behind it were even smaller. There was more to leaving than simply heading away, Asha realized, and she had no idea where she could go.

She knew that somewhere beyond the horizon there were other lands, though none had visited them since the people had come to these islands, fleeing death and persecution in their great ships of wood and metal. Yet even in the great ships many had died on the long voyage; it was certainly not a trip that one girl could make in her homemade boat with only a single honeycake in her stomach and one goatskin bottle of water, already more than half drunk, for supplies.

She could turn around and head towards the sunken island of Drift, she thought, the third point in the triangle that had once been formed by the three islands. But the waters above the drowned island were said to be treacherous, the currents sly and unpredictable. More than one treasure hunter had gotten himself in trouble when a rock or rooftop hiding just below the surface had ripped open a hole in his boat. Besides, Drift was a diversion, not a life.

She hadn't thought this through very well, Asha thought with chagrin. She hadn't thought it through at all.

Still, the idea of going back to Peak of the Ocean was more than she could handle, and not even the thought of her mother, worried at her absence, could make her change her mind. But there were other places on the islands she could stay. She knew a few of the Té of Oren, the sailor's god; some of the priests had taught her to sail as a little girl. She smiled at the thought of their reaction to her small but functional boat. Yes, she was sure that they would give her a place to stay for the night.

And, she thought, flushing, they would let her send word to her mother that she was all right.

Nodding once, she stood and began raising the sail. The fabric fluttered and belled out, catching the strong breeze. She would go to the far end of the island to the busy trading town of Precipice and the temple of Oren that stood on its shores. Resolutely, she set the bow of her boat towards Rise.

Returning, however, proved to be far more difficult than leaving had been. On her journey out, Asha hadn't cared which direction she'd sailed and had allowed herself to play, tacking and turning, skimming across the edges of waves, but now she wanted to get back as quickly as possible. She found it nearly impossible to keep her little boat running in a straight line, and constantly readjusted the ropes and angle of her sail in hope of making the trip a little easier. She hoped in vain. Within a few hours she'd drunk the last of her water and Rise seemed little closer than it had when she'd made her decision. The afternoon sun beat down, and the water she'd drunk seemed to pour from her skin as sweat. Soon she found herself almost dizzy with heat and thirst, and the ocean still separated her from her goal.

It was almost dark by the time Asha managed to bring her little boat into the wide cove that sheltered the port of Precipice. The fishing boats had long since returned to their docks, the catch had been hauled in and the men and women were home eating their dinners. The shops that lined the waterfront were closed, while warm candlelight shone through the slats in the shutters of the houses that dotted the cliffs. She could see the main docks, the warren of floating walkways and bobbing boats that she'd have to navigate before she could get to shore. With her luck and the temperament of her boat, Asha knew she was more likely to ram into another vessel than she was to land safely, likely damaging someone's livelihood and sinking her boat in the process.

Unfortunately, the docks were the only part of Precipice that came within twenty feet of the water. The rest of the town was perched on a series of small cliffs that gave the town its name. There was only one other place Asha could think of to land.

Before the flood, Precipice had been a much bigger town that both perched upon the rocky cliffs and sprawled out across the sandy lowlands. The town's main trading port had been a much larger, more elaborate affair that sprawled along the waterfront. Houses and shops had dotted the shore, too, sheltered from the wind and waves within a large protective curve of rock. When the waters rose, the lower levels of the town were lost until only the parts of town that clung to the steep slopes remained. Of the port and lower town, only the curve of rock remained, with a single metal staircase, once used to help transport goods, bolted to the side. The steps leading down into the empty water were the only sign that something more had once stood below.

Asha guided her boat towards the stairway. As soon as she passed within the shelter of the low cliffs the wind left her sail, and she was forced to duck under the sagging fabric, lean over the side of the boat and paddle with her hands. With much splashing and frustration, she at last made her way to the iron stairs.

With a spare bit of rope she tied her boat to the railing, leaving enough slack in the line so when the tide went out her boat wouldn't be left hanging. Wearily, she clambered over the side and onto the cold metal stairs. The water lapped quietly around the mesh of the bottom stair, licking her hot and tired feet. The stairs continued downward; she could see a few more of the stained metal treads just below the surface of the dark water, vanishing into the black. Shivering with what she told herself was only the chill of the evening, Asha wrapped her arms around her chest and hurried up the stairs towards the town.

Her feet rang hollowly on the metal, the vibration quivering along her callused feet and the palms of her hands. As she climbed wearily, Asha wondered how she would find her way. It had been a few months since she'd last visited the temple of Oren, and never had she needed to navigate the streets of Precipice at night. It was growing dark; the sun was already below the horizon, and the sky above the distant island of Wake was a deep and sullen red. The few people who wandered the town streets were above her and far away, unlikely to come close enough to offer her guidance; few ventured close to the rocky edge and its metal stairway, even in daylight.

Which was why the sudden sound of hushed, angry voices from the ledge just above her head was enough to startle Asha into stillness. She hesitated, crouched so that the top of her head would not be visible to those above her, and listened.

"We told you not to say anything," a male said, and his wavering voice held the uncertain timbre of one not long out of adolescence. "You chose not to listen."

"Quiet," said another, and he sounded older. The younger boy muttered something that Asha could not hear, and then there came the sound of a muffled sob. Startled, Asha peeked up, careful not to be seen.

There, farther down the ledge towards the docks, stood two teenaged boys. One – the first speaker – seemed to be all arms and legs, while his companion, though smaller, seemed stronger and more composed. Between them, her back to the water and the edge perilously close to her heels, stood a girl not much younger than Asha herself. The girl trembled, her eyes darting from one boy to the other then down to the round, heavy object she clutched to her chest.

"Please," the girl said, her voice little more than a whisper. "I'm sorry. Please…"

Asha felt anger boiling up inside of her and moved. It was only the sound of the younger boy's retort that hid the sound of her bare feet running up the last few steps.

"You should have thought of that before," he said, and laughed nervously.

"Shut up," said the older boy. "Both of you."

"Hey!" Asha said, and was almost startled at the volume of her own voice. Both boys stiffened and spun in her direction. "What are you–"

"Now – run!" the younger boy cried, as the older boy, still silent, reached out and pushed the trembling girl.

The girl screamed as she toppled over backwards, her arms flying out, releasing whatever it was that she held. It was only as the girl fell towards the dark water that Asha realized that what she had been holding was a rock, tied to her hands and feet with a length of thick rope. There was a splash, and the girl vanished beneath the surface without another sound.

The boys ran towards the town, the sound of their feet and the girl's scream echoing off the rock walls; Asha ignored them and ran, skidding to a stop as she came to the place where the girl had fallen. Only an expanding ripple remained, widening over the dark water in a ring. Bubbles floated to the surface.

Without thinking, Asha dove. It was a long fall, and the impact of the water was almost enough to push the air from her lungs. It was dark underwater, the faint light of candles and the dying sunset unable to penetrate the nighttime ocean. She could barely see her hands or arms as she pulled herself down into the water. Her chest felt tight, and she could taste salt. Her ears squealed from the pressure of the water, but she forced herself deeper.

Even as she dove, Asha knew it was hopeless. How could she ever find the girl in this darkness? She had no idea what the bottom was like, or how far down it lay. And even if she could swim far enough, how would she ever find the strength or the time to cut the girl's ropes and carry her back up without drowning?

In desperation, Asha called out with all her mind and spirit, with every burning muscle of her body. In the dark and swirling water she opened herself as she never could in prayer, laying herself empty and bare.

Save her! Asha cried to her goddess. *Please, please, save her.*

Through the dark water, Asha saw light. There seemed to be no source, only a cool, wavering radiance that dimly illuminated her surroundings. Dark shapes loomed all around her, muddy mounds in rows with holes in their sides. They were houses, Asha realized. The drowned houses of Precipice, buried beneath the water since the flood. Some had almost washed away to nothing, while others were only missing their roofs and shutters and doors. Row upon row of sunken houses lay about her, windows staring like dark and broken eyes. Below her, she could see a girl's body sinking, her wide eyes closed and small mouth open, her long dark hair trailing behind her.

She couldn't breathe, her lungs were screaming out for air, but Asha forced herself deeper still, reaching out for that pale, sinking hand. The girl landed on the bottom, sediment billowing out from her in slow clouds. Her hair drifted about her face, and she was still.

Asha swam those last, struggling strokes towards her and grabbed her by the arm. She pulled but could not drag the girl from her place on the ocean floor. She struggled against the weight and the water and her own weakness, the slow-motion struggles of one who is drowning.

Her lungs screamed for air. Spots danced before her eyes, and the darkness threatened to claim her.

Please, Asha prayed. *Take me, take my strength, take anything I have – but save her.*

The pale light around her suddenly seemed calm, and the water that she had struggled against held her gently. Asha felt herself relaxing, her body sinking to the sand beside the girl. She was lost in that long, black hair. Their hands drifted with the gentle current, fingers entwined.

And through the stillness, a woman's voice spoke. *I had thought to save you from this.* The voice sounded so young and so sad. *Would you truly sacrifice yourself to save but one life, Asha?*

Yes, Asha replied, and she drifted.

I should be glad that I made the right choice, the voice said, the youthful tone turned haunting by the wisdom and fatigue that it held. *But it brings me no comfort. Remember that, Asha. I, too, feel regret. Not for my choices, perhaps, but for the sorrow that they cause.*

Unbidden, an image rose in Asha's mind, that of a young man crumpled at a girl's feet, his hand in her hand as he sobbed in the mud. Aeyen, Asha thought, Narelle's lost love – and the man who helped find the Té'ahn who gave Narelle the strength to keep the water from rising again.

Would you fall as I have fallen, if that was the only choice left to you? Narelle asked her quietly. *No, don't answer, my friend; I hope we will never have to know. But this burden I place on you now is a heavy one, and for that I am sorry.*

Again Asha saw the great wall of water, and as in her dreams she reached her hands out towards it. She was so weak, but she had to try.

She felt a wave of warmth and love from the goddess. *Live, then, my Té*, Narelle said. *The road ahead of you is long, but you go with my blessing, and where I can, my help.*

Asha was in total darkness, and there was water rushing into her mouth, down her throat and into her lungs, and she was choking. But there was something in her arms, something soft and heavy, and she pushed up from the murky bottom with all her strength and she was rising. Like a bubble she was rising, and then there was air, and a shout, and hands grabbed her, and for a time that was all she knew.

Asha came to lying on hard rock, choking and coughing up salt water. A shape loomed before her in the darkness; she thought of the great wall of water from her vision and raised her hands in panic before the shape resolved itself into the figure of a man with a kind face and a full beard. He caught her hands in his.

"Easy, Té," he said in a low, warm voice. "You're safe now."

It was full dark; above her Asha could see a wash of bright stars appearing across the sky. She lay in a puddle of water on the cool stone ledge by the stairway where she had tied her boat. There were others on the ledge with her, townspeople bearing lanterns. Blinking, she tried to clear the gritty feel of sand from her eyes. Her chest ached, and her throat burned. When she coughed, Asha tasted salt.

She struggled to sit up. "The girl," Asha said. "Where is she?"

"Just there," he said, gesturing. Asha turned, leaning heavily on her elbow, until she could see the girl lying prone, surrounded by a cluster of kneeling figures in a warm circle of lamplight. The girl's eyes were open, and she was speaking weakly. Someone was untying a rope from the girl's wrist; the end of the rope was neatly cut, as if it had been sliced with a sharp knife.

"Poor thing," the man was saying. "Caught some of her father's workers stealing from his shop, and was going to tell her father. She almost died for having the courage to tell the truth. Lucky for her you were here – and that she screamed loud enough to near wake the whole town."

Asha frowned in confusion. The girl – even in the lamplight, her hair should not seem so gold. It was too short, too, falling to just below her shoulders. And hadn't her eyes been larger, the shape of her face more mature? Asha struggled to remember the face she'd seen in the water.

Memory washed over her, and elation, and fear. It hadn't been the girl that she had seen falling through the water in that pale silvery light,

Asha realized, but Narelle. Asha remembered that pale, outstretched hand.

She was so young, Asha thought, heartbroken. So young, and yet she'd done the only thing that she could to save the islands – and Asha. She looked again at the ropes that had bound the girl's hands and feet, tying her to the rock, and knew she'd had no way to break the ropes that cleanly.

"Thank you," she whispered to the empty stretch of water, to the wide and empty sky. "Thank you."

There was no answer, only a growing warmth in her chest that felt like joy.

"Té," the man at her side said. "You should rest. You are welcome at our temple for the night, if you wish."

Asha smiled slowly. "Thank you for your hospitality, Té-Oren," she said to the man, accepting both the offer and his outstretched hand. He helped her rise to her feet. "May I ask of you one more favor?"

"Name it," the priest of Oren replied.

"Would you please send word to Peak of the Ocean?" she asked. "Tell them that Ashanté Té-Narelle is coming home."

≈•≈

When Dragons Dream

by
Kevin G. Maclean

D
o it again, Brynelle! Do it again!" The children bounced excitedly up and down on the sleeping dragon.

"Huuuuunh! Go away and let me sleep!" Brynelle rearranged her limbs in repose, carefully, so as not to dislodge any of the children. "One sunset is enough for one day."

"Awww, Brynelle!" they complained together.

"Now is the time that little humans should be heading for bed, to have dreams of their own. You must have your own dreams – you can't use mine forever."

Slowly, the children trailed away homeward, only one little girl remaining, her thin face almost elfin in the twilight.

"Brynelle?"

"Yes, Eleanor?"

"Thank you for dreaming us the sunset. It was lovely." The girl smiled wistfully.

"You are very welcome, Eleanor, and thank you for thanking me. You are the only one who does, you know," she said.

"I know, Brynelle. Thank you for sharing your dreams. I must go now."

"Goodnight, Eleanor." Brynelle watched her tenderly as she made her way from the cave, then settled back down to the serious business of dreaming.

They came again that night, the Stealers of Dreams. Brynelle, ever watchful, rose to meet them with a vengeful roar. They scattered, and Brynelle hunted them, until she had hounded them back beyond the realms of Dream.

Tired but victorious, Brynelle sank back to her cave. Her charges still slept, but some of their parents were awake, so Brynelle dreamt a thin line of red through the sunrise before sinking into deep and dreamless sleep.

She woke in the afternoon to find a semicircle of children seated before her.

"Tell us a story, Brynelle… *please*," asked Roger, remembering his manners at the last moment. The others murmured their approval of the request.

Brynelle smiled. "First, I want to hear your stories. One from each, let us share, and grow strong in our minds."

So the children told their stories: Roger, a tale of heroic derring-do; Lyzette, a tale of romantic longing; Josef, a tale of good triumphing over cunning and treachery; and so on, children's tales all, until at last it was little Eleanor's turn.

"Come on, Eleanor, surely you have a story for us," Brynelle said.

"I have a good one, but it's not ready yet. May I tell you a different one?"

"Of course, Eleanor. Come on, sweetling, tell us your other story then," Brynelle said.

So Eleanor told her other story, a simple tale of love lost, and found, and lost again, but in a happy way, so that when she broke the spell, the other children did not know whether to cry out in joy or shed tears or both.

"You have the gift for certain, child. You will be a mighty dreamer indeed, when you come into your full power." Brynelle let a tear roll down one smiling cheek.

"Thank you, Guardian." Eleanor blushed and sat down. "And now, will you take your turn, Brynelle?"

Brynelle searched the faces of the children, so trusting and innocent, and judged the time was right. So she told them the tale of Poor Mad John, who stood alone against the Stealer of Souls and his children, the Stealers of Dreams.

She told of his victories, and of the terrible price he paid so gladly for each. She told of the valor and the hidden glory, and how he finally fell, alone – unbroken at the end.

There were tears in the eyes of the children.

Brynelle told last of John's victory in defeat: how even as he fell, his fall enheartened others, so that Thom the Rhymer stepped into the breach, and Ben Talespinner, and great Leonardo, and how these three of his disciples strode forth and chased the Stealer and his Children from the Realms of Dream. And she saw hope return to the little faces, and smiled.

"But if the Stealer is gone, why do we need strong dreamers, Brynelle?" asked Roger.

"He always returns, Roger. No victory over the Stealer is forever. At most, he goes for a generation or two, then creeps back. That's what he did when John's students passed on in their turn. As long as there is life, we will keep needing dreamers." She looked around at her own disciples, noting a smile here, a tear there, and brightened, "And now, would you rather have another story, or a sunset?"

"A sunset, a sunset!"

"Very well then, a sunset it shall be. Now leave me to dream." Brynelle shooed them out of the cave, all except young Eleanor, who stood quietly to one side.

"Brynelle, why do dragons dream for humans?" she asked.

"Because humans dream for dragons, too. You remind us when we are losing our dreams, so we remind you when you are losing yours. Sometimes we forget them completely, and have to learn how to make new dreams. That is what I am doing now, but the beginnings are slow."

"Are we the only creatures that dream, then? The humans and the dragons?"

"No. Many races dream, but their dreaming is so alien that it means nothing to us. Others we can understand, but their dreams are not safe or useful for us." Brynelle shrugged.

"I think Socks dreams."

"Yes, she does. Cats dream with power, like us, but any cat I would sooner trust with my dinner than with my dreams."

"Thank you, Brynelle," Eleanor said, and started to leave, then turned with a second thought. "Brynelle? Poor Mad John wasn't mad at all, was he?"

"No, dear. He was the sanest man I ever met. Now run along, so I can dream for you."

"Yes, Brynelle." And Eleanor trailed out to watch the sunset with the others.

Brynelle dreamed it pink and gold and streaked with grey – pretty, but not one of her best.

They came again that night in greater numbers. The Stealers seemed almost cheerful, in as much as their kind can be. There was a dull light in their dead eyes, and hints of smiles on their slack faces. They mocked her, singly and in groups, saying "Flee now, Dreamer, for the Master comes! Flee now, or you shall surely die!" And while they avoided direct confrontation, they did not flee, but boldly dodged and persisted in their attempts.

By the time the children woke, the Stealers had still not been banished, but it no longer mattered – the children were safe as long as they were awake. Brynelle allowed herself to collapse into a deep, dreamless sleep.

She woke to find her students seated in a semicircle in front of her. It was late afternoon. She had not dreamed the sunrise.

"Are you all right, Brynelle?" asked Eleanor. The small wrinkle on her forehead betrayed her concern.

"I'll be fine. Just give me a minute to wake up and then you can tell me your stories."

"Yes, Brynelle." The children waited patiently for Brynelle to begin the class.

She stretched and shook herself, but the children were already fidgeting and noisy by the time her mind cleared. She cleared her throat for silence, and the noise abated. "Now, children, tell your stories."

So Josef told a story of horror averted, and Lyzette a story of true love triumphing over adversity. Roger told a story of loss and redemption, and so on, until they came to Eleanor.

"Is your story ready yet, Eleanor?"

"Not yet, Brynelle. May I tell a different one?"

"Of course."

So Eleanor told the tale of a knight who traded away everything that made him a knight in a quest for a lady, and how what he got in return won her hand. It was a tale of such sweet longing that the other children sat in silent awe with tears unshed in their eyes, none of them wanting to be the first to break the spell.

Brynelle did not dream that day's sunset – the sky was sullen and grey.

The Stealers came in force that night, mocking her guard, and making her twist and turn, exhausting herself to catch those that tried to sneak past her to steal the dreams of the children.

And in the darkest hour, He came – the Stealer of Souls. Brynelle's heart sank, and she flew at him in a desperate fury of teeth and claws, but he laughed and slapped her away. She fell, and the Dreamthieves mocked her. She retreated slowly, snapping and snarling – thwarting his advance, until the night was over. The children were safe for one more day. She retreated back to her cave.

She woke in the late afternoon, to find her students seated in front of her, and young Eleanor gently stroking her giant head.

"Are you all right, Brynelle?" Eleanor asked tenderly.

"No, Eleanor. The Stealer of Souls comes, and I cannot stand against him."

"Hide then! Run away!"

"I cannot do that. To let my spirit die while my body still lives would be his ultimate victory. It is better to die fighting him." She sighed. "I fear this night will be my last alive, yet my greater fear is for you. You are too weak yet to stand against him."

"Then let us stand with you! Surely we can help at least …"

Brynelle shook her head. "I cannot protect you in the Dreamland. Only your own strength will suffice there."

And that was all there was to say.

The children's tales that evening were subdued and tinged with sorrow, and Brynelle did not dream them a sunset, saving her strength for the coming fray.

As she entered Dream, the Stealer was waiting for her in the form of a great grey ogre. She tried to use her speed, slashing and swooping, but he was too quick. Finally, he caught her and dragged her down, smashing her wings and crushing her body as a child does a rag doll.

"And now," he gloated, "your soul is mine." And he bent over to rip out her heart.

He stopped suddenly, surprised, then slowly looked up along the blade of the shining sword pricking his throat.

"I think not!" said the knight at the other end, a cold hard look on her deadly-calm face. "Get you gone, leech – you and all your kind. This land is not for the likes of you." She stepped back into a guard position, poised and confident, ready for attack or defence.

"Oh ho!" said the ogre. "A new and very junior Guardian." He grinned horribly. "Well, as you can see, I know how to kill Guardians."

He reached for her, but she was too quick. The sword of light bit deep into his arm as she spun inside his grasp and passed behind him in a single blur of motion. She cut twice more before he could turn: once behind the ankle, once behind the knee. The leg collapsed as he tried to turn toward her, and, off-balance, he crashed to the ground at her feet. Her fourth slash was through his throat as he hit the ground, and she leapt back into a guard position out of reach.

"Not while *I* live, you don't!" she said.

"Maybe not," came a voice from the grey fog dissipating above the dying ogre. "Nonetheless, I shall return."

"And we shall be ready."

The ogre's body crumpled to dust and blew away in the non-existent wind.

The knight sheathed her sword, and went to kneel by the dying dragon. "Oh, Brynelle," she breathed, "how could you let it come to this?"

"Eleanor? Is that you?"

"Yes. It's me."

"And you have won?"

"Yes."

"Then it was worthwhile." Brynelle sighed.

"But why? Why couldn't I help before?"

"You needed two gifts yet," the dragon whispered, "the gifts of Passion and Grief. Without them, no Guardian can be strong and no child can be an adult. And they cannot be given without pain. Now take me home. I have some goodbyes to say."

The children sat in a silent semicircle in front of the shattered dragon. Eleanor sat to one side, a little removed. Each had been farewelled, and instructed firmly to keep dreaming.

"And now, I think I may just have one more sunset in me," Brynelle said, and smiled weakly.

"Yaaay!" cried the children and ran outside.

Eleanor moved and sat down cross-legged by Brynelle, resting one hand on her head.

Brynelle waited until she was sure the last of the children were out of earshot. "They're not going to miss me, you know."

"Of course they will," Eleanor said.

"No, they'll miss the stories and the sunsets, but none of them will miss me … not the person, Brynelle … Children are like that, totally self-centered, and carelessly cruel. They have butterfly cares and woes, always hither and yon. In a week, they'll have forgotten me, and that is as it should be."

"*I* will miss you."

"Ah, but you're not one of them now, are you? If you ever were …"

"Maybe not. I don't really know any more." Her hand dropped from the dragon's head. "Why don't you save your strength? You know this sunset will kill you."

"And gain a couple of days more of pain? No, thank you. But there is one more thing I must know."

"Yes?"

"Have you finished your story yet?"

"Yes, Brynelle. As much as it can ever be finished …"

"Am I in it?"

"Oh, yes. You, and Poor Mad John, and Thom the Rhymer and all the others … It's true, you see." Tears streamed down Eleanor's face.

"Good company then."

"The best."

They stayed silent together for a few moments, then Brynelle said, "Why don't you go out and watch the sunset with the others?"

"I'd rather stay here with you, if that's all right."

"That's fine." After a few seconds, she added. "Thank you."

A few minutes later, Brynelle said, "Look after them!"

"I shall."

Brynelle closed her eyes, and dreamed. Eleanor sat beside her and waited for the breathing to stop, and then after that, until it was quite dark.

And all the children agreed that this was the finest sunset they had ever seen.

About the Authors

❧ • ❧

MARIE BRENNAN is the pen name of Bryn Neuenschwander. She holds a bachelor's degree in archaeology and folklore from Harvard University, and is currently pursuing a Ph.D. in anthropology and folklore at Indiana University at Bloomington, where her field of study is fantasy literature and its fan culture. Her education provides her with endless fodder for story material, and she hopes her two chosen careers, academia and fiction writing, will continue to influence each other for years to come.

Her short story "Calling Into Silence" received the Grand Prize in the 2003 Isaac Asimov Award for Undergraduate Excellence in Science Fiction and Fantasy Writing, and another story, "The Legend of Anahata," received an Honorable Mention in the same year. "White Shadow" is her first professional sale.

ED GREENWOOD has been hailed as "the Canadian author of the great American novel," and "an industry legend." A writer, game designer, editor, and magazine columnist, Ed is the creator of the Forgotten Realms® fantasy world, and has written over a hundred published books and more than six hundred magazine articles and short stories. He's also designed or inspired several bestselling computer games, including the popular *Baldur's Gate* series. His writings have sold millions of copies worldwide in more than a dozen languages, and he's received many game industry awards, including election (in 1992) to the Gamer's Choice Hall of Fame.

Ed is a Life Member of the Science Fiction and Fantasy Writers of America, and has been Guest of Honor at scores of literary and gaming conventions from Stockholm to Melbourne. He's even appeared (as himself) in comics published by Marvel, DC, and TSR, Inc.

Most of Ed's twenty-some fantasy and science fiction novels have made the New York Times bestsellers list and other major American lists. They include *Spellfire*, the popular Elminster Saga, and the Band of Four series. Ed's latest books include *Elminster's Daughter* (from Wizards of the Coast) and *The Silent House* (from Tor Books). His forthcoming games include a new fantasy world setting called Castlemorn™ from Fast Forward Entertainment, Inc.

In real life, Ed is a large, jolly, bearded guy who lives in the countryside near Cobourg, Ontario, and likes reading books, books, and more books (which more than fill his farmhouse). Ed has worked in libraries for over thirty years.

TANYA HUFF lives and writes in rural Ontario with her partner, six cats, and a disinterested Chihuahua. Her nineteen published novels – most from DAW Books Inc. – and three short story collections cover the course from quest fantasty, through contemporary fantasy, to horror and science fiction. When she isn't writing, she gardens and believes in magic.

KEVIN MACLEAN lives in Auckland, New Zealand. He gives his profession as "freelance computer geek." His short fiction has been featured in *Andromeda Spaceways Inflight Magazine, Millennium Nights*, and a number of *Pipers Ash* collections, but this is his first professional sale. He has yet to complete a novel, which he puts down entirely to his own slackness.

MT O'SHAUGHNESSY was born and raised in Ontario. With sheep. Among other barnyard animals. Early reading experiences were less than thrilling and it was only under a dire threat that he found J.R.R Tolkien's *The Hobbit*. However, as a result, he suddenly realized what other people do with those stories in their heads, and began to put pen to paper. This all led, eventually, to Michael's first professional sale, his science fiction short story "Skeeters," in *Tales from the Wonder Zone: Odyssey,* ed. by Julie E. Czerneda, Trifolium Books. Generally, Michael tends to work on at least one short story and one (never-ending) novel at a time. Although he is loathe to admit it, he loves writing and hopes never to be forced to stop.

JANA PANICCIA was born in Windsor, Ontario, but grew up in the country – just outside the town of Essex. She is the youngest of four children (the only girl!), and has parents who believe she can do anything (Thanks Mom, thanks Dad!). Never one to get bored, Jana's dream is to spend the rest of her life going "somewhere else." To that end, she's traveled in Europe with Girl Guides, headed off on student exchanges to Australia and Japan, and even studied International Business so she can become a Canadian Ambassador one day. Of course, she is also never far from her bookshelf, because the places she really wants to visit are unreachable any other way: Valdemar, Darkover, Athera, and Pern. Jana has been writing stories practically since she learned how to write – after all, the dragons were very hard to ignore when they started whispering tales in her ears. "Offering of Trust" is her first published story. Her second will appear in the DAW anthology *Women at War* edited by Alexander Potter and Tanya Huff (2005).

KARINA SUMNER-SMITH is a Canadian science fiction and fantasy writer who has lived in and around Toronto, Ontario for most of her life. Her first short story was published in 2000, and other short fiction publications have followed, with works appearing in *Strange Horizons, Challenging Destiny, Lady Churchill's Rosebud Wristlet* and *Far Sector*, among others. Karina attended the Clarion Writers' Workshop in 2001 and was a finalist for the Asimov Award in both 2002 and 2003. A recent graduate of York

University, she is learning to balance her writing and reading habits with the requirement for financial income. Though a degree in Humanities seems to qualify one for little, she is grateful for four years that allowed her to study everything from religion and culture to history and speculative fiction. Karina is currently at work on a novel about Ashanté Té-Narelle and the islands.

RUTH STUART is a Canadian fantasy writer, with her first novel presently under consideration by a major US publisher. Her short story "Memories Underfoot" can be found in the anthology *Haunted Holidays*, edited by Russell Davis (DAW Books). Ruth has been very active in the Canadian SF/F community for many years. When she isn't playing with words in her work at a major insurance company, Ruth enjoys playing with words in her own worlds. She lives with her geriatric cat and many, many books.

One day, she'd also like to be a Bard.

MICHELLE WEST has written twelve novels, all fantasy, and dozens of short stories. She's worked in bookstores since she was sixteen, loves reading, is allergic to cats (very, which means they crawl all over her), is happily married, has two lovely children, and has spent all of her life in her native Toronto – none of it on Bay Street. Her newest novel is *The Sun Sword*, the sixth and final volume in the series of the same name, from DAW Books. She started reading fantasy almost as soon as she could read, and fell instantly in love with Narnia. She moved on to *The Hobbit*, which led to her discovery of the life-changing *The Lord of the Rings*. Her greatest hope for her writing is that someone will read it and be moved by the same sense of magic and mystery that she finds in the books she loves.